Stormy Hill

Nancy Clarke

Illustrated by Penny Muire

Strategic Book Publishing and Rights Co.

Strategic Book Publishing and Rights Co.
12620 FM 1960, Suite A4-507
Houston, TX 77065
www.sbpra.com

ISBN: 978-1-62212-568-5

Book Design: Suzanne Kelly

Dedication

To my parents, Betty and Jim Bodine,
without whose encouragement this book
might never have been completed.

And to Murphy (Pequest Mihran),my own Arabian, whose
entry marked a turning point in my life. For the past
eighteen years we have shared adventures wherever the
trails of life have taken us. Because of you, I now
understand that mystery of a bond shared with a horse.

Table of Contents

CHAPTER 1   The Foaling 5

CHAPTER 2   Trouble! 16

CHAPTER 3   Decisions 28

CHAPTER 4   Panic! 42

CHAPTER 5   Exploration 56

CHAPTER 6   Summer 68

CHAPTER 7   The Bill 77

CHAPTER 8   The Solution 86

CHAPTER 9   The Yearling 96

CHAPTER 10   Stolen! 108

CHAPTER 11   Flight! 124

CHAPTER 12   Freedom 136

CHAPTER 13   The Girl 142

CHAPTER 14   The Whip 158

CHAPTER 15   Kentucky 173

CHAPTER 16   Derby Day 180

CHAPTER 17   Ted's Story 196

CHAPTER 18   Si'ad 203

CHAPTER 19   The Return 214

CHAPTER 20   Heritage 230

CHAPTER ONE

The Foaling

Lightning flashed across the sky in almost continual streaks, while thunder boomed incessantly. Rain poured down in steady sheets, acting as a wall of water, flooding the low spots and causing many roads to become impassable. Most of the fury of the storm seemed to concentrate its force on that part of Kentucky known as the Bluegrass Region. As the old year was being given a roaring sendoff, nowhere was the storm worse than at one particular little farm, less grand than her sisters, but Bluegrass all the same. Stormy Hill by name, it took the brunt of the storm stoically, as it had other such catastrophes in the past.

For tonight, its occupants were concerned with other, far more important matters. This was the night their most valuable broodmare had chosen to deliver her first foal. Within one of the barns a light burned as a somber group gathered to witness the foaling, their thoughts far removed from the gaiety that usually welcomed another year. One look on their faces made it evident that all was not going well with this particular birth.

Outside a small, slightly built woman ran anxiously from the house, across the courtyard to the barn. Frantically pulling the door open, she hastened inside lest the wind pull the door from her grasp. Even so, Jessica Collins made a wet, bedraggled figure as she came up to the stall.

"Doc Hawes can't get here," she announced, wishing she were not the bearer of such grim news. "The roads out his way are under water. He can't get off his own property. I tried the clinic also, but the lines are down." She looked from one to the other, knowing how upsetting her words would be taken.

Her husband, Michael, nodded dully, his eyes meeting hers briefly before returning to the mare lying in the straw. In that one glance she read all the despair he could not put into words. She sighed for she did not have to be told the obvious.

"That settles it, Michael, if Doc can't make it I'm going in," the weather-beaten, gruff little Scotsman beside him spoke up. "Don't worry, we'll pull her through."

"Sure, Scotty," Michael murmured without confidence. His handsome, rugged face bore the strain of the past long hours he had worried over Dawn of Glory's labor. His broad shoulders bent under the pressure as he hovered beside the heaving, lathered mare. His thick, black hair was damp with sweat and a lock of it fell across his eyes. Impatiently he kept brushing it away, only to have it fall back again.

Jessica looked away from her weary husband, across to Scotty, officially their trainer, but more important, Michael's closest friend. Scott McDougal did not give up easily. He had known much hardship in his life and had learned not to give in to self-pity. Scotty was no quitter. A veteran of innumerable foalings, he had grown up on this farm. He knew as much about horses as most vets. She felt a strong need to lean on Scotty's strength at a time like this.

Jessica's eyes traveled to the third member of this solemn group, her daughter, Ann. Ann sat quietly, stroking the mare, yet her concern showed on her tight pale face, her gray eyes large and emotional, though she uttered not a sound. Ann was only fourteen, so young to witness this possible tragedy. Yet so serious, so like her father in her strong commitment to the affairs of the farm. How could she have kept her away?

Physically, Ann was a near replica of her mother, small, light-boned and tomboyish, just as her mother had been before she had matured. Ann had the same pixie-like face topped off by an upturned nose, in her case offset by those large gray eyes and thick dark eyelashes, giving her face character. But her hair was all her father's. Unlike Jessica's light brown, soft, almost wispy, hair, Ann's was thick and black, tumbling in an unruly mass of curls to her waist. It was her most arresting feature. At the moment she had tied it back in the barest hint of a ponytail, but renegade strands had broken loose and hung relentlessly in her eyes.

"Is Jock back yet?" she spoke up suddenly to no one in particular. Jock was Scotty's son, two years Ann's senior, and her closest friend. He had gone to the house to sterilize the equipment. It was only a matter of time before the foal would have to be pulled out.

As if to answer her question, the barn door banged once again as Jock made his appearance. Water dripping from everywhere, he pushed a strand of wet brown hair from his face as he threw off the poncho he was wearing and handed his father the box of instruments he had been protecting underneath. Without a word he went to the back of the mare and settled down beside her. Pulling a fresh tail wrap from his pocket, he efficiently replaced the old one with this new clean one. Then he continued to hold her tail out of the way, stroking her wet dark rump as he did.

"Thanks, son," Scotty acknowledged, smiling at the boy. "Well, here goes." As he spoke, he pulled on a pair of sterile gloves and lubricated his hands. He was just beginning his examination when she suddenly began another heavy contraction. Scotty stopped, watching critically, but this one, like the others, was unsuccessful.

"Something's twisted," he told them. "I'm going in." Collectively they all nodded in silent agreement, unaware that each of them was holding his breath.

Glory gave a grunt as Scotty eased his hand up along her canal, probing gently for the twisted position in which he expected to find the foal, for surely there could be no other reason why she had failed to pass her foal after so long a time. It was past midnight and she had been having contractions off and on since early evening. By now she was showing signs of weakening.

At first he could find no abnormality. "The foal doesn't appear to be crooked," he relayed back to them as he found the head and forelegs in the right position. "No wait, one of the forelegs is bent. It's caught behind the pelvic bone." Gently, he felt along the leg, finding the tiny hoof and easing it around until it slid into position alongside the other one. As he eased his hand back out, he looked up at the silent, tense faces surrounding him.

"That should do it," he told them in his usual taciturn manner. "I've straightened the twisted leg. Up to her now." As one, they all let out their pent-up breaths-the only audible response given.

Ann continued to stroke the mare's damp neck, willing her to push. As she did, she thought of the importance of the foal she was carrying. Her eyes traveled across to those of her father, so like her own. Though young in age, she was well aware of the significance of this breeding he had made. It was, in effect, his last shot at producing a winning racehorse from their Stormy Hill line. He had, as the saying goes, put all his eggs in one basket. It was a mighty big gamble.

As far as they were aware, Dawn of Glory was the last available mare from the bloodline founded by a horse named Stormy Hill. In any event, she was the only direct granddaughter they had living on the farm. Stormy Hill had been their most famous racehorse. Racing toward the end of the Depression, his wins were legendary. He had gone on to sire a dynasty worthy of his fame. The combined earnings of his get had set the farm in good stead for years to come.

But then the hard times had come and most of the horses had been sold to pay debts. Now they were left with merely four mares, and only Glory was good enough to pass on her incredible heritage. An injury her second time to the post had prevented her from racing, but had not kept her from broodmare status. Here would be where she'd prove herself. Or so Michael had thought.

He had searched far and wide to put her to the right stallion. A quirk of fate had brought him Si'ad, a grey Arabian, bred and born in the desert and imported from Egypt at great expense.

It was through his old college roommate, with whom he'd continued to keep in touch, that Michael discovered the existence of such a horse as Si'ad. His friend, Roger, worked for an oil company and as such, was sent all over the world, one place being Egypt. Knowing of his friend's interest in racehorses, and having more than a faint one in them himself, he immediately recognized the value of a horse like Si'ad when he was offered. Roger quickly got in touch with Michael, who without hesitation bought him and had the horse shipped to the states. It took nearly every cent Michael had but he never regretted the expense from the time he saw his beautiful extravagance.

Ann would never forget the first time she saw Si'ad, as he stepped out of the trailer nearly one year ago. He was all fire, having been penned up for so long. Used to his freedom, he balked at such confinement. He stepped forth, hooves ringing on the wooden ramp, tossing his long, dark mane, snorting in anticipation as he drank in the air, sensing mares near. Si'ad was tall, much taller than the average Arab, belying the blood of his dam who herself was out of an English racing mare. He carried himself proudly on long, tapering legs, each one as black as coal and without a blemish. At three years of age, he was a dark, steel grey, the hint of dappling covering his rump, a strong contrast to the silver tips that sparkled when he swished his long tail or tossed his heavy mane.

While his body showed the Thoroughbred influence, his head was pure Arabian. Set on an arched, somewhat slender neck, his head was wide between the large, round eyes, and tapered down to a small, almost dainty, muzzle. His pointed ears nearly touched when alert, and his nostrils flared red as he swung his head around, mindful of everything within his vision.

From the moment Si'ad arrived, Ann set out to befriend this only partially tamed desert-bred stallion. Her father had thought only of the fine foal he and Glory would make, but Ann, loving

9

horses all her life, saw her childhood fantasies coming true right here and now.

Seeing Si'ad running free, the wind blowing back his glorious mane and tail, Ann was ever aware of the potential power and speed within the stallion. She must capture that spirit for herself and know what it was like to ride such a magnificent creature. But it took longer than she thought to win his trust. Only partially broken, Si'ad had never worn a saddle. Ann set about her project slowly and patiently. She spent many hours just talking to him as she stood beside his stall or brushed him, often leaning against him, resting her arm across his back. Eventually he learned to wear the bridle and saddle. At long last, she was rewarded by his whinny when she entered his stall. Then she knew she had his trust.

The first time Ann rode Si'ad, he was everything she had imagined he'd be. Now indeed she could race the wind. All other horses paled in comparison to the beauty and speed of this grey Arab. To own such a horse, to be able to ride him, to care for him, love him, was enough for Ann.

Yet she understood her father's wish for more. She was not too young to appreciate what living on a Thoroughbred-breeding farm in Kentucky meant. Each year the new crop of foals brought renewed hopes for the next stakes winner. Her father lived for that dream. The mating of Glory to Si'ad was, for him, the culmination of all he had planned. This foal could put Stormy Hill back on its feet, from a struggling farm to a successful one, if only...

Ann awakened from her reverie by Jock's shout. "There, I see a hoof," he cried. The mare gave a mighty contraction and more of the front feet slid into view, stopping at the knees.

Excitedly, Ann urged her on. "Push, Glory, push, " she murmured anxiously. "You can do it."

For what seemed like hours, but was in actuality was only seconds, nothing happened. Silently they all willed the exhausted mare to release her burden. Then, as though summoning all of her remaining strength, Glory's sides contracted into one last convulsion and her already overstrained muscles made one final effort. Ever so slowly the foal made its entrance into the world, as first its nose, followed by its head resting between its two forelegs, then its withers, back, and finally with a whoosh, its hind legs slid into view, until it lay, a wet mousy-colored bundle, in the thick straw. Glory gave a final grunt, before falling back, her energy now spent, too tired to be aware of the life to which she had just given birth, the burden she no longer bore. Glory was dying. Michael rushed to her head, holding it tenderly in his hands, stroking her forehead gently as he watched her lifeblood oozing out of her. His longtime experience with horses told him he could do nothing for her now.

But Ann did not give in to despair. "Quick, Jock, give me some of those towels, " she said. "Let's get this little fellow dried off." Vaguely, conscious of the mare's fate, her main concern was rather directed toward the newborn foal—a colt, she happily noted. Immediately grabbing for the thick white towels Jock handed her, she began to rub vigorously all over the foal's body, especially around the nostrils as she pulled off the remains of the mucus membrane that had protected him in his mother's womb.

"Here, I'll help," Jock volunteered, rubbing the colt's nose and mouth, as he bent over and checked his breathing for any fluid in the lungs, but luckily they were clear. Then they both sat back and looked at him.

He was a big colt, strapping, especially in the light of his early birth. Big even for a normal term foal, his size had certainly contributed to Glory's difficulty in delivering him, especially in lieu of the fact that she was a maiden mare. In color he was a dark, mouse shade all over, except for a funny, crooked strip of white down his forehead. This nondescript color pleased Ann for it meant that he would turn black, like his dam. Black horses were never born black, but rather mousy at birth. She rubbed each long perfect leg in turn, finding not a speck of white on any of his straight, slender legs.

Then he raised his head, small and dish-faced for the size of his body, and shook his long neck, making the short, stubby mane bob up and down. Ann laughed then, the sound

a sharp contrast against the still-howling wind. Jock looked at her and smiled.

"Oh, you wonderful, beautiful creature, you," she sputtered. The colt's large, liquid eyes held a surprised, almost comical look to them, situated between that crooked blaze as they were. He focused on Ann, as if trying to interpret the sound. She laughed again with delight. "You are something." She renewed her rubbing of the wet spots, as the foal struggled to raise his forelegs, his incongruously long legs unwilling to cooperate.

"Oh, look, everyone," Ann cried. "The foal. He's trying to stand already."

Her father turned desolate eyes toward her and muttered, "What good will that do now? Glory's not going to last the night and he'll never survive without a mother."

Ann suddenly became aware of the mare's labored breathing, at once so loud it seemed to block out even the storm raging outside. For the first time, she turned her attention away from the colt to become aware of the gravity of the situation confronting them.

"Oh, no, not Glory," she cried out, looking first at her father's anguished face and then down at the mare he was holding.

Glory was indeed dying. Although Scotty had immediately administered a high dose of steroids kept on hand for such emergencies, it appeared that nothing would help her now. She was too far gone to as much as raise her head. She lay in the straw, her wet, matted dark coat dull and lifeless, eyes glazed as though she had already accepted the inevitable. Michael continued to stroke her neck uselessly. His shoulders were slumped in defeat. Ann had never seen so much pain in her father's face. She could almost see the image before them as their dreams went up in smoke.

But, no! That could not be, she decided. With the determination born of youth, she cried out, "But look at him! He's strong and vigorous. Even now he's trying to stand. He cannot die, too!"

Fearfully, she glanced from one another's face for confirmation of her words. But her father only looked skeptical. Her mother appeared sympathetic, but she'd seen too much sorrow on this farm already to believe any different this time. How she wished her daughter was not so intensely wrapped up in their farm. Perhaps it would hurt less.

Ann turned to Scotty, so practical, so experienced. She could lean on him. He'd know what to do.

Scotty met her hopeful eyes. Well aware of the odds stacked against what she wished of him, he was also unable to refuse her. Ann was as much a daughter to him as Jock was his own son. She had seen so many setbacks for such a young life. Perhaps there was a chance. He said, "Ann, we can only try." At the sudden joy he saw burst across her face, he added cautiously, "But I have to warn you, it won't be easy. He'll have to be bottle-raised. The other mares are nearly two months away from foaling. And I doubt we would have much luck finding a wet mare from any of the other farms at this time of year…"

"I'll do it!" Ann interrupted, excitedly. "I know I can."

Scotty continued as if he hadn't heard her. "He may reject the milk. Some foals do."

"He'll take it from me," she said, doggedly.

"That's not what I mean," Scotty persisted. "His body may not take to it. We can't give him mare's milk. We'll have to use a formula, and then, in spite of everything we do, he may die anyway."

"I'll take that chance. Oh, please, Scotty, can we at least try? Look at him. He's so determined to live." She rubbed the foal's neck as he again tried to rise, only to lose his balance once more, collapsing on his too-long, stilt-like legs. Yet each time he tried, Ann could see that he was gaining strength. Soon he would be standing on his own.

"Okay, okay," Scotty gave in. Then suddenly mobilized by his proclamation, he roared into action, firing orders at everyone. "Well, if we're going to save this foal, we'd better work fast. Ann, you can help me move him into another stall. The one on the end has clean straw in it. Jessica, go turn on the infrared light to warm it up. Then can you prepare some formula? This baby's going to need it soon, if he'll drink at all." Jessica never questioned Scotty's authority but hurried off to do her part.

Scotty then turned to Jock, "See if you can collect some of that colostrum before we lose her, son. It sure would help if we can get some of those important anti-bodies into him. Sterile pails and bottles should be in the feed room. See if Michael will help while Ann and I carry the foal down to the other stall. And hurry," he added unnecessarily, more for Michael's benefit than any other. He could see his friend still bent over the mare in a trance, as though he'd not heard a word spoken.

Reluctantly, Michael did help Jock, though he would have preferred his mare die a natural, uninterrupted death, while he was left alone to mourn her passing. Forcing Glory to give up her all-important milk seemed so cold-hearted to him, as though her feelings were no longer considered. Deep in Michael's subconscious, the hard-bitten, practical side of him saw the need for this action, but right now his emotional side won out. Even as he aided Jock, he muttered, "Won't do any good. Only going to prolong Ann's heartbreak if she gets attached to him and then loses him. It'll be that much harder on her. Besides, of what use to us is a hand-raised foal, anyhow? Won't ever make a race horse out of an orphan," he continued, grumbling to himself.

14

Jock knew only too well the truth of his words. Not knowing how to answer his logic, he only replied softly, "Gotta try, though, Michael. Gotta at least try."

Michael was unaware that his daughter heard his words as she helped Scotty move the foal into the clean, empty stall. However, it only served to make her more determined that ever. I will save this baby, she told herself, I will. And he will amount to something, she added optimistically.

CHAPTER TWO

Trouble!

Ann was to remember those words time and time again as she struggled to succeed in the challenge she set for herself. It would not be easy. The first obstacle she had to overcome was getting the foal to accept the bottle.

When Jock rushed in, breathless, a bottle of colostrum in his hands, the black colt was still trying to rise on unsteady legs. He had just about succeeded in standing when the sudden appearance of a new person, coupled with the banging of the stall door, surprised him and down he went yet again.

"Here," Jock handed her the bottle, "I got all I could. Hope it's enough," he added.

"It better be," Ann took it gratefully, her attention returning to the foal, still lying in an awkward heap. "Easy, boy," she coaxed. "Come on. You can stand. Try again. Look what Jock brought for you." As she gently kept up a soft, soothing chatter, once more the baby struggled to his feet. This time he held his precarious stance as Ann steadied him with her arm around his body. Slowly she pried open the side of his mouth and slid the bottle in, tilting it as Scotty had taught her. She carefully squeezed a bit of milk onto his tongue. When he didn't swallow right away she tried tickling his throat, but still he refused to cooperate.

Not undaunted, Ann tried raising his head to allow the life-giving liquid to flow down his throat, but it only trickled down the side of his mouth instead. Knocked from his shaky balance, the foal took a step backward and went down once more.

Frustrated, Ann turned to Scotty, who'd just come in, a questioning look on her face.

"Don't bother getting him up again," he advised. "That will come later when he has more strength. The important thing is to get as much of that colostrum into him as you can. Let's try something else. It may be the taste of the rubber nipple he doesn't like. It's not like a mare's. Try putting some on your fingers and rubbing them against his lips. Sometimes that works."

"Okay, Scotty," Ann agreed, dipping her fingers in the milk and rubbing them across the foal's lips. At first he refused to open his mouth, but she persisted with soft, gentle touches until he finally moved his lips reluctantly. Ever so slightly the pink tongue snaked out curiously as she hastened to dab more of the white liquid on it. It was almost comical, if it hadn't been so critical, to watch his face as he rolled his tongue around his mouth as though deciding if he liked the taste or not. Eventually she guessed he did, for he opened his mouth for more. Ann was quick to give him what he wanted as he pulled against her fingers.

"Hey, greedy, not so fast," she laughed in relief. "Scotty, Jock, I think he's catching on," she spoke, excitedly.

Scotty nodded encouragement. "Now as you're offering him your fingers, try to slip in the bottle, too. See if he changes over."

It was easier than she thought; for once the foal caught on to the fact that he liked the taste, instinct took over. The urge to nurse, built into all newborns, helped him switch over to the nipple once he realized it, too, would give him the nourishment he craved. And faster, too. Eagerly he began to pull the vital milk into his throat.

"Hold it higher," Scotty advised, growing as excited as Ann at the results. "Just like he was getting it from his mother. It's more natural that way."

17

Ann did and the foal responded even faster. In no time he had finished the bottle. "I believe he wants more," she said, pulling the now empty bottle away as he followed her, stretching his neck as far as he could.

"I'm afraid he'll have to wait a bit. Your mom's making up some formula now, but I doubt it's ready yet."

"Perhaps he'll he strong enough now to try standing again."

"Especially with the colostrum in him," Jock reflected.

"You're right, son. Nothing can quite replace the value of the first milk in saving a foal. We're mighty grateful to you and Michael for getting what you could."

Before Jock could acknowledge his father, there was a flurry of movement, as the foal scrambled to rise. Stronger now that he'd had his first meal, he quickly stood, four legs spread for balance, but as he took his first step, he lost that balance and collapsed, only to rise again, this time with more confidence. Several more tries, each one stronger than the last, and finally he was able to make it across the stall to where Ann was now standing, watching with baited breath. The miracle of birth was something none of them ever tired of witnessing. Hardly an hour old, and this baby was on his way.

When the colt reached her, he immediately began nuzzling her for food. "Look, Scotty," she laughed, excitedly. "He thinks I'm his mother." She stroked the soft muzzle, adding, "Hang on little one. Mom will be here soon with more goodies for you."

Hardly were the words out of her mouth when her mother did appear, pulling a bottle from beneath her wet trench coat. "Just in time, I see," she panted, handing the new bottle to her daughter. "Well, you've got him up and on his feet. That's a good sign," Jessica observed from experience borne of a lifetime spent around horses.

"Yes, Mom, he's doing quite well, in fact," Ann told her as she offered the new bottle. Immediately, the foal began sucking, hesitating only slightly when he realized the taste was a bit different than the mare's milk he'd downed earlier. But hunger took over and soon he was greedily consuming this milk, also.

During this Ann brought her mother up to date on their progress so far.

"And what of Glory?" she then asked softly. Ann's face was a mask of pain. She only shook her head.

Scotty answered for her. "I've done what I could for her, but she was too weak from loss of blood. I doubt she'll last the night. Michael's with her."

Jessica nodded sadly. Knowing the colt's needs were being met, she moved quietly down the hall to slip silently into Glory's stall where she came up beside her husband and placed her hand on his shoulder. He looked up at her and, though neither spoke a word, the look that passed between them spoke volumes.

So much sorrow, Jessica thought, as she knelt down next to Michael and watched the mare, her tortured breathing marking the end was near. Her eyes glazed, Glory was beyond pain now.

"Perhaps, if the vet -" she heard Michael whisper.

"No, Michael. There's nothing even he could have done. Scotty's as good as any vet. You know that. Why, I doubt even the clinic could have saved her, had we been able to get her there. We've done all anyone—It was just not meant to be," she finished lamely, holding him as she would a small child.

Michael only stared blindly at the mare. "Why?" he moaned, though not expecting an answer. Tears ran unashamedly down his face.

Jessica only sat beside him in silence. In her thoughts, too, she was asking 'why?' as she watched her husband's dreams dying with the mare. It's not fair, she thought angrily. He's tried so hard to succeed, to bring the farm back to what it once was, back when his grandfather was alive, before Michael's father nearly bankrupted them. And now this had to happen. Was there nothing left? She, too, knew with the realism and experience of adulthood, what little chance they had with the newborn colt, even if they were to save him.

Her mind raced back in time as she remembered the first day she came to the farm, an eager young bride of twenty, bursting with happiness, anxious to start her new life with her handsome husband. Michael had missed the war, being called up and in training when peace was declared only days from his orders to ship out. He had met Jessica while stationed in Maryland. She had come from a fine moneyed family nearby and they were drawn together by their mutual backgrounds. Jessica's family was against a hasty marriage, but was unable to prevent them from eloping. This caused a split from her family that had never quite been bridged. Yet in spite of the often-turbulent years to follow, Jessica never regretted her decision to marry Michael. She was still as in love with him as she'd ever been.

And they had been hard years. Little did Michael realize, upon returning to his home with his new bride, how swiftly his life would change.

The family home was a huge horse farm located right in the heart of the Kentucky Bluegrass Region, outside of Lexington. It had been in the Collins family for five generations.

The first Collins had settled there in the days following the Revolutionary War. At the time of the Civil War old Colonel Collins and his four sons owned it. They were split between loyalties to the North and to the South, causing brother to fight brother, father against son, until when the war was finally over, only the youngest, Sean, was alive to carry on the farm, now a mere shell of its former grandeur.

Sean was just twenty-one when he returned from the war to rebuild his home. Together with his new wife, he set about doing just that. A son, Sean Jr., joined them a scant year later, much to Sean's delight, for he wanted very much to have an heir to whom to leave his empire. However, the war had left its toll on Sean, who disillusioned and suffering from failing health, did not live to see the fruits of his efforts.

Sean Jr. was eighteen when he inherited the Collins farm. Nurtured by his father's dreams, he was to carry out those plans and turn the farm into one of the finest showplaces in the Bluegrass Region by the turn of the century. He had a natural skill in breeding Thoroughbreds. With his expertise many fine-blooded horses were to run and win under the blue and gray colors of the farm, colors that Sean had chosen in memory of his heritage.

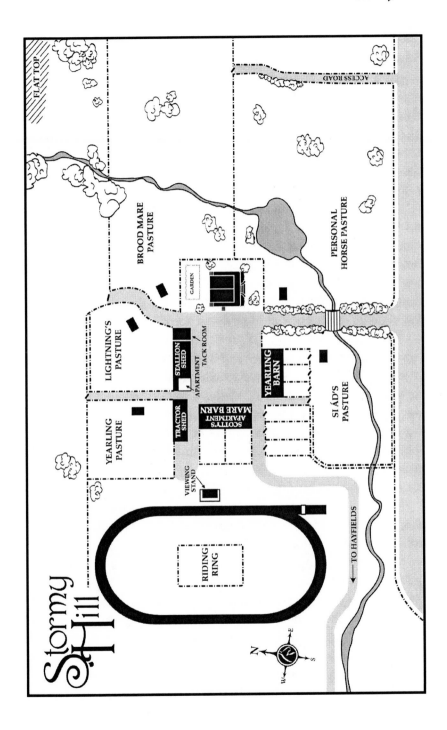

The Collins line culminated in the great Stormy Hill, who, though he failed to win the Kentucky Derby, still sustained a lengthy, successful career. Stormy Hill so altered the farm's acceptance as a racing power and more directly as a breeding force, that the farm was renamed after him. Though Stormy Hill rose to its greatest heights during this era, Sean's fondest desire, that of winning the Kentucky Derby, was never realized, for though Stormy Hill was to be a prepotent sire as well, his progeny would never win that race either.

Sean's only son, Harris, was to be an even bigger disappointment to him. Harris lacked his father's interest in horses. Nor did he have the drive his father had. He was a lazy, indulgent boy, content to live off his father's self-made fortune, preferring his fast cars, gambling and a playboy style of living. He cared nothing for learning the workings of the farm that had provided so much of the money he now spent so freely.

Though Harris proved a great frustration to his father, Sean lived long enough to see the birth of his two grandsons, Mark and Michael. While Mark seemed to take after his father, showing little or no interest in the farm, Michael, ten years younger, became the joy of Sean's later years. The boy adored his grandfather and was often seen toddling after him as he went about his business on the farm. Patiently the old man explained all about horses to his worshipping shadow, holding him up to stroke their soft, velvety muzzles. They were a familiar sight around Stormy Hill.

Sadly, Sean was not to see his favorite grandson grow up. He died when the boy was but seven years old, a wealthy, successful, but an unfulfilled man. Michael was devastated.

After that things changed drastically. Harris Collins was only to run the farm less than fifteen years, yet in that time he would destroy nearly all that his father and grandfather had built. Through his inept hands the money fast disappeared, spent on his gambling debts and a series of faster and faster cars. It was the latter that proved his undoing. When he and his wife died in a disastrous auto accident, he left behind a farm full of debts.

Of his two sons, Mark, like his father, had no interest in raising horses. At the time of his parents' deaths, he was already living contentedly in Chicago with no intention of returning to Kentucky. Michael, who'd just returned with his bride scant months before, was welcome to it.

And so to Michael fell the task of restoring the Stormy Hill he'd remembered and loved from his past. Having reached the early promise his grandfather had seen in him, he had not only the love of fine Thoroughbreds, but also the skill to go with it. For years he'd seen the systematic destruction by his father of all he loved and his heart had cried out against the injustice of it. Now it was his.

Sensible and mature beyond his years, he made a decision that was to change Stormy Hill's future irrevocably. With Jessica's willing consent, he gave up their life of false grandeur and set about to pay off the debts his father had incurred over the years.

In order to clear those enormous debts, he and Jessica came to several conclusions. They realized all the help must go and much of the land would have to be sold, along with all but the most valuable of the horses. It was a hard, painful option but after much debate, they both admitted it was the only way to keep Stormy Hill off the auction block.

Michael then became the first Collins in five generations to go to work off the farm. He opened up a grain and saddlery shop in town to help defray the costs of operating the farm.

The parcel of land, several hundred acres, that was sold off, was bought by the newly rich Ralph Garrison, who set out to build one of the finest showplaces in the Bluegrass Region. Complete with just about everything a successful breeding and racing farm could possibly need, Garrison and his farm still failed to buy the respect of the long-time residents of the area. The other farm owners looked down upon his gaudy, garish home. He would never fit in, nor gain the much-desired acceptance that folks like the Collinses took for granted. To others their misfortunes were considered only temporary. Michael was a highly respected horse breeder. Stormy Hill had been in existence more than one hundred fifty years, its owners fifth generation Kentuckians. The Collinses, poor or not, belonged.

While the remaining acres left Stormy Hill only a modest farm now, there was plenty of pasturage to support the many horses they currently owned. But Michael saw the need to cut back to only the most irreplaceable ones to continue his breeding program. Besides he could no longer afford the help to care for such a large herd.

The Stormy Hill Stock Reduction Sale became the most well attended sale of the year, vying even the famous Keeneland sales in its quality, as well as its attendance. Stormy Hill bloodlines had been known for years among the racing community. Sean's expertise as a horse breeder was legendary. And even though Harris had been at the helm for nearly fifteen years, all the horsemen around knew that the breeding decisions had continued to be made after Sean's death by his right-hand man, a tough, wiry little Scotsman by the name of Angus McDougal. He in turn had passed his knowledge onto his son, known to all as Scotty.

Michael had consulted with his friend, Scotty, about each and every horse that was put up for sale. For hours they had poured through pedigrees, records, and notes on each and every horse on the farm, Michael, as always, deferring to Scotty's judgment for the final decision. With the few they kept, Scotty assured him they would be able to rebuild one day.

The sale horses brought good prices, as many breeders coveted the Stormy Hill bloodlines, noted for their speed as well as stamina, especially the mares that had the reputation for being consistent producers. Michael should have been proud of his standing in a community to whom horses were everything, but all he was conscious of was a strong feeling of sadness. An era was over. Would it ever come again?

Jessica remembered that day well for when the gavel fell on the last horse, she ran, coward that she was, to the seclusion of the upstairs study. There, hidden from everyone, especially her husband, she bawled inconsolably, her brave front abandoned. She cried for the anguish she knew was in her husband's heart, in spite of his outward appearance. She also cried for the fears she dared not exhibit in his presence, and, too, the life of comfort they had always known that they must now leave behind.

And finally, she cried for the unborn child whom she had yet to tell Michael she carried, for she knew not what the future might hold for them.

When she could cry no more, she rose dry-eyed and visibly shook herself. It is done, she told herself, and now I must be strong for Michael, for the farm, and most of all, for this child I carry. From that day on she never gave Michael any indication that she was anything but supportive toward his decisions concerning the farm or their future. He was never to know about what she thought of as a weakness in her character.

But the day turned out to have one bright note. With the sale over and the horses gone, there was no reason Scotty should stay on, Michael told him. He had not reckoned with Scotty's obstinacy. Scotty's father had been head trainer during much of the glory years of Stormy Hill, due mostly to his expertise in management. Scotty had spent every free moment growing up, at his father's side, learning all he could absorb. He had seen and handled such greats as Stormy Hill and his famous sons, Stormson and Storm Warning. Like a sponge he soaked up all he could from his father who was only too delighted to pass on his knowledge to his only son. When his father died, it was only natural that he would take over as head manager in his stead. Now he had a motherless son not quite two years to raise. This was his home and he was staying, regardless of the incontrovertible truth that there was no money for his services. Stormy Hill was the only home he'd ever known. He would stay. Besides Michael needed him. He still had other horses to care for and breed.

It was decided that he would work part-time at Garrisons place, but Stormy Hill was his home. He and his son would continue to live in the apartment above the broodmare barn, while Jessica would help raise the baby, Jock, along with her own baby. Michael could not put into words his sincere gratitude to his friend. Losing Scotty would have been an insurmountable blow. He had never realized how much he'd come to depend upon him until the moment he'd asked to stay on.

Soon Michael was deferring all major decisions involving the horses to Scotty. He often wondered how he ever would have managed without him. Although ten years his senior, Scotty would become his best and closest friend, even as their two children, Jock and Ann, born soon after, would grow up together as close as any brother and sister could have been. Living as isolated as they were out on the farm, it was good they had one another as childhood playmates, for unfortunately Jessica was unable to have any more children.

As the years went by, Jessica watched the two grow up, glad for the joyous sounds of youth, for the farm had not prospered as well as they hoped it would. A series of setbacks always seemed to plague them so that they never quite got ahead. So many things had gone wrong, mares who missed or lost their foals, freak accidents, injuries on the track that stopped a promising career, equipment that got old and worn out, its replacement costing more than they could spare, droughts or severe storms. Whatever, it always held them back one more year.

But there had been some good memories over the years, too. Races won, a good profit at the yearling sales, bumper hay crops and most of all the birth of the promising near-black filly on which Michael set such high hopes that he named her Dawn of Glory. In her veins flowed the blood of champions. Her breeding had been so carefully planned. Stormy Hill, himself, was her paternal grandsire. Even when a race injury prevented her further career, Michael saw it as merely a minor delay. Immediately he made plans to put her to the best stud he could locate.

Finding Si'ad was an omen. One look at the stallion and he knew it was meant to be. When she caught on the first cover, Michael knew he'd been right. For this he'd waited so long. This would be the foal to turn their luck around. Everything had gone smoothly until tonight.

From the moment Glory had gone into premature labor, throughout the long desperate night, Michael had begun to believe his dreams were not to be answered yet again. And now it was over, Jessica suddenly realized, shaking herself back to reality, another loss to overcome. She saw by her husband's sagging shoulders and bowed head that he saw it, too. Could he recover from this latest blow to the farm?

Outside the storm was abating as the dawn struggled to break in the east. Realizing how exhausted they all were, Jessica tried to coax Michael to return to the house and get some sleep. Though he argued with her, he finally relented when she convinced him that Scotty would take care of the mare's burial later that day. Relieved, Michael knew he really wasn't capable of handling that gruesome chore. With a final pat on the neck of the mare that had meant so much to him he reluctantly left the stall with his wife. On the way back to the house, Jessica became aware that he had not even asked after her foal.

CHAPTER THREE

Decisions

Ann, unaware of the passing of Glory, was too busy discovering a new life just starting. By the time the young colt had completed the second bottle, he had caught on quite well. Ann let him drink until he was satisfied, then watched as he lay down in the fresh straw to sleep.

"He should be all right for a couple of hours now," Scotty whispered, yawning himself. "Why don't you try to get some sleep yourself? You must be exhausted."

"And leave him?" she complained. "No, it'll be fine if I just lay down here beside him and sleep. Then if he wakes up hungry I'll know right away. Mom left some extra bottles I can heat up on the hot plate in the feed room."

"That doesn't sound very restful," Scotty remarked.

"Really, I'll be fine. You and Jock look beat," Jock was nearly asleep on his feet, she noticed. "You can come and relieve me later."

"If you're sure. We'll only be right upstairs. Call if you need us..." Scotty was half out the stall door, looking reluctant still, tired as he was.

"Please, just go," she laughed softly, laying down beside the sleeping baby. "Lightning and I will be just fine."

"Lightning, is it?" Scotty murmured, smiling. "You've named him already?"

Ann replied, "The name just came to me as I was feeding him. See his funny, crooked blaze. Doesn't it remind you of a streak of lightning?" She yawned, barely able to keep her eyes open, now that the tension was over.

"Okay, well I guess you really don't need us then. You and, uh—Lightning get some rest." But his words fell on deaf ears. Ann was already asleep, beside the foal, one arm draped across his neck.

Ann was awakened later that morning by the soft exhaled breath of a dark muzzle as the colt nuzzled her cheek. She rubbed his forehead affectionately. "Suppose you want me to get up and get your meal, huh, fella?" she murmured, rising. The colt tried to follow her out of the stall but she gently held him back. "I'll be right back with your food," she told him, aware of how much stronger on his feet he was this morning after food and rest.

As she hurried down the hall, she heard his whinny, a funny little high-pitched squeal. In the feed room she found a bottle in the small refrigerator and began to heat it up on the hot plate kept for such emergencies. When the milk was warm enough, she hastened back to the stall where an impatient foal awaited her.

"Here you go, you little pig," she laughed as, without hesitation, he grabbed hold of the nipple and began to drink.

As he gained nourishment, Ann observed him, lost in thought. She had seen dozens of foals born over the years on the farm and knew what to look for. Already she could see he was perfectly formed. His long legs were straight, toes pointed neither in or out but forward and true. Pasterns sloping yet strong, there would be plenty of spring there to later absorb the pounding a running horse must be able to take.

His neck was long and nicely arched, flowing into a well-laid back shoulder. The back was short and arched up over a slightly higher rear that rounded out in a gentle slope to the hindquarters. Later this would muscle out and provide the drive needed to carry him great distances.

29

His brisket and chest were deep and well rounded, essential for heart and lung room. Every part of his body was as near perfect as any she ever seen, but the head was her favorite. Huge liquid, dark eyes with such long lashes were set in a wide skull topped by small, pointed mobile ears. The somewhat dished face, a characteristic coming from his Arabian sire, tapered down to a muzzle so dainty she could hold it in the palm of her hand. The whole picture was completed by the unusual blaze. She hoped it was an omen.

Deep in her heart, Ann felt that this was the foal that they'd been breeding for. Still she wondered if the others would see it, too, or be hopelessly colored by the loss of Glory.

Glory! Suddenly she realized she had not given the mare a thought since they had brought Lightning to this stall. Surely by now—but, no, she would not think about endings. That was behind them. Only beginnings now.

The colt, Lightning, had finished his bottle, and contented, stomach full, laid back down in the fresh straw and fallen asleep. Ann, still tired herself, curled up beside him, one arm protectively across his back.

She suffered no false illusions when it came to this colt, albeit perhaps the forgivable high intensity of youth. She had grown up around Thoroughbreds all her life. She had seen many a promising youngster fade in the harsh reality of the track. Scotty and her dad had been good teachers, teaching Jock and her what to look for in a potential winner. Avidly they had absorbed every bit of knowledge they could.

Lying beside Lightning, she let her mind wander back in time, thinking over her life growing up. Unlike most of the other farm kids, she and Jock attended public school. Living out of town and being needed at home so much, they never developed strong friendships with their classmates. Instead they had each other, growing up as brother and sister. They loved the farm, not minding the isolation at all, sharing in its successes and failures. And in the never-ending workload, cleaning stalls by the time they could yield a pitchfork, mending fences, operating the manure spreader and other farm machinery, dressing wounds, stacking hay, these and other chores were all part of their days.

Of necessity, Michael spent the majority of his day with the feed store, which left them short-handed on manpower. Ann and Jock, as they grew older, had had to take over some of the burden of the farm.

Yet there were many chores that to them were not work at all, socializing and halter breaking the foals, preparing the yearlings for the sales, breaking and training youngsters that were kept, and foaling season.

Ann had ridden from babyhood, first on her own pony then graduating to full-size horses. Early on she had begun helping break yearlings and by the time she was twelve Scotty had begun using her to exercise their colts in training. Not only did she weigh practically nothing, an essential to young horses, but she also had natural balance and quiet hands and was able to get the most out of her mounts without a fight. She could maintain the exact speed Scotty requested, from a gallop to a breeze. It was too bad girls couldn't be jockeys, Scotty had remarked more than once, for Ann might have been a good one.

It was this very same issue that had caused the only real split between her and Jock, not withstanding the usual scraps all natural siblings go through while growing up. Still, their friendship had always prevailed until a gelding named Tag-along went to the track.

This Storm-along son had always been a favorite of Jock's, especially after an injury kept him from the yearling sales, and Scotty had decided to race him after all. At first he did not show much promise and being a plain brown, rather homely horse, he was gelded and left home a year. For a while Michael thought he might have to sell him but when he turned three, he blossomed. Jock had done all the schooling on him and begged his father to let him ride. Scotty agreed, seeing the potential in the pair.

How upset Ann had been, ranting and raving about the unfairness that allowed boys to ride and not girls. Of course she was jealous of Jock's luck. It took her a while to accept the

31

inevitable, but when Jock and Tag began to win races, she did come around. While he did not burn up the track, he did win a couple of respectable races, even a stakes or two. By then Ann was genuine in her feelings of happiness for her dearest friend, though she still resented the fact that she herself could not ride.

Tag only ran two seasons when an injury caused his retirement. Since Jock had no other horses to ride, he was temporarily sidelined. However, a sudden growth spurt put him beyond racing weight anyway. Still, Jock felt no regrets. His moments with Tag had been good ones, ones he'd remember the rest of his life.

One of the nicest things to come out of Tag's winnings was that when Si'ad became available to them, they had been able to pay the purchase price.

A head poked over the stall door, "Sun's out. No more storm. Want to go for a ride?" It was as if thinking of Jock had made him appear.

"Do I? You have to ask?" she smiled up at him, getting to her feet. "I think he can do without me for a little while. I do feel the need to stretch my legs and I'm sure Si'ad would like the exercise." Just the thought of him made her long to take him out for a run. She could almost feel his tense coiled power ready to explode into flight when she gave him the word. She looked down at his sleeping son. Yes, Lightning should be fine for another hour or so. A ride was just what she needed. As she slipped out of the stall, the colt never stirred.

As she passed by the birthing stall, she glanced briefly in, seeing Glory's still form. A questioning look to Jock only confirmed what she already guessed as he shook his head.

"Poor Dad," she sighed. "He must be heartbroken. He put such hopes in her." She turned away and hastened to follow Jock toward the barn door.

"I know he did," Jock was saying. "What a tough break."

"At least we saved her foal."

"Don't think that'll matter to him, at least for a while. First he'll have to get over his loss."

"But the colt, he's so beautiful-"

"I agree. He is a gorgeous baby. And I think Michael will see it, too. Just give him time." He stopped outside the tack room door. "Hey, cheer up. Come on. Let's go riding."

Ann nodded, smiling. She grabbed her bridle from its peg and ran for the stallion barn. Skidding to a halt in front of Si'ad's stall, she opened the door and stepped in, reaching for the head that turned toward her. A soft whinny greeted her and she stroked his velvet soft muzzle with one hand and rubbed his neck under the thick mane with the other.

"You have a son," she told him. "A feisty, strong young fellow who will grow up just like his father. I've named him Lightning and you should be very proud of him." She spoke as if he understood, though it was more the sound of her voice to which he responded. As she spoke she slid the bridle over his head and led him out to the courtyard. The stallion stepped out briskly, eager to be off, anticipating the ride to come. Once outside, she grabbed a hunk of mane and swung lightly up on his bare back. Jock was not far behind her and together they turned their horses toward the lane that led out to the back fields.

The storm of the night before had passed leaving behind a lovely, crisp, breezy day, not too cold, perfect for riding. They both felt revived in spite of their lack of sleep. For a while they rode along in companionable silence, each lost in thoughts and dreams.

Si'ad felt like a coiled spring. His muscles rippled beneath her legs as she bade him to stay at a walk. Crow hopping and shaking his head so that his long mane sprayed out in a silver shower, the stallion could barely contain himself.

"Not yet," she murmured. "You must stretch your legs and warm up first before you can run." She was as keyed up as he, though and just as eager to fly. Looking over at Jock and Tag, she saw that they felt it, too.

As the gate at the end of the lane came in sight, Ann finally relaxed her light hold on the stallion's mouth. Si'ad sprang forward as Ann grabbed a handful of mane to steady herself.

33

Reins were useless now. Already Si'ad was in full gallop as he sailed over the gate so smoothly it was as if there had been no four-foot obstacle in their way. Ann barely moved on his back as she became one with her horse. Behind her, Jock and Tag also cleared the gate, though not quite as handily, as they strove to keep a respectable distance between them before Si'ad's ground-eating stride left them in his wake.

On the other side of the gate lay the huge back pasture, a rolling land, which gradually led up to a flat peak at the far end. Between lay several erratic stretches of woods, at least one gully and a quiet, slow-moving creek. Its natural riding terrain made it a popular place to ride their horses.

Ann let Si'ad have his head, enjoying the feel of the wind whipping mane back in her face and tossing her own long black hair straight out behind her. The stallion ran on smoothly, without effort. They cut through the part of the woods where a well-worn path opened up before them, Si'ad never slowing his wild, ground-eating stride. Jock and Tag were now barely visible behind them.

As they turned a bend, Ann saw a tree had fallen across the path, probably a casualty of last night's storm. Si'ad never faltered, skimming over the lowest part as if it wasn't there.

Bursting from the trees to open land once again, Ann began to ask Si'ad to slow so Jock could catch up. Still they were nearly to the creek that lay in the middle of the field before the grey stallion settled into a walk. He was scarcely breathing hard, his coat only slightly damp. Tag, on the contrary, when he caught up with them, was blowing quite hard. By tacit agreement they both walked their horses for a while, letting them cool down.

The path they were on began to climb up a rise leading to a large flat bare area named aptly 'Flat Top,' for it was, in addition to being flat, also the highest terrace for miles around and offered a spectacular view of the surrounding area. Once at the top they jumped off their horses and let them take a few bites of the lush thick grass that grew there, while they enjoyed their favorite spot. Neither Jock nor Ann ever tired of coming up here to gaze at some of the prettiest country in all of Kentucky. All around them sprawled other horse farms, green seas of grass carefully tended and contained by miles and miles of four-plank fencing, either painted white or creosoted, yet all beautifully maintained. Here and there were clusters of barns, often painted in the farm's colors to set them apart from the rest. A clump of tall shade trees might hide the main house from view, but Ann, who'd been in many of them, could visualize their luxurious environs. More interesting to them were the dark dots that moved within those pastures. Love of horses was not limited to their own.

Remembering her own horse, Ann ran her hands along his neck and under his brisket, noting satisfactorily that he was just about dry. Si'ad was in great shape, she thought, walking slowly about in a random circle to keep him moving.

"I've named him Lightning, you know," she spoke up suddenly, breaking their silence.

"Who? Oh, you mean the foal?" Jock looked up, his own thoughts broken as he grasped what Ann was saying. "Do you think that's wise? I mean, suppose something were to happen to him? It's kind of too early to know for sure," he finished lamely, not wanting to upset Ann.

"I don't see where a name should make a difference."

"Sure, it does. You get more attached to something when it has a name."

Ann laughed, "Oh, Jock. I can't imagine being less attached to the little fellow, can you? Besides, we're not going to lose him. He's so strong and determined. I just know he's going to be a good one. That's why I named him Lightning."

Jock caught her enthusiasm. "Because you want him to run fast?" he asked.

"That, of course. But also because of his funny crooked blaze. It's the only white on him and it reminds me of a streak of lightning. Besides he was born in a storm. And there's always the tradition of Stormy Hill, his great grandfather."

"Yes, I guess with all those things going for him, 'Lightning' is just about perfect."

"So you see, we just have to save him. I know he's going to be a good one for us. With his breeding and conformation, he has to be." She was rubbing the side of the stallion's head absently, but when Si'ad nickered softly, she took that as an omen. "See, Si'ad agrees."

Jock smiled, "Well, then it must be so," he said.

"And speaking of Lightning, he's probably awake by now and wanting his next meal. We better be getting back." Putting her words to practice, she swung back up on the grey, followed quickly by Jock on Tag, and they headed back down the trail. This time she only permitted him a light canter on the way back.

As they approached the gate leading to the lane behind the house, she reached down and opened it instead of jumping it. Jock closed it after her. Off in the distance they heard the sound of the backhoe. Looking in that direction, they saw Scotty. He was taking care of the gruesome task of burying Glory before Michael got up. They both turned away.

Off in the other direction grazed the remaining mares, three now, all heavy in foal, though none were due for another six weeks or more. Two of the three bore Stormy Hill blood, not of the quality they had lost with Glory, but capable of producing foals that should command a decent price as yearlings. Their current yearling crop grazed in an adjoining field.

Upon reaching the courtyard, Ann and Jock leaped off their horses, now completely cooled out, and turned them loose in their respective fields. Ann had barely reached the barn door when she heard the plaintive cry of a very hungry colt. By the time they arrived, Lightning had worked himself into quite a fit of temper, his needs not having been met.

Ann sighed, as Jock went to heat up a bottle. "My, aren't we the demanding one," she laughed. "You'll just have to wait, though. It isn't quite ready yet." She stepped inside as the baby rushed up, pushing against her, eager for his food. She could hardly fend him off before Jock got back with a warm bottle, which he ravenously took into his mouth, sucking greedily.

"He thinks you're his mother," Jock commented, grinning.

"I guess so. He sure is hungry now. Look at him pull the milk down. One bottle's not going to be enough."

"Then I'll just go and get another one made up. Won't take but a minute." Jock left to take care of it.

Before he came back, Scotty appeared to check on the foal's progress. He looked tired. She knew he had not slept much either.

"How's our young fellow today?" he asked, showing a real interest in the colt's progress. "Looks like there's nothing wrong with his appetite. That's a good sign."

"Can't keep the milk coming fast enough," she smiled, as he pulled down the last of the bottle. "Jock went to heat up some more for this greedy pig." Lightning pushed against her as he realized the bottle was empty and he was still hungry.

"So I see," Scotty observed. "Jock better get here soon."

"Here I am," Jock came into the stall, panting.

"And not a moment too soon. Thank you." Ann took the bottle from him and offered it to Lightning who took it immediately.

They all watched him drink, each pleased with the results of their efforts. For it indeed looked hopeful for saving him at this point. After a while Scotty spoke up, "Ann, you've done a fine job with this youngster. Though it's too early to predict, I think we've overcome the worst hurdle, getting him to eat. I'll get Doc out as soon as he can to check the vital signs, but baring anything unforeseen, we just might save this foal yet."

"Oh, I know we will," she confirmed happily. "See how strong he is already? He's going to be just fine. I'm sure of it."

"Let's hope you're right," Scotty was still unwilling to commit himself all the way. "Meanwhile, Ann, I think you should go to bed and get some real sleep. You look exhausted and I'm sure Jock and I can handle the next feeding for you."

"But-"

"No, buts. You look dead on your feet, lass."

"Dad's right, Ann. We can take care of his next feeding. You really look done in," Jock said.

Between them they finally convinced her to go lie down and at least take a nap. Ann thought she would to be unable to sleep, given all the excitement of the past twenty-four hours, but as she passed through the large kitchen to her room at the other end, she realized just how tired she was. She flopped down across one of the twin beds sandwiched into the little room and was asleep before she had her clothes off.

It was mid-afternoon when she awoke. Following a quick shower and a change of clothes, she headed back out to the barn, feeling much refreshed. She could hear Lightning fussing before she got to the stall. As she opened the door she told him, "What's the matter, Lightning? Didn't Scotty and Jock feed you enough?" Then she saw that they were both already there, in the stall, Scotty holding the bottle, a grave look on his face. Jock was trying to hold a very stubborn, recalcitrant youngster.

"I wish that was our only problem," Scotty said, grimly, as Ann entered. "We've been trying just to get him to take it. He won't have anything to do with either of us, no matter what we do."

"And we know he's hungry," Jock added.

"You mean he hasn't been fed since I fed him this morning?" Jock shook his head. "Why, that was hours ago." She looked distressed. "Here let me try. He can't go so long between feedings, can he, Scotty?"

"It's not good, but…" he stopped as they all watched the colt fairly lunge to take the bottle from Ann's hands, so hungry was he. "Well, I'll be," Scotty exclaimed in wonder. "I thought I'd seen everything, but this is one for the books. Seems we've been had, son, and by a mere slip of a girl yet." But he was smiling as he said it. He was well aware of Ann's way with horses. Hadn't she gentled the half-wild Si'ad?

"Awfully fickle, for a newborn, isn't he?" Jock remarked. "Guess you'll just have to be in charge of feeding him from now on."

"Oh, I won't mind," she countered.

"You will when you have to get up every two hours to feed him. You'll get pretty tired after awhile," he teased.

"What other choice do we have?" Ann asked. "It won't be a problem. I can stay right here in his stall so I'll be sure to hear him when he gets hungry."

"I'm sure your mother will approve of that," Scotty scoffed.

"Why not? It won't be for that long."

"Well, for starters you and Jock have to go back to school next week. That's only three days away."

"Don't remind us," they both groaned simultaneously.

"Still you can't stay home and miss school just to feed a foal. But," on seeing their faces, he amended, "We'll cross that bridge when we come to it. Hopefully by then he'll be accepting it from one of us. In the meantime, if we're going to try and save this foal at all, I guess it's up to you, Ann."

"I'll do my best, Scotty," she replied, looking down at the foal that, stomach satisfied, had lain down in the deep straw to take a nap. "I've got a good feeling that he's going to be just fine, though." She looked over at Scotty and caught his skeptical expression, a sudden insight causing her to know what he was thinking. "I know you and Dad don't think orphans can amount to much, but, I believe this time, this one is different-"

"I'd like to think so, but unfortunately we gotta look at the practical side, too." Scotty was torn between his love for Ann, wanting to protect her from reality, which could often be cruel, and the need to confront her with the odds of what she was trying to do. For him honesty won out. "Ann, lass, you're going to spend a lot of time and energy trying to save this colt who in the end may be nothing more than a fancy pet. I mean, look at the odds of normal foals making it to the track. Ann, I don't have to tell you. You've grown up on this farm. You know how it is."

"Yes," she said softly, looking at the sleeping colt with such naked love that it scared Scotty, "I know all that, but, well, couldn't this time be the one?" She looked at him for understanding.

"I can see what's happening to you," he sympathized. "You've already fallen in love with this foal and you think you can will him into something he may or may not be. It's hard to see reality when your heart's in the way."

"You're right, Scotty. I'm trying to be objective but I keep having this strong feeling that this time will be different for us." She reached out and stroked the sleeping colt under his fuzzy mane. "Didn't you ever have that feeling?"

Scotty smiled. "Once or twice, when I'd see a particularly good one born here," he reflected. "And some of these hunches turned out. But of course they were older youngsters. Ann, remember it's my job to select the ones who will give us the best chance as racehorses. That doesn't leave much room for sentiment."

"But, look at him, Scotty, really look at him. Have you ever seen a more perfect foal born on this farm?"

Scotty once again tried to see the foal from Ann's eyes; after all she did have an eye for a horse and a natural talent around them. And he had to admit, even to himself, this was an awfully nice baby. "Okay, I can agree with you that he's a finely built foal. But-" he added as he saw the look of triumph cross her face, "he's a long way from being a winner. We're not even sure we can save him yet. And if we do, he may end up just another riding horse to be gelded and kept around here as an extra mouth to feed." Seeing Ann's stricken face, he added, "Oh, what the heck. What's one more horse? It's not like we don't have the room. We've already got Jock's Tag and your mom's old hunters, Cedardale and Banshee. What's one more?"

"Oh, thank you, Scotty," she hugged him.

Afraid to be seen as too soft, Scotty finished by saying. "Ann, in the interests of this colt, I'll try to be as open as I can. If things go as you hope, I'll give you every aid I can. And that's a promise."

"Thank you," she said humbly. Then she had sobering thought. "But what about Dad? I can't help but feel that he resents Lightning, like he's responsible for the loss of Glory."

"Right now your dad's hurting. Glory was very special to him. He might indirectly blame the colt, but I think he'll come around eventually. Then he'll be mighty glad to have him to remember her by. You'll see," he said with more conviction than he felt.

It was enough for Ann. When Jock and Scotty left to do other chores, she sat back next to the sleeping Lightning, feeling grateful that whatever the future held, Scotty would be on her side. And maybe, just maybe, her father's faith in his mare would be vindicated in her son.

CHAPTER FOUR

Panic!

Still tired from her day's exertions and lack of sleep, Ann lay down beside her colt and slept until he nudged her awake. Automatically she got up, heated his bottles and fed him, falling asleep again before he had quite finished the second one. However by the next time he woke her for his feeding she felt more rested.

"This is it," she told him. "Guess I'll have to go into the house and make some more." But as she started out of the stall, she saw her mother coming down the aisle with more formula.

"Thanks, Mom. You must have read my mind. I was just coming in to make up some more."

Jessica looked at her critically. "Ann, honey, how do you feel?" she asked with a mother's concern, for her daughter's face looked tired and drawn, pale in contrast to her normally healthy tan.

"Oh, I'll be okay. Once I get used to this routine."

But her mother had her doubts. "You really can't go on like this, dear. I know you want to save the foal but not at the risk of your health. You look so tired. You need to come in and sleep in your own bed where you can get some real rest."

"I know, Mom, but this morning when I tried that, Jock and Scotty tried to feed him for me and he refused to accept the bottle from anyone but me. He's totally bonded to me now. He thinks *I'm* his mother. If we have any hope of saving him, I'll have to be the one to feed him." As if to emphasize the fact, Lightning came up and nuzzled against her, snuffling his lips along her arm. Ann scratched along his neck in return. Jessica could not help but see the dependence was already formed.

"I see your point," she agreed. "But if you are to do this then you must get more sleep. The rest of us should be able to help out by taking away some of your responsibilities for now."

"Why, Mom, you've already done your part by making the formula for me. All I have to do is heat it. I don't know what could be more convenient, unless he moved into the kitchen," she finished smiling.

"Go ahead, if you think it will help," Jessica startled Ann by saying.

"Are you serious, Mom?"

Her mother nodded. " If it means my daughter will get more sleep, I am. Honey, I long ago gave up thinking that anything would ever come first in this family before these horses. If it's the only way to save this colt and your health, why not give it a try?"

"Oh, Mom, you're the greatest," she hugged her mother. "But what'll Dad say?"

"He's so upset over Glory that I doubt he'll even notice. Just be prepared for your father's disinterest for a while. He's not ready to accept anything that reminds him of her, so it'll take time. Perhaps this will bring him around faster."

Ann nodded her head. "I understand."

So Lightning was brought in and made comfortable in one corner of the spacious kitchen that ran across the back of the main house, where Ann and her parents lived. Fortunately Ann's room, formerly used as a den, was just off the kitchen, making this very convenient for her to heat up the formula and feed him each time, while allowing her to sleep in her own bed. She'd get more rest this way. As the foal grew his feed times would lengthen, but for now this looked like the only way, short of Ann living in the stable.

A corner of their oversized kitchen was turned over to Lightning each night and for the next two nights Ann only had to get up twice to feed him. It was so much easier for her than before. Her mother rose early to prepare the first morning bottle so that all Ann had to do was get up and give it to him.

The vet had stopped by the day after Lightning was born and pronounced him to be perfectly normal. He agreed with their regimen for him and could see no reason why they would not be able to save this foal, barring anything unforeseen. They were all elated.

As the weekend progressed, each of them tried to feed Lightning but he would only accept the bottle from Ann. By Monday morning there was some concern since Ann had to return to school and he was too young to go all day without eating. As she was giving him his last meal, Michael having offered to run her in so she could leave at the last possible second, she voiced her anxiety.

"He'll come around. Once he gets hungry enough he won't care who gives him the bottle," Michael said. He had shown very little interest in the foal, still grieving as he was for Glory. But at least he did not stand in their way.

"That's what I'm banking on," Ann replied.

But four hours later he still refused to eat from any of them. Scotty and Jock, who had gotten home early that day, tried everything. Lightning appeared hungry but would not eat. Finally, in desperation, Scotty told his son, "Get a couple of freshly warmed up bottles from Jessica. You and I are going to put Mr. Stubborn here in the wagon and take him to school. Ann will just have to come out and feed him herself."

When Jock looked surprised, he added gruffly, "I'd never hear the end of it if anything happened to her colt while he was in my care."

Though he suspected it all along, Jock then knew his father was as concerned for this foal as he and Ann were. Quickly, he helped bundle up the youngster and got him into the old sta-

tion wagon before Scotty changed his mind and thought he was being too soft.

As they drove the several miles to the high school, Scotty told his son, "I suppose he could hold out 'till she got home but that's stretching it a bit much. He could get mighty weak. Then we'd be all night making up for it. This way if we get a mid-day feeding into him we stand a better chance of keeping his strength up, so that he'll gain weight like a normal foal. Besides, he needs to be strong to fight off anything to which he might come in contact."

Jock couldn't agree more.

They pulled into the schoolyard and Jock ran in to have Ann paged. She came out at a run, a look of concern across her face. She had been on her way to lunch when she was contacted, but she had not been told what was wrong. Reaching the car, she gasped, "Is something wrong?" She glanced at Lightning, swathed in blankets behind Scotty.

"Just a case of misplaced bonding," Scotty assured her. "He still won't let us feed him so we brought him to you. Seemed the wisest thing to do under the circumstances," his casual words belying his concern.

Ann immediately took the bottle Jock offered and they all watched him hungrily attack it as though he couldn't drink fast enough.

"Can you beat that?" Jock grinned, relief flooding his face. " What a little stinker."

"After everything we did, too," Scotty added. "Guess this means I've got to run him over here each day so he can have his noon meal. Will that be a problem?"

"Not if you coincide it with my lunch period like today. I'm just sorry you have to come out here, busy as you are."

"Can't be helped. Besides it should only be temporary. As he gets bigger and stronger, he'll be able to go longer between meals. Couple-three weeks should do it. Fortunately things are at their slowest at home right now. Wait till the other foals arrive. Then we'll be plenty busy."

Ann nodded, "When I get home I'll try to pitch in more."

"Forget it. You've got enough to do now. Don't worry, we'll work it out."

"Don't forget, you've got me, too," Jock added.

Scotty smiled gratefully at him. "You go back to your classes now, Ann. I'll pick you up later so you can make his next feed. He should do fine."

Ann reluctantly left them with a final pat for her colt. She knew time would crawl before school let out and all she wanted was to be back home watching over Lightning until he was old enough to take care of himself.

Later that afternoon, Ann had finished feeding the black colt and was sitting beside him, her books spread out before her, when Jock came in and sat down next to her.

"How's it going? You look tired."

"Fine. Oh, I am, a bit. Just wish there were either more hours in the day or more of me to go around."

He smiled, "Let us help. You're trying to do too much. I know you can't be getting enough sleep when you've got to get up a couple of times each night."

She nodded, glad for the sympathy if nothing else. "I'd like that, but I can't. There's always too much work around here regardless of what Scotty says."

"Well, don't take so much of the burden on yourself. We'll make do."

"Perhaps if I stayed home from school the rest of the week…."

"Your folks will never allow that," he smiled.

"Probably not," she conceded, "but honestly, I don't know what good it's doing to be there. I only think about him all day anyway. I can't concentrate on any of my classes."

Jock nodded, "I know. I'd feel the same in your shoes." Then he brightened. "I know what you need. A quick ride before dark. That'll clear your head."

"Of course. Let's go." She jumped up, making for the door, just as her mom came in, arms loaded with groceries.

"Where are you two off to?" she asked, setting the bags down on the table.

"Riding," was Ann's short answer. "See you in a bit." But her words were lost as she was already out the door and halfway across the walkway leading to the drive by then.

Moments later, on Si'ad and Tag, bareback as usual, Ann and Jock headed their horses across the courtyard and up the lane. Si'ad seemed frisky and eager, but this time he was more willing to stay beside the brown gelding. They rode along silently, each absorbed in the rhythm of his horse.

Though well aware of how outclassed Tag was against the superior Si'ad, Jock could think of riding no other horse. Since his late growth spurt had left him too heavy to make jockey weight, he had come to grips with his retirement, realizing he'd likely never enjoy racing other horses as much as he had Tag-along. Now that riding was over and he was in his junior year, he needed to think about what he wanted to do in the future. But there had never really been a doubt in his mind. Being an outstanding trainer like his father had always been his plan anyway. In the meantime he was still lean enough to exercise horses in training, something he enjoyed doing.

Thinking ahead to summer he knew he'd spend part of his time each day exercising horses at the Garrison place next door, as he had the previous summer. His father also put in time over there for extra money, though his work was seasonal as well. Lucky for them he was not working now. This was the best time for Lightning to have come along.

Jock glanced over at Ann, noting the easy, sure way she sat the magnificent stallion. She looked very relaxed and content right now, and he knew without saying that she felt better, not as tired or as emotionally drained as before.

"Dad's taking quite an interest in your colt," he began, breaking the silence. Already all of them had begun to refer to Lightning as *her* colt. "He was very concerned this morning when he wouldn't eat."

"Was he?" Ann's face lit up.

"Oh, he tried to brush it off, you know how gruff he can get when we catch him being sentimental, but I know he wants to save this foal as much as we do, else he'd never have been so concerned with getting him to school today."

"You think so? Oh, I'm so glad to have Scotty on our side, especially with Dad…" she stopped, thinking sadly of her father who still showed barely any interest in the foal Glory had left them. He hardly noticed him and never asked about him. "But I guess Glory's memory is still too painful for him to accept," she concluded.

"He will. Give him time." Then as if noting the time, he added, "Guess we'd better head back. It gets dark fast this time of year."

"O.K." Suddenly she grinned. "Race ya," she challenged, urging Si'ad into a full-blown gallop. Jock let Tag have his head also, as he burst, laughing, after her, even though he knew there was no real contest. But as they reached the head of the lane, they both remembered, a little belatedly, Scotty's rule about always walking the last stretch on the way home. That way they'd be cooled out by the time they reached the barns. Of course Jock and Ann slowed down and walked the last few feet to the courtyard, but their horses were still wet when they got back and they were forced to walk them out anyway, much to their dismay. Still they had avoided getting caught for their slip up.

Or so they thought. Actually Scotty had seen them and smiled when he saw their prank, for it back-fired when they were forced into extra work for themselves, walking their horses out. When would those two learn, he thought to himself, that his rules had a practical side as well as a serious one?

After that, things settled into a routine for the next week or so. Ann somehow managed to juggle her schedule a bit better, though sleep always seemed to come up on the short end. She got her studies done with the bare minimum requirements, most of it beside the sleeping colt.

Sometimes she helped her mother make the ever increasing supply of formula that the growing colt required, his voracious appetite demanding more and more to satisfy him. Other times she helped around the farm with the endless rounds of cleaning stalls, feeding horses, and so many other chores that needed to be done.

On Tuesday, Jock returned with her to school and so was able to take the car on the days his lunch period coincided with hers. It was cutting it close, but they could just about make it home, feed Lightning, and get back to school before the next class, bolting a sandwich Jessica handed them as they ran out the door.

Other days Scotty took the time to run the now lively colt over to meet Ann during her lunchtime, returning to pick them up after school unless Jock had a later class, in which case he'd take the bus. It was terribly confusing as well as time consuming. All of them felt the strain yet no one complained for as Lightning entered his second week of life, it was obvious he was responding well to their concern.

Already he was filling out as a normal foal would. He was becoming quite active and soon would no longer be confinable in the kitchen. By the following weekend it was unanimously agreed that he be returned to the barn when he repeatedly got out of his confines and made messes in the kitchen. Even the long-suffering Jessica finally reached her breaking point when he learned to open cabinets and spilled several bags of dry goods all over one day. She had only stepped out to hang some wash when she returned to the mess and quite emphatically told all of them at dinner that a kitchen was no place for a horse, even an orphan one. Lightning was banished to the barn.

So Ann returned to the barn with him where she spent each night on a cot outside his stall.

The following Sunday turned out to be an unseasonably warm day, with only a slight breeze blowing, so Scotty suggested to Ann that she bring her foal out for his first introduction to the paddock.

Already Ann had taught Lightning to wear a halter so she just hooked a light lead shank on him and led him outside. This was no trouble as he was like an adoring puppy with her and would have followed her anywhere. In essence he wasn't even aware of the rope for he stayed so close to her, it never grew taut.

Ann, followed by Scotty and Jock, took him out behind the broodmare barn, the middle of the three bigger barns, and opened the gate to the first of three paddocks, Lightning following curiously behind. He carried his little head high, his crooked blaze dazzling white against the dark face. As soon as she shut the gate, she unhooked the lead and turned him loose. Then they all waited to see what he would do. At first he only stood still, unsure of what to do next. Soon his curiosity got the better of him and he walked out into the middle of the paddock, ears quivering and eyes darting everywhere as he took in his new surroundings. He looked back at Ann but she only laughed, "Go on, silly, try out those long legs of yours." Then she started to run herself as one would playing tag, Lightning watched her dart past his line of vision. Suddenly, with a little crow hop, he broke into a funny trot, trying to keep up with her. She ducked past him, making him change course rather awkwardly. Yet after a couple of twists and turns he began to gain more control over his long legs and was soon running about the paddock in an admirable pattern. Panting, Ann returned to the gate beside Scotty and Jock.

"Boy, being a mother sure is hard work," she sighed. "Hope I don't have to teach him to run, too."

"I don't know who looks funnier, Lightning learning how to trot or you trying to teach him," Jock teased.

"Enough out of you," she took a swipe at him but he only ducked away from her, laughing at her discomfort. Then Lightning came charging up and butted her playfully, making her turn away from Jock to pay attention to him. "Want me to play with you, huh?" Ignoring Jock's grin, she streaked off, first chasing then being chased by the foal. It was a wonderful game, and though she came back winded, she returned smiling in spite of her exertions.

"Best bring him in now," Scotty said after a bit. "Weather's beginning to turn cooler and we don't want him to get a chill."

Ann immediately snapped on his leadline and led him back to his stall, the colt shaking his head impatiently this time as he realized for the first time he was tied to something. "Sorry, Lightning, you'll have to get used to this. But you'll get plenty of freedom. If tomorrow is nice you can go out again. It *was* fun, wasn't it?" As if in reply, the colt whinnied shrilly.

But the next day turned quite nasty and a cold, freezing rain began that later turned into snow, blanketing the area with a thick layer of white. Ann and Jock were not at all displeased when they were let out of school early Monday, followed by two more days home as the snow lingered, a heavy wind making clearing the side roads nearly impossible.

Finally by Thursday the snow had been cleared or melted sufficiently to get buses through and two very reluctant Stormy Hill residents returned to school. By the time Scotty came over with Lightning that day, the sun was shining and the roads were drying up.

The next afternoon was pleasant enough for Ann to consider bringing the now two-week old colt out again to the paddock for a brief run. Full of energy from his long enforced confinement, he tore about kicking and bucking happily. Scotty came up, a foaling blanket over one arm.

"Here, you might need this," he told her. "He's apt to be sweaty from his exercise and this'll ward off a chill."

Gratefully Ann accepted it. "Thanks, Scotty, I should have thought of it myself. Of course I don't want him to get chilled." She called him over and slipped the blanket on him. It was made just for newborns but it barely fit around Lightning's girth, so big was he already. Both of them remarked about his size.

"Why this young fellow has been growing on us. Didn't realize how much he's filled out until you put that blanket on him. It this keeps up he's going to be a big boy."

"Think so?" she trusted Scotty's knowledge explicitly in anything that pertained to horses. Secretly she was hoping he'd be of good size.

"I've seen foals like him top out at sixteen hands or better," he said noncommittally, making her smile.

"That would be wonderful. Oh, I do hope he ends up that big."

"Well, I suspect if the way you're feeding him has anything to do with it, he just might. You're doing a terrific job with him, I might add."

Ann glowed at the praise as she took him back to his stall. But later she had only that praise to hold on to when tragedy struck.

Lightning appeared fine when she got up to give him his midnight bottle. He drank it all and went back to sleep. With his first two weeks behind him they had begun to stretch his feedings out to three hours or better, as he was able to take in more at each feeding. Therefore Ann didn't check him again until nearly four o'clock. It was getting harder and harder to wake herself as she had been without a full, uninterrupted sleep for so long now. But as she brought back the heated bottle, upon entering the stall, she immediately noticed the heavy, difficult breathing.

"Lightning!" she screamed, running to him. He raised his head but his eyes were glassy. He only attempted a little bit of his milk, then quit as though it were too much effort for him. His neck and flanks were sweaty but every now and then he'd shiver involuntarily. Ann didn't need Scotty or her father to tell her what had happened. He had caught a chill after all and was going into, or possibly already had, pneumonia!

The first thing she did was turn on the overhead infrared light. Thank goodness they hadn't changed him out of one of the foaling stalls yet. Then she grabbed for the blanket he'd worn earlier. It was still hung across the stall door. Wrapping him as tightly as she could, she ran and found some towels and blanket pins, tucking them around his exposed neck, before racing to call Scotty.

Hurrying up the stairs on the side of the broodmare barn that led to their apartment, she banged on the door, yelling for them to hurry. A sleepy-eyed Scotty had only to see her face to know there was trouble.

"Lightning! Pneumonia!" she gasped. In two words she'd told them all they needed to know. Jock was already past her, throwing on his coat as he ran for the main house to alert the Collinses. Ann turned, leading Scotty back to the stall, where he fully assessed the situation, noting Ann's quick thinking handiwork. As comical as he looked, she had diagnosed the problem correctly and done what she could. Looking more closely at the foal, he confirmed her prediction.

"It's pneumonia all right," he answered her unspoken question. "Or will be. Perhaps we … correction, *you* caught it in time, though. Smart thinking to wrap him up right away like that. Good thing you had the infrared light, too. Stall's already feeling warmer. Good girl."

"I only did what you've taught me to do over the years. Oh, Scotty, is he going to—I mean -" she stopped, her throat choked with tears as she began to realize the seriousness of the situation.

Scotty, who was now listening to the colt's breathing, looked up. "Hey, don't fall apart on me now, lass." He put his arm around her. She tried to smile bravely but her shoulders heaved with fear. "We'll pull him through, but we've got to work fast.

53

These lungs are filling with fluid. What I need you do now is to run into the feed room and look in the refrigerator. There should be some combiotic on hand. Bring that and a fresh needle. They're in the drawer next to it, or if not, then they'll be in the cabinet up over the sink. Got that?"

When she nodded hesitantly, he added, unnecessarily, "And run, hurry!" She scooted.

It didn't take her long to find what Scotty had requested. On the way back from the feed room she ran into Jock and her father, coming down the aisle. Surprised at the concern on her father's face, she dismissed it in her own anxiety for her foal.

Jock was carrying a vaporizer. "Your mom said we should use this to help clear his lungs," he explained as he and Michael went about hooking it up. Ann returned to Scotty, handing him the combiotic and the needle. He quickly filled the syringe and inserted it into the foal's neck. "Now, go and see if you can find some I.V. equipment," he told her. "He obviously won't be able to take a bottle until his lungs are clear, so I'm going to start the intravenous." Once again Ann ran back to the feed room where she was able to locate one bag with a current expiration sticker on it and brought it back to Scotty. With the help of her father they rigged up an I.V. pole, just as Jock got the vaporizer going.

"Jessica said she put a little mentholatum in the water to open up his lungs," he said as he turned it on.

"And my sinuses as well," Scotty laughed, as the full effect of the vaporized water hit them. Suddenly they all laughed, breaking the tension in the air. Jock still looked a little sheepish, but his father consoled him. "Thanks, son, it's a great idea. Sure worked when you kids were small and had bad colds. Hopefully it'll help him, too."

"What can I do now?" asked Michael, his voice sick with worry. Suddenly aware of his presence, Scotty didn't stop to question it. He just pointed to the I.V. bag and said, "We'll need more of these. No telling how long we may have to supplement before he can eat on his own."

"I've already put a call in to Doc Hawes, but I'll run over there myself. It'll be faster." He was gone before they knew it.

Everything that could be done immediately had been taken care of. The three settled down next to the sick colt to begin their long fearful vigil.

CHAPTER FIVE

Exploration

How could this have happened?" Ann asked Scotty. "I blanketed him like you told me. I took real good care that he wouldn't get a chill. He was fine when I fed him at midnight."

"Don't blame yourself, lass," Scotty tried to comfort her. "I know you did and it's not your fault. We've had a lot of wet, cold weather lately. It's been real hard to keep out drafts and such. Just one of those things that happen, I guess. But we caught it early and thanks to your swift response, we've been able to do as much as we did. Now what he needs is time, time to heal."

"I never should have taken him out so soon after the snow," she continued to admonish herself.

"Ann, stop blaming yourself. I'd have put him out, too. Yesterday *was* a lovely day. And we can't treat these babies like they are fragile dolls. They do need lots of exercise and fresh air if they are to grow strong and healthy. Coddling them is worse."

"But …."

"No buts. Listen to me. Your Lightning is going to be fine. But right now he needs his rest, and so do you. Get some rest, Ann. You're going to need it."

Doubtfully she lay back down beside the now sleeping colt, her arm across his side, and closed her eyes. Though she didn't intend to sleep, exhaustion caught up with her and she drifted off.

Reluctant to leave, Jock, too, lay back and dozed fitfully while his father kept watch. The colt was too sick at the moment to object to his intravenous that was giving him the nourishment he needed. For a while the only sound to be heard in the close confines of the stall was the still-raspy breathing of the colt and the soft hiss of the vaporizer.

The sky was just turning a pale gray as Michael entered the barn. He set the new I.V. bags in the refrigerator before hurrying down to the stall where a red light burned eerily. Surveying the scene, he questioned Scotty, "Is he ...?"

"Holding his own, fortunately. Breathing has not worsened. Shivering has stopped, though. Thank goodness. We've done all we can at this point. Were you successful?"

Michael nodded. "Doc gave me all he could spare. He'll stop by later with more, and to check on the colt."

"Good, we'll probably need them. I don't think he should go back to the bottle until his lungs are clear. If he swallowed wrong it could send him right back into pneumonia again," Scotty said.

"What are his chances, Scotty?" Michael whispered, seeing that both kids were asleep.

"Pretty good, I think. We caught it early, thanks to Ann's quick intervention. Good thing she was here with him. She of course spotted it right away and knew what to do, even before I got here. Had the infrared on to warm the stall and got him blanketed right off, even to a towel wrapped around his neck. Looked quite a sight, he did. Quick thinker, your little girl. If he makes it, it'll be because of her."

"He'll pull through," Michael stated emphatically. "He's got to."

"I thought you didn't care," Scotty said softly.

""Me? Why, that's the problem. I probably care too much."

"I don't understand?" Scotty looked puzzled.

"It's been hard, losing Glory. I guess I just withdrew from all of you for a while. But I never stopped caring. Oh, it was hard, at first, to look at this foal. Each time I'd see a part of her. But that's what's kept me going. He's all we have left of her now. No, I don't want to lose him, too."

"Then you'd better tell her," Scotty nodded toward Ann, "when she wakes up. She's been doing all this to save his life and all the time thinking you resented him and blamed him for the death of his dam."

"Nothing could be farther from the truth. I'm so sorry I gave her that impression. Yes, I'll tell her straight away."

Ann, who'd awakened at the sound of voices and heard most of the conversation, at least the part that counted, suddenly flew up and raced into her father's arms, surprising all three of them. "You mean it, Dad? You really like Lightning after all?" Her eyes were wet with emotion. Her father was so moved he could only nod his head.

Jock, awakened by the commotion, and Scotty, feeling a little bit like they were intruding on a private moment, started to slip out the door when Jessica stopped them. In her hands she carried a big tray loaded with fried egg and bacon sandwiches, coffee and juice.

"Figured by now all of you would be pretty hungry," she explained, offering the tray around. Ann pulled herself away from her father to go help pass out food and drinks. Jessica noticed right away Ann's change of mood, and seeing her husband there beside the foal, surmised without being told, what had happened between them. She smiled.

"Jessica, I thought you were still in bed," Michael said. "You didn't have to get up."

"And who would keep this family together through all these crises," she answered lightly, "if not for me and my coffee and sandwiches?"

"Umm, you're right, Mom," Ann said through mouthfuls. "These are delicious."

"Probably you're just hungry, dear," she smiled. "Lord knows if you've stopped to eat a decent meal since that foal was born." She shook her head in mock disgust.

"Face it, Mother," Michael said. "Horses just run this family."

"Don't I know it." She then changed the subject. "Now if all your stomachs are temporarily at bay, I will clear away the debris and go make phone calls. Good thing it's Saturday so you two don't have to miss school. I know neither of you are going to leave his side until he's out of danger. And Michael, I'll call your assistant and tell him he's on his own today. He can handle the store without you for one day."

Michael grinned, "That's for sure. Tells me I only get in his way, anyway."

Jessica continued as she got up to leave, "Want me to call Doc? Colt looks like he's doing fine so far. Must be my vaporizer."

Michael shook his head. "No need. He said he'd stop by this morning anyway. Just send him around. And as to the vaporizer. It looks like it just could be doing some good after all."

Jessica sniffed. "Could be, my eye," she grumbled. "It's what brought you two kids through many a sickness when you were little. And you, too, Michael, when you had that bad case of bronchitis several years ago. Don't see why it couldn't do the same for one small foal." With that she left the barn.

"Oh, oh, Dad, I think you've made her mad," Ann teased.

"I doubt that. Just your mom's way of asserting herself. I think sometimes she feels left out of all this horsey stuff we concern ourselves with."

"That's not true. She's the backbone that keeps us going."

"And often the only calm head among us," Scotty added. "Especially times like these."

"Oh, she knows it all right," Michael said. "She just likes to remind us once in a while how valuable she is to this farm."

"Well, I'll remind her anyway," Ann said so strongly her father smiled.

"Good idea. Now the rest of you get some rest while I stand watch. I'll call you, Scotty, when I need a break. Ann, I want you to get some sleep in your own bed for a change. He'll be on I.V. for a while so we won't need you to feed. I want you well rested so you can take up his feedings again when he's ready for you."

Ann smiled. Her father was back in charge again. "Glad you're back, Dad," she said, squeezing his shoulder as she went out. "We missed you."

Her bed felt so good after the hard cot and she was so tired that she slept way past the time she had planned to rise to check on Lightning. When she came running out to the stall she found Jock on duty. Lightning was pretty much as he'd been when she left him, the I.V. still working to grant him life-giving sustenance while his body fought off the pneumonia.

"How is he?" she asked upon entering the stall.

"About the same." Jock started when Lightning suddenly raised his head and whinnied when he saw her. He tried to rise but she pushed him gently back down.

"Not yet, boy," she told him, stroking his neck.

"Now that's new. He hasn't shown signs of interest in any of us, until you came in. That's great."

"He knows the hand that feeds him," she giggled, glad to see an improvement. Even his breathing sounded stronger, less raspy.

Still, it was three days before he was completely out of danger. By Tuesday morning, when Ann and Jock reluctantly returned to school, he was again eagerly taking the formula Ann offered him, anxious to be out of his confines. Suddenly the stall seemed too small to hold him. But Scotty insisted on another week at least before he ventured out to the paddock again. The weather in January was just too unpredictable.

The one good thing that came out of his illness was that when he was able to return to food again, he learned to drink from a bucket instead of the bottle, since he needed so much now at one feeding. And this he would accept from any of them, though he still showed a marked preference for Ann. This made life easier for all of them, but especially Ann. She no longer had to concern herself with the mid-day feeding, nor get up several times during the night to feed. Now she took turns with Scotty, Jock and her dad.

As his third week passed by, he gained all his old strength back. The weather had turned mild again so he was allowed out for short periods to run about the paddock, which he did with high exuberance, kicking and bucking all around the fenced-in area. And, while they all watched anxiously for any signs of reoccurring pneumonia, Lightning suffered no relapses. His lungs remained clear.

It was into his fourth week that he began to more than nibble at the grain that had always been available in his stall. Most foals, from a week on, will show some interest in picking at the grain their mothers leave behind, thus gradually switching over, until by the time of weaning they are able to eat fully on their own. Lightning, being an orphan, showed more desire to eat the grain over the milk at an earlier age. Along with the sweet feed, Ann was placing hay pellets in his feed bucket and seeing a healthy amount disappear each day. While he still got most of his nutrition from the formula, he would be ready to wean completely at a younger age than foals left on their mothers.

His feeding schedule was gradually lengthening, also. By now he was being fed every four hours, instead of two, giving them all more time to get their chores done with fewer interruptions.

Even though he followed Ann around like a puppy, she used the lead line whenever she took him anywhere just to get him used to it. She had begun other lessons in good manners as well. Each day she ran her hands down his legs and asked him to pick up his feet for examination. She used the hook pick lightly on his young hooves so he would be ready for his first farrier visit.

Brushing with a soft curry, she followed up with a rag rubbed all over his body, a preferred part of the grooming ritual for him. After she was done to the point his dark coat shone with health and vitality, she carefully combed out his stubby new mane and tail, scratching his favorite spots as she went. Lightning often nuzzled her with his soft nose as she worked on him.

One day, while she was teaching him to stand quietly tied to the fence as she groomed him, her father came up. Michael stopped and observed him for a few seconds before he spoke.

"Your colt seems to be coming along just fine," he commented.

"Think so?" Ann responded, as she rubbed him down with her rag. The rubbing was beginning to have an extra effect of removing the mousy outer fuzz to expose the sleek black coat beneath. "At the moment he looks a little moth-eaten until all this fuzz falls out," she said.

"Even so, he's turning into a mighty fine colt. Might be worth saving after all."

Ann looked offended. "Of course, he's worth saving!"

Suddenly realizing how his words had sounded, he apologized. "I'm sorry, honey, of course he's worth saving. I didn't mean it that way. Let me try to explain. You've done a super job here, pulling this orphan through, despite great odds. I'm well aware of your devotion and I appreciate it."

"But you still don't think he'll be more than just another pet?" she said.

Michael hesitated, trying to pick just the right words for her to understand.

"No one around here, except maybe Jock, realizes what Lightning is, or what he's going to be," she went on doggedly.

Michael looked sad suddenly, as though the weight of the world was on his shoulders. How could he explain what he felt, or knew from the wisdom and experience that only age can grant, in words that she'd grasp? His daughter, for all her knowledge, was still so young. He leaned over the fence and sighed, "Ann, sometimes I envy you your youth and optimism. It would be great to be your age and have my whole life to look forward to. But, I'm afraid I can't. Age, and too many disappointments over the years, has taught your dad to be very cautious in life. I don't know if you, or Jock, can understand what I'm trying to say. You kids are so impetuous at your age."

"I'm trying, Dad, really I am." She put down her rag and released the colt, which dashed off, racing about the paddock in a moment of playful exhilaration before settling down to nibble at the sparse shoots of last year's grass. They both were silent a minute as they watched him. "I guess I don't see why you don't want to acknowledge how really good this colt is."

"Ann, honey, it's not that. It's just … Here, let me try to explain. Sure, I'd love for him to be a winner, just like you think he can be. He is, after all, Glory's son. That *is* why I did that breeding, after all. And I must say he does look promising at this stage, but," he added quickly at Ann's triumphant look, "and I don't want to burst your balloon when I say this—Lord knows, one of us around here should still have dreams—so much can happen between now and the winner's circle. So much can go wrong."

"I know that," she insisted.

"I know you do. I just have to say it again. I'm sorry if I'm being a 'Dad' but I've seen too much, I guess. I've lived through heartaches, near misses, hopefuls who came close but never quite made it. Sometimes I wonder why it keeps happening to us and if I'll ever bring Stormy Hill back to the position it once held in my grandfather's day. I don't know why, what I'm doing wrong, but I just can't find the key to the success we once had. Maybe it's not meant to be."

"Oh, but it is, Dad," she put her hand on her father's arm. "Don't blame yourself. It's not your fault. You've done all you can. We all believe in you."

Instantly sorry he'd revealed so much of his inner feelings to his young daughter, Michael hastened to say something positive. "I know, deep down inside I do. It's thanks to all of you, my wonderful supportive family, that I'm willing to try again. We are due, I think, for our luck to change." He laughed mirthlessly. "The eternal optimism of a horse breeder. Who knows? Maybe this colt's the one we've been waiting for, after all." He watched the youngster critically, noting the fine lines, the strong, straight legs, the well laid-back shoulders and powerful hindquarters. In all honesty he had to admit he hadn't seen a better-looking foal for his age in a long time. Maybe Ann wasn't far off the mark with her prediction. Only time would tell. "Guess I just need a little more of your faith, honey."

Ann glowed, "He's the one all right. You'll see."

"Well, I don't know about that, but if he continues to develop as he's doing now, he'll be impressive indeed. I *am* very pleased with the work you've put into him so far. He has wonderful manners and that will be very important later on if he shows racing promise."

"Really? You'll race him?"

"Wait a minute. I shouldn't have put it like that," he retracted. "Let's just say that at this point in time, he shows a lot of potential. But that's a long way from the track and anything can happen. Still, he's the finest colt we've had here in some years and, yes, if he continues to show potential, he'll get his chance."

"That's good enough for me," she cried, hugging her dad.

"After all," Michael added, "as Glory's son he's got a great heritage behind him. He should be a winner. Guess I can dream one more time."

Ann agreed, happily.

"So, what say, you and I put this future champion of yours, Lightning, you call him, back in his stall and go see what your mother has rustled up for dinner?" As she nodded, snapping a lead rope on the tall colt and leading him to the gate which Michael opened, he added, almost as an afterthought, "So what do you think about 'Stormy Lightning', huh?"

Taken back, she hesitated, "For what?" Then it dawned on her. "Oh, I mean for his name?" Excitement spread across her face. Many horses down through the years, all descendants of Stormy Hill, as was Lightning, were given the Stormy prefix, certainly most of the best ones. Still, it was an honor to be given the prefix, but more important, it showed Ann what the colt really meant to her father.

"Why not? It fits him and hopefully it will be an omen of luck."

"Thanks, I love it." A sudden thought crossed her mind. "Wait a minute," she said, looking at him slyly. "You've been holding out on me, Dad."

"Why whatever do you mean?" he said innocently.

"You didn't just think of that name. I know you." Then she smiled, thinking out loud. "And if you've been thinking up names for him, then you've had a bit more faith in him than I thought, am I right?"

He laughed, "Guilty. Guess my daughter knows me better than *I* thought." He hugged her. "Yep, I guess I've had my eye on this colt of yours for about a week or so, ever since I knew for sure he was going to live."

—⚡—

Lightning was six weeks old when the first of the other foals was born to Stormy Melody. Melody was a bay mare of later years and this colt was her tenth foal. A veteran broodmare, she had no trouble delivering and caring for her foal. Unfortunately since none of her other youngsters had proven to be big stakes winners it was doubtful this one would either.

Right behind Melody, by a week, came the last two mares, a couple of days apart. The first one, Tawny Dancer, gave birth to a rather ordinary looking bay filly, but healthy nevertheless. Finally Shelly's Song had another filly, a chestnut like herself. As this filly had a well-bred sire, she might bring a bit more come sale time, but neither Scotty nor Michael saw enough promise in any of them to consider keeping them for the farm.

With the coming of the rest of the foals, several things happened. As soon as they were all old enough the mares and foals were put out together in the large pasture next to the house. They tried putting Lightning out with them but the mares were too jealous of the strange baby and kept running him off. Because they kicked at him, Lightning had to be separated from the others for fear of being hurt. Thus, he was still very much an orphan.

This rejection of his own kind left him completely dependent on people for companionship. As this was not good from a social standpoint, since he needed to learn to get along with other horses, they decided to try him with the geldings. Tagalong, Banshee and Cedardale basically tolerated the lively youngster but at least they didn't drive him away. Actually, because of their patience with him he was able to learn the very important social lessons that would make getting along with his own kind later in life possible.

Lastly, and most important, was that as the other foals grew, it was becoming more and more obvious to all just how superior Lightning was, even though he was much older and likewise that much more developed. As he grew he seemed to get better, if possible, to the point that there began to be great excitement over him. Even conservative Scotty commented on his potential though he was reluctant to say anything before the fact.

There was no doubt that Lightning was a good-looking colt. He had completely lost the mousy covering he'd been born with, leaving beneath a shiny glistening black color that Ann loved to brush till it shone. In spite of his big size, he was well-proportioned, with straight legs and muscular hindquarters from exercise and good condition. His long, arched neck fit nicely into his sloping shoulders. The way he moved showed that he would be a smooth, pleasant horse to ride one day. Lastly, his rather small Arabian head still maintained the refinement and intelligence promised at birth, the dark eyes, large and bright, yet gentle, too.

The first people to see him outside the farm were those who had bookings with Si'ad for their Arab mares. Since he was the first foal Si'ad had sired, they were especially interested in him. They all agreed unanimously how impressive he looked and verbalized as to how they hoped to get one like him. One farm owner, who came all the way from Arizona to breed to Si'ad, was so impressed that he offered to buy the stallion on the spot, after seeing the colt he had produced. Michael, smiling, turned it down, of course, but the owner was not offended in the least, telling him the offer would be honored anytime he changed his mind. Just name his price, he was told.

Thus spring arrived with its lovely weather, green growth and planting time. The fields used for raising hay for the horses were plowed over and planted, a time-consuming but necessary chore. Yet one of the compensations was that with the better weather, the horses could be left out most of the time, allowing for fewer stalls to clean.

For Ann and Jock spring meant summer was just around the corner, and school would be out soon. For Jock, although he'd be working part-time for the Garrison's next door, he would still find plenty of time for summer fun with Ann at the farm. They both looked forward to the long, lazy days ahead.

CHAPTER SIX

Summer

"Ah, summer," Jock sighed as he swung up bareback on Tag and, taking Si'ad's reins in one hand, walked the horses across the courtyard toward the main house.

While he would be spending part of each day working next door, he was still very much needed right here at Stormy Hill. Even so, working with horses, that was not work at all to him, or Ann for that matter.

Ann was still in bed asleep when she heard a light tapping on her window, which faced out the back of the house. She awoke at once, not at all surprised to see Jock grinning impatiently from the other side. As she raised the sash he called out, "Wake up, sleepy head. Time's wasting. Summer vacation is here. Let's go riding!"

"Boy, you're up early. What time is it anyway?" She mumbled, rubbing her eyes as she noticed the two horses behind him, jingling their bits in nervous anticipation.

"Early. Who cares? Throw some jeans on and let's go."

"Okay, Okay. Give me a second, will you?" she stumbled toward the bathroom, situated between her room and the kitchen, grabbing her jeans as she went. Her mood was more for effect than anything else. There was nothing Ann loved better than riding at dawn, especially in the summer when the morning mist still clung in the air and the sweet smell of bluegrass rose as the horses moved through it. As they passed through the countryside, they would see the dark forms of mares and foals grazing peacefully in distant fields. The only sounds to be heard would be the chirping of birds and the occasional light rustle of leaves as a breeze passed through the trees lining the pastures. There was nothing quite like it, and both she and Jock knew it.

Suddenly, Ann couldn't wait to join him. Hastily she threw on her clothes, brushed her teeth and darted for the window. Whistling for Si'ad she swung off the ledge and onto his bare back. "Well, come on, I'm ready. Let's go!" she called to Jock, who also jumped back on Tag and followed her lead across the brief lawn behind the house, turning up the lane leading to the back pastures. This is heaven, she thought, shaking back her head and letting her wild, unruly hair blow free. She was out riding her favorite horse on this beautiful morning. They had the whole summer ahead of them. What could be better?

For a while they rode in silence, each in tune with the other's feelings. There's no place I'd rather live, Ann was thinking, than right here in Kentucky on this horse farm. While it was the only life she'd ever known, she was quite sure nothing else could top it. She had everything she could possibly want, her family, including Scotty and Jock, of course, the horses, a wonderful stallion like Si'ad to ride, and now Lightning.

Lightning! What a fine promising colt he was becoming. Surely, at least in her mind, he was the one they were waiting for. He was everything she thought a champion should look like. At five months, now fully weaned, he could be called a big, strapping youngster, yet for all his size, graceful and refined, too. So exquisitely formed, muscular and full of life, yet very tractable and easy to work around. Being an orphan had made him dependent on people, thus making him friendly and inquisitive. Nothing mean or arrogant about him. Living in the pasture with the geldings, he loved to put on bursts of speed. As soon as the other foals were weaned, Ann expected they'd all be put together so that he could have some playmates his own age, as well as competition as they chased each other in mock races. Ann already knew what the outcome would be.

As they passed the yearling field, Jock suddenly broke the silence by remarking, "We'll be working on those babies now that summer is here, getting them ready for Keeneland this fall."

"You bet," she nodded, observing the two bays and one chestnut grazing near the fence. Another, a chestnut filly, stood some distance away, watching them. She would not be going to the sales with the others, but would stay on as a potential broodmare, possibly replacing Melody, who was getting on in years.

"I do enjoy working with the yearlings, though," she continued. "That's one of my favorite jobs."

Jock nodded in agreement. "Not many jobs around a horse farm I don't like," he said. "Except maybe mucking stalls."

"No one likes that," Ann replied.

"But getting the yearlings ready for the fall sales, that's fun work."

"You bet. I do hope the youngsters bring a decent price at this year's sales. Dad so needs the money to run the farm."

Jock looked sympathetic. "No matter what we do, the expenses seem to exceed the amount coming in. You'd think we'd have been able to get a little ahead, what with the money Tag won from his races and Si'ad's stud fees, but the farm seems to absorb everything just like a sponge."

"Sure does," Ann patted the grey stallion's neck. "But imagine where we'd be if we didn't have Tag's winnings or Si'ad's stud services. I know Dad would love to pick up a few more broodmares, but he hasn't been able to scrape together the money it would cost."

"More mares would help," Jock replied. "We do need more foals to sell, that's for sure. But good mares are expensive, and there's no point in holding back yearlings just because they're fillies. Not when we can get a decent price for them."

"There haven't been any with the right quality and bloodlines for us to keep anyway, except for possibly that chestnut filly. Least that's what Dad and Scotty said."

"They know best. Dad's so wise when it comes to horses, I only hope some day I can be as good as he is."

"You will be. You already know as much as many trainers, and you've got a great teacher." They were walking their horses now, taking a path, which wound behind many of their neighbor's farms and eventually swung back to connect to a dirt road that ran between their property and Garrisons next door.

"True," he conceded, pleased by her faith in him. "I'll be so glad when school's over for me so I can concentrate on what really matters to me—training."

"Lucky for you, you've only got one more year," Ann moaned. "I've still got three and then I know Mom and Dad expect me to go to college."

"Don't say that. College is important. Besides, it's fortunate for you to have the opportunity."

"You could go, too, if you wanted to. Scotty'd find a way."

"Perhaps, but I really don't want to. I was never one for books and learning. You were always better at that than I was."

"Why do you say that?"

"Look at the way you were able to juggle raising Lightning and keeping up with your schoolwork. I could never have done that."

"Not easily. I barely kept up in school," she reminded him.

"Still, you did it. That's what counts."

Instead of arguing with him, Ann changed the subject back to a pleasanter topic, that of how they would be spending their summer, now that it was here. She was aware that schoolwork had always come easier to her that it had for Jock. Still, she, like him, found school a loathsome chore that they had to do. Any time spent away from the farm was to be resented by both of them.

Being in public school had always presented a problem anyway. Most of the children from the surrounding farms, those with similar backgrounds, attended private schools, so that Ann and Jock did not come in contact with them to make friends through the usual social medium of school. Besides the fact, Jock's status as 'family' at Stormy Hill would not be considered as such by many of the neighboring farm owners, who would look upon him as 'help'. Within this close-knit society, there still prevailed a certain class-consciousness.

On the other hand, the Collins family, as fifth generation Kentuckians, were granted all the respect of their wealthier cousins. Poor or not, they held a place in Lexington society, for as long as one had the land and the horses, the rest would roll around eventually.

Most of the students, who attended the public high school lived in town. Even if Jock and Ann had been inclined to visit, there was nothing in common for a friendship to grow. In the end they were both too busy at the farm to develop any lasting friendships and since they had each other, they were happy with the way things were. If they both were a bit too shy to encourage friends, it bothered no one, leastwise themselves.

One girl her age Ann did see was the Garrison daughter, Greta, though this was not by choice. She sometimes ran into her when she rode over to meet Jock and Scotty after they were done working. Often she and Jock would ride back to the farm together, leaving Scotty to follow by car. Greta, she found, to be nothing but a shallow, spoiled rich girl who loved to flaunt her many material possessions in Ann's face. Having taken a fancy to Jock, she often tried to be around when he was working there. On the other hand she treated Ann with cool disdain, possibly out of misplaced jealousy, delighting in making her feel uncomfortable. Consequently, Ann spoke to her as little as possible and always tried to leave as soon as Jock was ready.

Jock equally found Greta a very displeasing person, due no doubt to her treatment of Ann, so he was always just as anxious to get away as soon as he was done with his work. He seemed totally unaware of her interest in him and spoke to her only out of politeness. Not surprising, considering he'd shown very little interest in girls in general up to this point.

"Sun's getting higher. Must be time to get back to our chores," Jock's voice broke into Ann's thoughts. She nodded and turned Si'ad's head toward the distant barns. She looked over at Jock and smiled.

"What are you grinning about?"

"Oh, just glad to be alive on such a beautiful morning, living here, all of summer ahead of us. Isn't it great?"

Jock agreed, suddenly choked with emotion as he thought how lucky he was indeed to share this extraordinary life with such wonderful people as the Collinses. He was also grateful his father decided to stay on those many years ago, and help rebuild Stormy Hill. Otherwise he'd never have had the chance to know all this. They had their little apartment above the broodmare barn, he had Tag to ride, horses to train, even his job at Garrisons was not so bad since it involved working with horses and gave him extra cash. And of course he had Ann for a best friend. Life was pretty good to him so far, he thought.

They approached the barns from a westerly direction, riding around the half-mile training track. Within the track was a large pasture and an enclosed schooling ring. At the southern end of the track was a straightaway, which was used as a starting run-up. Across the end stood a rusting old starting gate holding three stalls. Tag had been the last horse to use this device. Currently it sat there, weeds sprouting, belying its neglect.

Beyond the track, a dirt road led back to the three barns, which formed the courtyard. On either side of the road several paddocks housed broodmares and their foals, while they were still young enough to be kept separate, or older horses in training. The road ended between the broodmare and yearling barns.

Jock and Ann came into the courtyard in time to catch Scotty on his way to bring in the yearlings. At this time of year all the horses were left out overnight and brought in only during the heat of the day, if at all. However, the yearlings would now be brought up to the barns each day to begin their conditioning for the upcoming sales.

"You two are up early. Did you have a good ride?"

They both replied affirmatively, slipping off their horses and automatically checking them to make sure they were dry before turning them loose in their pastures.

"I see you're bareback, again," he commented.

"We both prefer it," Ann responded.

"That, or you're both too lazy to clean tack," Scotty reasoned.

They both laughed at Scotty's insight. "That had nothing to do with it," Jock countered.

"I'll bet," his father snickered.

While Ann and Jock often groaned or made fun over Scotty's rules, they well knew the sense behind them. Caring for one's horse's physical well being always came before one's personal comfort. Besides, simple rules of farm safety had unconsciously become a part of their every day living habits. They hardly needed Scotty to remind them of these practices. Even so, being young, they couldn't help trying to cut corners every now and then.

Summer was the best time to be on the farm. Days were long, busy, yet fulfilling ones that left all of them tired and eager to fall into bed come nighttime. The growing foals needed to be worked and taught their manners as weaning time drew near. The yearlings had to be prepared for the annual fall sales at Keeneland. The hay crop had to be brought in and stored for the winter, with the extra bales set aside to be sold through the feed store. Fences must be checked and mended, acres and acres of the traditional four-plank fence to be examined and replaced if necessary. The horses they guarded were too valuable to be careless. Other equipment had to be checked for repairs, also. Throughout the summer Ann and Jock were kept occupied. They even aided Jessica in canning the fruits and vegetables from the vast garden that she grew every year. Ann lost track of how many jars were stored in the big pantry behind the kitchen. She only knew how good her mom's home-grown vegetables or fresh-baked pies would be on a cold night next winter.

But summer was not all work. There was still plenty of time for long morning rides on their beloved horses. And time for lazing away a hot afternoon beside the pond located just below the house in the big front pasture.

Years ago an earlier Collins relation had had the foresight to dredge out the small stream that wound through both front pastures, creating a pond near the house that would provide entertainment for the generations to follow.

Scotty and Michael later added a rope swing to one of the branches of the huge old live oak that stood beside the pond. Their favorite game was swinging it out over the water before jumping in. Both were fine swimmers and many hours were spent racing each other across the pond.

Still, none of these games compared with those involving the horses. Since the pond was within the pasture usually reserved for the geldings, the horses were often pulled into service as diving boards, as they leaped onto them bareback and rode them into the water before catapulting off them, shrieking with delight.

Another use for the horses was as ladders to reach high into the surrounding fruit trees for a particularly tasty treat. In all, the three geldings were considerably tolerant of such antics.

Lightning, who spent most of his days with the geldings, at least until the other foals were weaned, was often part of the pond games Ann and Jock played with the horses. It was quite comical to see him running alongside the bigger horses, bucking and cavorting, splashing about in the water without the slightest fear. He still followed Ann like a shadow. Once he was so intent on following her he even jumped off the bank into the water, when she swung the rope out over the water and dropped off. Though he was mighty surprised when he landed in the deep part it didn't deter him from scampering about in the shallower water.

As summer drew to an end, work on the yearlings intensified. Each of the three youngsters was handled daily in preparation. Their coats were brushed to a high gloss, manes and tails kept tangle-free, and hoofs trimmed. Each was led out into the courtyard and taught to stand foursquare to show off their best conformation. They were given much exercise to build muscle and tone. In all, everything was done to make them look their finest.

The Keeneland Yearling Sales was so famous it drew buyers from all corners of the globe. People seeking potential winners came to look at the foremost yearlings produced in the past year by Lexington farms. Each farm selected with great pride those colts and fillies they felt reflected their expertise as breeders. The farm whose yearling sold for the most money that year was honored indeed.

Those at Stormy Hill hardly expected to compete at that level, however. But they did desire to offer three healthy, well-conditioned representatives of their farm who showed the long-standing tradition of a proud heritage.

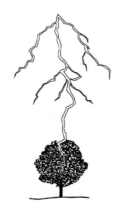

CHAPTER SEVEN

The Bill

Fall crept upon them before they knew it. Ann and Jock returned to school, and the days began to shorten. The time between school and nightfall was crammed with chores. There was seldom time for more than a quick ride.

Still most of the harvesting was done now. The haylofts were full to overflowing with their winter supply of hay and straw. Grain bins were also full. Jessica looked out at her now barren gardens with satisfaction, knowing her pantry shelves were lined with an assortment of foods to enjoy in the coming year.

The morning of the yearling sale, Ann and Jock arose early. With special care they gave each of their charges a final grooming before wrapping their legs with bandages as protection during the short trip to Keeneland. Coolers were placed on each, as well as neck wraps to keep their manes laying flat and tail wraps to prevent tangles. Then each was led out and loaded on the old van that had served Stormy Hill so well over many years. It wasn't much to look at but it got them where they needed to go. Jock elected to ride in the back to watch over the yearlings while Ann rode up front with Scotty.

As they pulled into the track, Ann eagerly scanned the scene all about her, excitement building inside. She loved this stately old track. The long tree-shaded drive leading in made one feel he'd gone back in time to another era. The drive itself gave way to a parking lot lined with more shade trees, overseen by an entrance way made entirely of stone. As one passed through the gates and into the track interior, one saw more of that fine old stonework in all the surrounding buildings, while everywhere stood those marvelous old oaks, as if guarding the track from modern intrusion. Ann had only to close her eyes to imagine the place as it once must have been, filled with gentlemen tipping high hats to ladies, hoop shirts swishing softly as they carried their parasols and sipped daintily on mint juleps. It must have been grand, indeed.

But now the place was alive with a different kind of activity as horse vans of all sizes waited impatiently to discharge their valuable passengers into awaiting stalls prior to crossing the auction block later that night. Grooms struggled to comply with trainers' directions. Trucks pulled in and out. Prospective buyers scurried about trying to get the first glimpse of what they hoped would be the best buy of the night. All the while some owners, unconcerned by the confusion, attempted to push the bidding up by loudly promoting the racing potential of their colts to possible future buyers. Awed by the spectacle, Ann and Jock tried unsuccessfully to take it all in.

Finally Scotty had their colts settled to his satisfaction and he suggested that they all get a bite to eat. Michael would arrive later that evening in time for the sale. Afterward there was nothing to do but sit around and wait. Instead Ann and Jock chose to fill the time walking around, looking at the other yearlings there for the sale and speculating which ones would draw the highest bidding. Like most of the people there they were just as curious about their competition. They also spent much of their time beside their own sale colts, ready to answer questions and show off the colts to anyone who stopped to see them. Sometimes the colts were led out and walked around for further inspection, thus showing off their conformation and manners. Ann and Jock felt a sense of pride that their work had paid off, for each of the colts remained calm and unruffled, in spite of the hectic atmosphere around them.

Two of their yearlings were listed to go toward the beginning of the sale. Michael showed up just as the sale began and he and Scotty, after giving Ann and Jock last minute instructions, left them to go watch from the stands. Bidding started off well but was so rapid, neither of them, standing in the holding area with their charges, could follow it. Then suddenly Jock's number was called and he was pushed out into the lighted arena. Ann tried desperately to see how he was doing, unaware that she was holding her breath as the bidding started out slowly. Suddenly, it caught on but when the gravel fell at last she wasn't sure what the final figure was. Then Jock was back, urging her out into the arena for her turn. Vaguely she remembered her instructions as to what to do to enhance her colt as much as possible. Once again bidding flew over her head in a familiar singsong chant. Too soon it was over and she was back at the stalls where Jock awaited her, preparing the final yearling who would go up later. Michael and Scotty soon joined them, both pleased with the results.

"Well done, kids," Scotty praised, giving each a hug.

"Did they sell well?" Ann asked. "I tried to follow the bidding but it went too fast."

Her father quoted their selling prices and her eyes widened. "You did well. Both colts went for more than I had hoped. Don't expect we'll get as much for the last one but it won't matter. Looks like I'll be able to buy that broodmare I had my eye on, after all."

"Really, Dad? That's wonderful," she hugged him. That would be good news to the farm, she thought happily. Last year they had barely broken even after the sales. There had been no money left for replacing any mares then.

Michael was right. The last of their yearlings sold for a much lower price but when all the fees were paid and Michael was able to figure in his farm expenses that the sale of the yearlings went toward each year, he was left with enough to add another broodmare to his small band.

Right before Christmas she arrived, a chestnut named Sassy Lassie. And she had some of the blood of the old Stormy Hill horses of the past. Michael had found out about her availability when an old friend stopped at the feed store and mentioned her. He was lucky to get her at a reasonable cost. He only wished he could have purchased several more like her.

"Perhaps we'll put her to Si'ad next year," he commented as she was unloaded and turned out in the paddock nearest the house. True to her name she sped off, racing about before settling down to sample the sparse grass left from the fall. "She's a maiden yet and while he's got a full booking for next season, one more won't bother him. Sure is a pretty mare, though."

"Pretty feisty," was Scotty's summation, watching her switch her tail and kick out at what appeared to be nothing. "Needs manners before we can put her in with the other mares, is what I think."

"Aw, she'll come around," Michael defended her. "Once she settles down and accepts this as her new home. She's a great addition, though. Perhaps things are finally changing for the better around here."

Michael was to regret those words when barely two months later once again their luck ran out.

The new year had come and gone. Lightning was now a yearling, a big, leggy colt that outdistanced the other yearlings in all ways. Bigger and stronger than the others, he easily outran them in all their mock races. As big as he was, he remained agile and quick on his feet. His distinctive black color and startling white crooked blaze set him apart from the other youngsters. More than once Scotty or Michael had remarked on the strength and potential of this young colt. While there had never been any doubt about keeping him when it became apparent they had saved this orphan, all of them were beginning to think that possibly he would be more than just Ann's pet.

Ann herself had never doubted it. From the beginning, her faith in her colt remained undaunted. As he grew she witnessed him developing into the champion she knew he would be, and she dreamed constantly of that day. Still it was gratifying to know that the others saw it, too.

She had actually been dreaming of him one night in January when she was startled awake by a terrific sound. She lay there a moment before a blinding flash of light caught her eye and she realized that they were having a freak winter thunderstorm. She was just about to slide comfortably back into sleep when a huge blast of thunder shook her fully awake. It was followed almost immediately by more lightning ripping at the sky. That hit somewhere, she thought as she rose to a sitting position. Normally she was not frightened by thunder but this was so close she knew she couldn't go right back to sleep.

Suddenly there was a deafening crack followed by a crashing sound. Ann leaped to her feet. That did strike, she thought, alarmed, hurrying out into the hall to see where. The hall was completely dark and for a minute she lost her bearings when she heard her mother's voice calling her. She sounded troubled. A flash of light showed Ann the front of the house where she was able to make out the shape of the front stairs. As she flung herself up them, anxious to reach her parents, she was suddenly met by an obstacle blocking her way. As she grabbed at it impatiently, she thought it felt like a tree branch. Thoroughly confused, for what would a tree be doing at the head of their stairs, she stopped. Then she felt rain hitting her face, quite hard in fact, and realized she was getting soaked. Completely scared now, she called out, still clinging to the banister.

"Mom! Dad! Where are you? Are you all right?"

Her mother's voice came from somewhere above her, in the direction of the landing. "Yes, Yes! We're okay. Neither one of us is hurt," she added to reassure her daughter.

"Then, what?" Ann called again, more confused then ever.

"I'm trying to get to you," Jessica called back. "Stay there. Your dad's looking for a flashlight. The lights seem to have gone out, I'm afraid." For the first time Ann became aware that there *were* no lights. She hadn't even thought to try them. Jessica continued, "I think one of the trees has crashed against the house. Or hopefully it's only a branch. Obviously there's been some damage. I can't tell what yet, except that the hall window is knocked out. This branch blocking the stairs must have gone through it."

Ann involuntarily let out a little cry as she began to realize what must have happened. Now thoroughly wet, she stood on the steps shivering, not knowing what to do next, when suddenly a dark form appeared above her, silhouetted against another flash of light. The scene was so eerie, she felt like she was in a spooky movie watching some tentacled monster about to devour her parents. She almost screamed but her father's calm voice brought her back to reality.

"Can't find the flashlight, I'm afraid. But it doesn't look too difficult to get through this mess." He pulled a long branch back and stepped over it until he reached the balustrade. "Are you okay, Ann?" he called down to her.

Ann assured him that she was, though scared.

"Hold on, then. We're both all right and we're coming down." He held out a hand to Jessica who took it gratefully as she stepped gingerly over the mess of branches between her and the stairs. At last she had reached her husband and together they tackled the last large limb keeping them from their daughter. Ann let out a yelp when they at last were beside her, flinging herself into their arms with a great sigh of relief.

"Thank goodness, you both are okay," she shuddered, looking back at the horrible mess behind them, still unable to define the extent of the damage, because of the darkness. For a long moment they all just stood holding one another, letting the relief that each one of them was all right take hold.

"Come on," Jessica said after a minute. "We're all getting soaked. There's nothing we can do until this storm passes and it's daylight."

"You're right, Jess," Michael agreed. "Without electricity we can't even ascertain what kind of damage has been done to the house."

"Gosh, I hope it isn't too bad," said Ann through chattering teeth.

"We'll worry about that later," her mother hastened, suddenly becoming aware of Ann's state. "First, you need to get out of those wet night clothes and get on a warm robe.

You're freezing, honey." Quickly, she bustled Ann down the stairs and back to her room where she could change into dry, warm clothes.

Michael, after one last look at the confusion left behind him, followed her back to the kitchen. There he found Jessica already fussing with the stove so she could make coffee. He, himself, began to search for flashlights and candles to create some form of light.

"What happened?" Ann asked softly as she returned from her room, swathed in a thick, warm robe. She immediately set about helping her mother prepare the coffee.

Before either of them could answer, the back door banged open and two wet figures burst in, flinging water everywhere. "Are you okay?" demanded Scotty as he and Jock stopped to take in the situation.

All three assured the McDougals they were fine. Suddenly everyone began talking at once, until Michael called a halt, throwing up his hands in despair. "Wait a minute. Let's all sit down, have some coffee, and tell our stories."

Once they were seated, Scotty started, "We heard this huge clap of thunder. It woke both of us up. Jock ran to the window first."

"I remember yelling at Dad," Jock interrupted excitedly. "I think I said 'That lightning hit. Oh, my gosh, it hit the tree next to the big house.' Anyway, next thing I saw it fall, right on your house."

"By then I got to the window," Scotty filled in. "But it was too dark to see anything. We had to wait for another streak of lightning. By then we could see what looked like one of your big oaks. It was lying right against the house."

"So we threw on clothes and came right over," Jock finished.

"How bad does it look?" Michael asked Scotty.

"From the outside, it looks like the whole tree is laying against the house, all right. Can't tell how bad it is, though. Too dark. We'll know by daybreak."

Michael groaned. "That's what I was afraid of. We woke up to the crash but it was on the other side of the house. Right away I tried the lights but the lines must be down."

"We have lights, though," Scotty interrupted. "The tree must have pulled down your house wires only."

Michael acknowledged his statement. "That's good. At least we aren't totally without power."

"Anyway," Jessica continued, bringing more coffee to the table. "Michael and I got as far as the hall but could go no further. One of the branches must have gone through the upstairs window by the landing. It blocked our way."

Michael went on to finish their story. "I wasn't able to locate a flashlight but I did break enough branches to at least get us through to the stairs where Ann was waiting for us."

"I was so scared," she cut in. "I didn't know what had happened. I'm just glad Mom and Dad are okay."

"As soon as it gets light enough we'll be able to see better. But right now everything's so dark there's no telling how big a mess we've got on our hands." Michael took a sip of his coffee, then added, "I'm really worried about water damage, though. The way it's raining and the water's pouring in through the broken window, that could be real serious."

"Dear, there's no sense in fretting yet," Jessica patted his shoulder. "Hopefully it won't be as bad as we think. I'll make breakfast while we wait it out. At least we have the gas stove. Things always look better on a full stomach."

As dawn broke and the rain finally ceased, they all gathered outside to ascertain the damage. The sight was shocking. Lightning had indeed struck one of the lovely old live oaks splitting it down the middle. One half still stood, while the other had fallen against the house. All the upstairs windows on that side of the house were shattered. Fortunately those two rooms were only used as guest rooms, but still, rain had caused extensive water damage, especially to the lovely wood floors. Part of the roof was also crushed, which would require major repairs. Finally the branch that had pushed through the upstairs hall window had wreaked its own havoc.

Besides substantial water damage, the halls and floors had suffered scratches and gouges that would have to be repaired or repainted. The final summation was not good. Besides, it being the middle of winter, it was imperative that it be rebuilt as soon as possible.

All of them spent the better part of that day cutting away branches and covering with tarpaulins as much as they could. The cleanup was extensive but by nightfall they had managed to salvage what they could and at least prevent further loss.

Michael immediately put in a call to his insurance company but it was dinnertime before they were able to get back to him. The news was not good. Their policy had expired the previous month and no payment had been made to continue it. They were not covered.

"How can that be?" he questioned Jessica, still in the state of confusion as he got off the phone. " I was sure I paid it. I always pay those things the minute they come in. Or try to at least."

But after much searching, it did turn up, unpaid, still laying on the desk in the den with the other mail. Somehow it had gotten mixed into the wrong pile, too late to be of help to them now.

So there they were facing a cold winter in a very badly damaged house, needing a considerable sum of money to restore it. Though Michael solicited estimates within the week, he was well aware that they had no means of paying for the repairs.

CHAPTER EIGHT

The Solution

I t's the only way," Ann overheard her father say, as she prepared to enter the kitchen, after riding Si'ad the following Saturday morning. Her mother was busy making pancakes for breakfast, always her favorite. But a sickening feeling of dread suddenly hit her stomach and took her appetite away.

"It'll break Ann's heart," she heard her mother reply, softly.

"Don't you think I know that?" Her father countered in a pain-filled voice. "It certainly doesn't make me any too happy either. I wish there were some other way." Apprehension gripped Ann as she stepped into the kitchen.

"What's wrong?" she looked from one to the other, seeing their grim faces, terrified of what they might be about to tell her. "What are you talking about?"

Michael looked at his daughter, knowing that in the next few minutes she just might hate him for what he was about to do and wishing beyond hope that he could avoid this moment. This may well be the hardest thing he'd ever faced. Not sure how to begin, he started weakly, "Ann, honey, please believe that what I have to tell you, well, I wish there could be any other solution but this. It's the last choice I'd pick, but you know we've got to get the house fixed and soon."

"What are you talking about?" she broke in again, near hysterical now with fear, wishing her father would get to the point.

"Ann, we've had an offer for Si'ad," her mother cut in, quietly. "A good offer."

"No!" Ann screamed, covering her ears. "I won't hear it! You can't mean …."

"Wait," her father stopped her. "Hear us out. You must know how I feel about Si'ad. He's the best horse on the place. I would never willingly give him up."

"But you are," she glared at him, accusingly, the statement hanging in the air. Michael would have given anything to take that look away from her face. He knew only too well the pain this choice was causing her, all of them.

"Not completely," he added.

"How's that?"

"Let me explain. They're willing to lease him instead of buying him outright. They're proposing a three year lease."

"Three years!" To Ann three years seemed like a lifetime.

"Ann, hear me out. I know you don't want to give up Si'ad. None of us wants that, but just think about it for a moment. We've got a serious problem here. The house must be repaired, and soon, before more things go wrong. We've done what we could temporarily but it's not enough. It's winter. We can't keep living like this. It's got to be fixed right. And that costs money. It's too late to complain about the insurance. That's unfortunate, but what's done is done and we can't do anything about it now."

"I know, Dad, and I'm not blaming you, but Si'ad?" she moaned. "Isn't there another way?"

"I wish there were. I've tried everything I could think of." He looked so devastated; Ann was suddenly made aware of the anguish her father must be suffering, too. After all Si'ad was his horse first. "Nothing seems to be the answer," he continued. "We need too much money and we need it now. I was beside myself when I got this call from one of the people who booked to Si'ad last year. They just had their foal, a filly, and called to tell us how pleased they were."

"For a filly? Not a colt?"

"Arab people prefer fillies. Not like us Thoroughbred people," he said. "Fillies are much more valuable to them. Anyway, they've booked two more mares to him this year and were calling to make arrangements, as well. In passing, Mr. Haines reminded me he was still interested in buying Si'ad, if we ever chose to sell."

"But you said 'lease'?"

"I know I did. You see after I hung up, I got to thinking about it and called him back, explained our situation to him, and asked him if he'd consider a lease instead. We agreed on a three-year lease to be about equal to the amount of money we'd need to fix the damage to the house. After that time he'd be returned to us."

"But, three years. It's so long," she sighed. "And can you get along without the revenue his stud fees are bringing in for that period?"

"I guess I'd have to. Anyhow, we've done without before." He shrugged. "Look, honey, the bottom line here is how you feel about this. If you can bear to part with him."

"I thought you'd already made up your mind. I thought you'd already agreed."

"Not exactly. I told him I'd get back to him after I spoke to my family. Honey, I know what that horse means to you. I won't do it if you don't want me to."

"You would?" she suddenly looked hopeful.

"Of course. I couldn't stand to have my own daughter hate me over this."

Ann suddenly dissolved into tears. "Oh, Dad, I'd never do that," she ran to him, hugging him. Then she knew, sadly, what she must do. "Where is this farm?" she asked through choked tears.

"Arizona."

"Arizona! But that's so far away. We wouldn't get to see him and three years is a long time."

"It seems so now," he said as he patted her on the back, "but it'll pass quickly. And in the meantime you do have Lightning to raise. Another year and you'll be riding him."

Ann hesitated, "I know, but I'd miss Si'ad so much. You sure it's the only way?" She wailed, tears welling up in her eyes and spilling down her cheeks.

Michael felt as though his heart were breaking as he held his only child. He'd give anything not to cause her this pain. "I know what you're going through," he said, lamely. "I know it won't be easy. If you really can't give him up, I'll understand. Maybe we can find another way."

Ann only shook her head, "Please, let me have some time to think about it," she choked. "I just have to get used to the idea..."

"Of course, honey. Take all the time you need."

Without another word, Ann rose and ran for the kitchen door. She did not stop until she had reached Si'ad's pasture where she whistled to the stallion. Si'ad raised his head and came up to her. She leaped over the boards and ran up to him, throwing her arms around his neck. Patiently he stood there, not understanding the sudden hysterical tears being shed into his neck, as Ann poured out her emotions in the only way she knew. As she stood beside him she slowly came to grips with what she must do. In her heart she felt there was no other choice. Finally, she removed her arms from around his neck and turned back to the house.

Though considerable time had passed, she found her father still sitting at the table in the kitchen, while her mother prepared their lunch. He looked up at her, noting her solemn expression through the now-dried tears. Before she could utter a word, he began, "Honey, I've made a decision not to send him. This is just too hard on you. We'll just have to come up with another way to fix the house."

At first Ann brightened. Si'ad wouldn't leave after all? She thought. Her elation was quickly spent. But at what cost? She sighed. No, there was no other way. "No, Dad, not without risking the farm, or putting ourselves in too much debt, we can't. I've been thinking, too. And now I see that it is the only way. It wouldn't be right of me to demand you not to send Si'ad away when to do otherwise would jeopardize the farm. I guess I'll just have to grow up and stop being so selfish. At least I'll still have Lightning. And three years will pass, eventually." Tears began to blind her eyes again so that she missed the look that passed between her parents. Suddenly unable to stand there any longer, she turned and fled, calling over her shoulder, "Go ahead and make your call, Dad, before I change my mind."

Her parents watched her go in silence, each understanding how painful this decision was for her. In that moment their little girl had come a long way toward accepting the cruel realities of adult life.

"If there was only some other way," Michael said wearily.

"I know, dear. It's not your fault. And she really doesn't blame you. It's just … It's so hard on her. But then, it's hard on all of us. Si'ad means a great deal to this farm." Jessica bent her head in acceptance for what she could not change and put a hand out to her husband. " She's young. She'll get over it. At least she's still got the colt." Michael nodded, reluctantly picking up the phone to make the one call he wished he never would have had to make.

Later, when Ann returned to the house for the second time, she asked her father only one question, "When?"

"Next Sunday," he replied.

"So soon?" she responded incredulously.

"They're sending a van out from Arizona. If they can take him now they can still get in this breeding season. They didn't object to handling the mares already booked to him for this year, either. We were lucky on that score. They must want his blood pretty badly."

"Lucky? Why do you say that?"

"Why if he can fulfill this season for them, he'll only have two more out there. That means we'll get him back that much sooner."

"I suppose so," she replied, still thinking it would be a long time, regardless.

"I'm sorry," he suddenly realized how Ann saw it. "I wish it wasn't so soon, either. Doesn't give you much time with him."

Ann merely shook her head and went on into her room.

Early in the week men arrived to work on the house. Michael had wasted no time starting repairs to their storm-damaged home, for it was now the height of winter, not the time to have one whole side of the house open to the elements, as it were. Though that part of the house had been closed off and they were actually living in the downstairs area consisting of the kitchen, living room and Ann's room with adjoining bath, there was constant threat of water damage and frozen pipes. The heat source basically came from the huge fireplace in the living room, along with the wood stove in the corner of the kitchen. It was imperative that the exposed part be sealed off as soon as possible so that central heat could be restored.

As the work progressed, Ann tried not to notice, as it was a constant reminder of her upcoming loss. Instead she sought out Si'ad's company as much as possible, even to the temporary neglect of her colt, Lightning. She would have him later to fall back on. For now she needed Si'ad. In many little ways, the rest of the family made it easier for her to spend these last moments with her horse, knowing that she, more than any of them, would suffer the most when he was gone. No one doubted the wisdom of this decision, but that did not alleviate any of the grief.

Too soon it was Sunday morning. Ann rose at dawn for one last ride on her beloved horse before he left. As she entered his stall, bridle in hand, he came over to eagerly nudge against her, keen for the forth-coming ride, anxious to stretch his legs. His reactions were so predictable, so familiar, a sharp pain ran through her as she slid the bridle over his head for the last time. Opening the stall door, she led him out and vaulted on his bare back. If this was to be their last ride together, she thought, let it be the way she preferred, natural and free like the wind.

Dawn was just breaking as she walked him past the paddocks and out around the track, striking across the large field beyond it. She had no set plan in mind, but let Si'ad have his head.

The stallion, upon seeing the field open before him, shook his head, restless to move out faster, anxious to run. Ann's spirit, too, was restless, so when he fought the bit, she gave in, setting him free. At once he burst into a full gallop, stretching his powerful muscles as he lengthened his stride. Wind tore through his mane, whipping its long strands back in Ann's face, mingling with her own wildly tossed black curls as she bent over his neck and urged him on. Relishing the feeling of power beneath her, she experienced a sense of freedom. Exhilarated by the speed and unleashed fury of the half-wild stallion, she let him run.

Then the gate at the end of the field was upon them. Without hesitation, Ann put Si'ad to it and while it was easily four feet, he cleared it so smoothly she hardly felt it. Just before his take off, she buried her hands into his mane and gave him his head. Reins were useless now. She could not have controlled the grey's flight had she wanted to.

Si'ad had nearly crossed the length of the adjoining field before Ann felt any visible slowing of the horse beneath her. Bringing him down gradually she bade him walk to cool himself out, subconsciously picking a path that would eventually lead them to Flat Top. As they wound their way through the stands of tall shade trees, she let her stallion pick his own pace, one hand stroking his now-damp neck. She spoke to him little for the communication between them was such that words were not necessary. This is how it will be when your son gets old enough to ride, she thought.

But that was far into the future. Lightning would not be ready to break to saddle until next winter. For a youth of fifteen, that time seemed endless. Faced with the three years she must wait for Si'ad's return, she saw the time as too long to fathom. Worse, a premonition gnawed at her deep down inside she couldn't erase that even when Si'ad did return to them, things would not be as they were right this minute. There would never be the bond between them that existed now. Though she had no basis in fact for this, in her heart she knew it to be true. She was reluctant to voice her opinions to anyone, lest he fail to understand.

Si'ad reached the trail leading to Flat Top and she let him continue up it, stopping as she always did when they reached the top. Sliding down from his back, she checked his chest before turning him loose to graze, but it was dry already. The stallion was in wonderfully fit condition, having cooled down quickly after his exertions. Easing the bridle off but keeping the reins around his neck, she allowed him a couple of bites of grass as she gazed distractedly out at the familiar scene, lost in thought. It was not until she felt the impatient tug of the reins, that she was jolted from her reverie.

"Sorry, you've eaten too much already," she admonished, sliding the bridle back in place and drawing the reins up before swinging upon his back.. The grey shook his head, fanning out his heavy, dark mane. "Time to head back, but let's take the long way," she added, trying to prolong this ride as much as possible.

The sun was now high in the sky when she finally returned down the lane behind the house. She could not resist putting him at the gate at the head of the lane one last time, reveling as he cleared it effortlessly. But even as she silently cheered his strength, she was met by a strange van with Arizona plates, parked in the courtyard, as she rode up. Her heart sank. They had not changed their minds, nor had they wasted any time getting here to pick up their valuable charge. Her loss had become a reality.

Michael and Scotty came out of the stallion barn with a stranger whom Ann assumed was the van driver. "Oh, here she is now," she heard her father tell the man. "Ann, is he cooled out enough to load?" he asked, coming up to her and checking Si'ad, nodding satisfactorily. "He wants to leave right away, I'm afraid."

"Now?" she asked faintly, sliding off the stallion.

The driver was not without compassion. "It's a long trip," he explained. "I'd like to put as many miles behind us as possible before nightfall. It'll be easier on him," he added, looking slightly embarrassed. Obviously, her father had explained the situation to him and he was feeling very uncomfortable about being the one chosen to take the horse away.

Without a word, Ann turned and led Si'ad into the barn where she cross-tied him. There, with infinite care and love, she rubbed him down for the last time. Jock entered the barn and

93

started to volunteer his assistance, but thought better of it, intuition telling him this was something she must do alone.

Once he was cleaned up to her satisfaction, she put on his leg wraps and bandaged his tail. Then she eased a blanket over him and buckled it to fit. At last he was ready. She could stall no longer. Slowly she unsnapped the cross ties and re-snapped the lead rope back on his halter, before leading him out to the trailer. Si'ad walked confidently beside her, but with each step she felt as if she were betraying his trust. Even as he followed her without hesitation into the van, she fought back the tears that threatened to engulf her. As she tied him into his stall, automatically checking to make sure everything was safe, she again struggled against the desire to suddenly scream out "No!" and flee with him away from this, somewhere safe where they could be together as before. But there was no place safe. She'd made her decision and now she must keep her promise. She had no choice but to live with things are they were. Flinging her arms around Si'ad one last time, she hugged him tightly.

"Be good," she whispered into his mane. "We'll be together again." With that she fled the trailer, leaving them all behind, not stopping until she reached Lightning's stall where she threw herself down in the straw, tears that she had held so tightly in check, now pouring forth in a torrent of misery.

"Will she be all right?" the driver asked, shocked by the show of emotion on the young girl's face. He did not know the whole story about why this horse was being shipped from Kentucky to Arizona, but one thing was for sure, that there was one member of this solemn family that bitterly opposed the stallion's leaving. Suddenly he wished he were a long way from here. He had a soft heart, especially when it came to animals and kids, and he wasn't sure he wanted to know this story.

Michael only nodded. "I think so. You'd better leave now, though. This is hard on all of us, so the sooner he's gone the better, I'm afraid." The driver couldn't agree more. He jumped into his cab and started the motor. Seconds later he was heading down the driveway, leaving a thin cloud of dust in his wake.

Ann heard the motor as it pulled away, taking with it her beloved horse. She looked at the black colt before her. "I guess that makes you an orphan for sure, Lightning," she murmured, hugging him. "And you're all I have left. From now on it's just you and me." Though deep in her heart she knew she'd be ultimately grateful for Lightning's presence, she could not soon forget her loss of his father. Si'ad may return three years hence, but somehow she felt that life would never be the same. It was as if he were already lost to her.

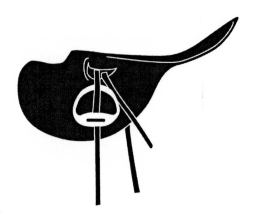

CHAPTER NINE

The Yearling

With Si'ad gone, Ann poured all her energies into Lightning. Now the big black yearling was all she had, so he came to mean that much more to her. He had become her shadow, following her everywhere, just like a huge puppy. Over the winter he had gained in stature and as spring approached, Scotty remarked one day that he'd bet the colt leveled off at close to seventeen hands, if he continued as he was growing. In the yearling pasture, he towered over the other babies in size. None of them could touch his speed and agility either. Ann was so proud of him.

Often she would just stand at the fence watching the youngsters at play. Lightning stuck out so obviously from the rest that Ann was sure he was an exceptional colt. When she got to see the yearlings from other farms, she convinced herself all the more that none were as good as her Lightning.

Now and then she felt her throat restrict when he did something or looked a certain way that was so reminiscent of his father. Sometimes the way he carried his head or swished his long black tail so arrogantly, but mostly it was his head, that finely chiseled delicate version in black of his grey Arabian sire. When he flared his nostrils and cocked those fine ears of his forward so that they nearly touched, Ann could feel tears sting the backs of her eyes for just a moment.

There was one way in which Lightning was his own individual, not like Si'ad at all. Whereas the grey stallion had always maintained a certain aloofness, a certain untamed desert wildness that no amount of handling could remove, Lightning was completely the opposite. His orphan upbringing had given him a docile, gentle nature around people. Anyone could handle him. He was fully well-mannered and so easy to work around. Ann continued his education to the point of spoiling him. At the sight of any one of them, he would rush over to the fence, whinnying for attention, for like as not they would each stop to give him a pat and possibly a treat.

Perfectly behaved, he would stand quietly to be groomed or to have his feet worked on. He led so easily one barely needed a lead rope. He even backed on command. What more could anyone want? Yet every so often Ann would remember a certain wild trait that his sire had shown and just wish, if only for a moment, to see that wild look come into Lightning's big, soft eyes. She missed him still, though she seldom if ever made reference to him. It was as if he were dead to her. And though she might have loved to see a little spark of untamed fire in his son, she knew far too well that any wildness had no place on a race track. Besides, with all the attention he had received as an orphan, Lightning's temperament had been molded to the docile, spoiled pet he was now. Far different from the wild desert upbringing that had shaped Si'ad.

Jock often asked her to go riding, and many times she did ride with him, though they both knew it was not the same any longer. Of the horses they had left, she chose her mother's near-black gelding, Banshee. He'd been a gift from her mother's family a couple of years ago, a kind of atonement following years of coolness after she had married Michael. Banshee, a finely bred hunter, was to replace her Cedardale, who was getting too old to ride. But Jessica seldom had time for riding these days, so too often Banshee just lazed about his pasture eating grass and getting fat. Now Ann took him over.

If she had never known Si'ad, she could have enjoyed the gelding. He was beautifully trained, with excellent gaits and able to jump like a bird. He was even quite pretty to look at with his shiny black coat and high, evenly matched white socks on the hind legs. A large, straight blaze splashed down his foreface running into seal-brown nostrils. Because of this he was considered a brown by Thoroughbred color standards even though the rest of him was mostly as rich a black as Lightning. He was an enjoyable horse to behold as well as to ride, but he wasn't Si'ad.

Still, she and Jock had many pleasant rides together, albeit at times the fun was a bit too forced. Jock tried hard to make her forget, or at least not to regret so much. He spoke often of Lightning and his potential. In many ways he let her know he had the same faith in the colt she did. And she was grateful, even though she did not always show it. Fortunately they were so close in spirit and friendship that Jock understood and accepted that she was still grieving. Eventually she would need to talk and he'd be there for her.

Long about late spring, as summer was once again fast approaching, Ann and Jock went out for one of their rides. It was Saturday morning so there was no rush to get back right away. This time they chose to take Lightning with them. He ran about them like a giant pet dog. So comical was he that they found themselves laughing at his antics and for the first time in a long time, Ann suddenly realized she felt good inside. She tried to express that feeling to Jock.

"In spite of everything that's happened to us lately, I wouldn't ever want to live anywhere else but here," she sighed, contentedly. "Can you imagine any other life but ours?"

Jock turned his head toward her, surprised to see a smile on her face for the first time since Si'ad left. Pleased, he shook his head in agreement. "Never. This is the only home *I* ever want to know." They watched Lightning race on ahead of them, choosing to jump a log in his way with a big, disdainful leap, bucking as he landed. They both laughed.

"He's got all the makings of a winner, he does," Jock remarked.

"I agree. Is that what Scotty thinks, also?"

"Oh, you know Dad. He seldom says much one way or the other. But he watches. He watches Lightning all the time. I don't think he'd do that if he didn't like what he sees. Besides, you know Dad's look when he really approves of something, but doesn't want to say anything out loud?"

Ann nodded, how well she knew that look. Excited, she questioned him, "Is that how he views Lightning, do you think?"

"Hard to say for sure. I suspect so, though he won't actually come out and voice any opinions."

"I guess that's just because things around here have a way of not panning out. I guess your Dad and mine kind of lose hope after awhile," she added in a rare moment of insight. She was pensive for a minute, lost in thought, remembering. "I know I did, when Si'ad … well, you know," she stopped, unable to go on.

Jock nodded, expressing with his eyes what he couldn't trust his voice to speak.

"Anyway," she went on after gaining control of her voice again, "it's better now. I mean, it'll never be the same. Not like it was. But I think I'm beginning to cope."

"He's not dead, Ann. He *will* be coming back." Jock tried to choose his words carefully. This was the first she'd opened up and tried to speak about her loss. "Look, one season is already behind us. Two more and he'll be back here to stay. It's not that far off, really." He knew she really needed to communicate to someone and he didn't want to stop her once she got going. It was time to face it and put it behind her.

"I know that, but ... oh, how can I explain?" she sighed, looking at the black colt who also meant so much to her. Her feelings were torn and she didn't know how to explain, even to her best friend Jock, what she was really feeling inside.

"Try me. I'll understand."

"Yes, but I'm not sure if *I* do. Things, feelings are happening inside me and I'm not sure what I feel or how I'm supposed to feel."

Jock remained silent, instinctively knowing this was not the time to voice his opinions. She was hardly aware of him now, as she wrestled with her problem aloud, trying to come to an understanding. His presence alone was reassuring enough to Ann. Patiently he waited for her to continue.

The two horses moved along in a companionable walk for a considerable distance. Just when Jock began to doubt that she was ready to discuss it after all, a small, barely audible voice began again. "When everything happened to us last winter, I was so angry. At first I couldn't understand why. I wanted to blame Dad for not paying the insurance, but deep inside I knew I really couldn't. It was an honest mistake and knowing Dad I was sure he was blaming himself enough for all of us. And our debts are too high to try for a loan. Even if we could get one, it would be too risky. Suppose we couldn't pay it back? We couldn't put the farm in jeopardy. Finally I had to accept that Dad was right.

The house had to be fixed immediately and there was no other way. Si'ad was the only answer.

"But even after I understood that, it was hard to face. I know he meant so much to the farm, the income from his stud fees alone … Still, I guess I was just being selfish. I only saw my loss. He was really my horse, wasn't he?" Jock nodded, choking back the emotion he felt, even now, after all this time. She went on in a somewhat ragged voice, "I tamed him. I'm the one who rode him and looked after him. The thing is, now he's not mine anymore. Once he left our farm, I lost my exclusive right to him. Do you know what I'm saying?"

Jock concurred, "Yes, I think I do. Kind of like when Tag here was racing. How I'd have felt if anyone else got to race him."

"Yes, that's it, exactly. He may come back here someday, but he won't be mine any more. Not the same as before. Now he belongs to other people. The bond we shared will have been broken. It will never be like it was."

"I know. Even though he'll remember you, that something special you two had together will have changed."

Ann nodded. "But yet I still have Lightning and he's special, too. Maybe more special because he's our future. And my feelings start getting mixed up because I have him and I love him just as much. Sometimes I think I love him even more. Maybe that's on account of he's here and I have him to look forward to … breaking, riding, and, hopefully, one day racing. I get excited about the future and then I think maybe I'm being disloyal to Si'ad. Maybe I'm forgetting."

"No, you're not being disloyal," he said slowly, picking through his words. "You are learning to get on with your life. It is important to look toward the future, not back to the past. And Lightning *is* your future. You're not forgetting Si'ad. What you are doing is putting his memory in its proper place. You'll never forget him. You're just learning to live with what you cannot change."

"And when he comes back?"

"You'll remember. The good times will all come back to you. But by then things will be in proper perspective and you'll be ready to accept him back. It'll all work out. You'll see."

She smiled shakily over at him. "Suddenly I don't feel so guilty anymore. Jock, how do you get to be so wise?"

"I didn't. It's just called growing up."

"No, it's not. You've always been so much more serious than I. I don't think I'll ever be that smart, if I live to be one hundred."

He grinned. "Well, you always were so emotional about everything, always leading with your heart. Maybe you're right. Maybe you'll never be as smart as me."

She looked up, suddenly ready to argue, when she saw a big silly grin on his face. "Oh, you," she laughed.

"Feel better?"

"Lots."

"Good, now if you think we've had enough of an emotional catharsis for one day, how about a race to the back gate?"

"You're on." She dug her heels into Banshee's sides and tore off, whooping with glee, Jock in hot pursuit. These two horses were much closer matched than Tag and Si'ad had been, and these races more often than not ended in a tie or so close neither could call it indisputably, as was this day when they came up to the gate in a dead heat, still laughing and name calling. Actually Lightning won, beating both of them by scampering ahead, not burdened by the weight of a rider.

They rode into the courtyard, Ann and Jock talking animatedly about the upcoming summer while the big black colt followed them like a faithful dog, Scotty looked up from his work, repairing the hay bailer, and smiled at them, immediately aware of the change that had come over Ann, and pleased by the result. It was not good to grieve excessively when one was so young, and a full life awaits, he thought.

From then on Ann did feel much better and showed it. It was as if she'd been released of her guilt in letting Si'ad go and now was able to give her attention fully to Lightning without feeling disloyal to Si'ad.

Lightning as well seemed to sense the very subtle change to come over Ann. While he had always been closest to her and accepted as her horse, now, without the competition of her loyalties toward any other, he grew even more bonded to her than before. His very docility allowed him more freedom than the average horse and Ann often took him about the farm with her as she did her chores. She treated him much like a beloved dog rather than the large beast he was. He could be found almost anywhere Ann was, from helping stack hay onto the wagons in the hay fields to swimming with her and Jock in their pond by the house. Scotty remarked more than once about having the large colt under foot. In fact he added that he was so spoiled he'd be not much use for anything but an expensive lawn ornament. But Ann caught him smiling when he said it, so she knew he really was as fond of the only offspring of Glory and Si'ad as any of them.

As summer approached once again, Ann began to look forward to her busy summer schedule. This year's crop of foals, four in all, were nearing their weaning time and would need individual training in handling and manners. Plus there were the yearlings to prepare for the fall sales. Best of all, this year she had Lightning to break to saddle and bridle.

That she enjoyed most of all. All summer she worked with him, teaching him to wear a bit and bridle, until she could easily slip it in and out of his mouth. Then she worked with the long reins, lunging him in both directions at all three gaits, walk, trot and canter. She taught him to turn and back via the rein pressure on each side. It was not long before he was completely tractable to each command. He could even switch gaits by voice alone. Ann was quite pleased with the result of this, her first attempt to completely break a colt on her own.

By fall she had him wearing a light racing saddle and getting used to the tightening of the girth, thus completing his groundwork. All that remained now was for him to learn to bear the weight of a rider. Through it all he had never shown signs of rebellion or refusal to do what was expected of him, a remarkably compliant young colt, showing none of his sire's wildness.

"Tomorrow's the day," Jock announced, as he swung his arms over Lightning's stall where Ann was finishing the colt's rub down.

She turned to face him. "What's tomorrow?" she asked.

"Why, silly, tomorrow you get to ride Lightning."

"Who said?" her face lit up as the reality of Jock's words began to sink in.

"Dad, of course. He thinks the colt is strong enough now to hold a person on his back, so since you've done all the work so far, you get to go first."

"Whoopee!" she shrieked as the news finally sunk home, startling Lightning as she did. The colt jumped but for once Ann failed to notice. "You mean it? Wow!" she kept saying, first hugging him over the stall door, then hugging her colt for good measure.

"Hear that, boy. I'm finally going to ride you. Not just here in the stall, either." The last couple of weeks she'd saddled him in the stall with the lightweight racing saddle. Starting with just leaning heavily upon his back, she had gradually increased her weight across him until she was sitting in the saddle. She had practiced mounting and dismounting until she was bored with it and secretly thought Lightning was, too. He had shown every indication that he was ready for a rider. All Ann was waiting for was the go ahead from Scotty. Now he had given it.

"Tomorrow!" she said again, as if she couldn't yet believe it. It seemed she'd been waiting all her life for this moment. Turning back to Jock, one hand still across the colt's withers, she said. "I just know he'll be wonderful to ride. It'll be just like having Si'ad back." She looked back at him as if studying his confirmation all over again. "He's so perfect and he moves so freely across the ground. Oh, I can't wait!"

"Well, you'd better," Jock laughed. "Tomorrow you'll probably only get to walk him. At least at first. You won't be running him for quite a while yet," he added, as if reading her mind.

"Oh, I *know* that," she grimaced at him as if he thought her a complete idiot. "I'm talking about later, when I can begin to let him run. I bet he can fly!"

"You're probably right," Jock agreed. "I wouldn't be surprised after watching him in the pasture. He outruns all the other colts his age. Still, it's a long way from that to the track."

"Perhaps. But this time we'll get there. With this colt. From the beginning I've always felt he was going to be the one for us. I've never doubted it. Lightning will be our champion. Don't you agree?" she said.

"Well, you've certainly always had faith in him. Yes, I will agree that I, too, have some high hopes for him. I can see what you see. Maybe this *will* be our turning point. Maybe this guy will finally be the winner we've been waiting for." he rested his chin against his outstretched arms, lying across the stall door.

"I think so," she went on, glad of his confidence, too. It was nice to have a friend who shared her innermost hopes and dreams and felt as she did. She leaned back against the stall. There they both stayed in comfortable silence, each lost in thought, until it was time to do the nightly chores.

When Scotty came into the barn to tell Ann of his plans for Lightning the next day, she was unable to keep a straight face and blurted out that Jock had already told her. "That son of mine," Scotty shook his head. "He was never any good at keeping anything to himself. I suppose he got you all excited and worked up for nothing. All I want you to do tomorrow is to mount him and walk him about the paddock, a nice even *slow* walk. Nothing fancy."

"Sure, Scotty. I know what you want. I'm just excited because at last I'm going to ride him, that's all."

"Well, your dad and I decided since you've put all the work into him so far, you might as well go ahead and be the one to break him to saddle. You're certainly as capable as anyone is."

"You mean it? Thanks for having such confidence in me." Impulsively she hugged him, making Scotty bristle at such a show of emotion. It always made him uncomfortable. "Aw, go on with you now and get your chores done before I change my mind. And you might as well leave your colt out tonight. It's going to be a warm night, especially for this time of year. I put all the geldings in the big pasture by the house. Put him in with them."

Ann nodded her assent. Now that the rest of the yearlings had been sold at the Keeneland sales last month, Lightning was the only yearling left on the farm. Therefore he was generally turned out with the geldings in the front pasture alongside the house. This pasture spread out across approximately fifty acres of good thick grass and was fed by a stream running through it. In addition there was a run-in shed to provide shelter from any inclement weather. It was so self-sufficient that horses could be left out there almost all year round.

Though it was late November now, the night promised to be a mild one, so the horses were turned out to enjoy the last of the pleasant tasting grass. Lightning, big as he was, walked content-edly alongside Ann, as graceful as a much older, more mature horse. In fact, he hardly looked a yearling as she released him to run off kicking and bucking in high spirits, trying to get the more sedate geldings to play with him.

"Just get all your energies out now, my pet," she called to him, "because tomorrow we get down to serious business." Lightning looked back once, whinnied, but kept on running, stopping only when he was convinced the geldings would not leave their grazing to play with him. Ann would have continued the enjoyment of watching her colt even though it was nearly dark, but she faintly heard her mother calling her to dinner and she reluctantly turned back to the house.

"Tomorrow," she thought dreamily, "tomorrow I get to finally ride my beloved Lightning. It may be only a walk but it's a beginning and soon, very soon we'll be free to run together. Just like I used to on Si'ad. And Lightning will be so fast, maybe even faster." For a moment the thought of Si'ad crossed her memory and she felt a sadness. But it was different now. She still thought of him, but not nearly as often. Lightning occupied her thoughts far more. Without realizing it, she had transferred her affections to his son. Jock had been right. Here was her future. She didn't love Si'ad any the less but she had come to grips with what she could not change. Her whole focus was centered around the black colt, her Lightning.

As she fell asleep later that night, her thoughts again returned to her colt and what it was going to feel like to ride him. Already she could feel the wind in her hair, the thrill of a strong, muscled horse beneath her, the sense of power he would generate as everything flew past them at an alarming rate. and she just knew he'd be the fastest horse ever, she just knew it.

CHAPTER TEN

Stolen!

Later that night a long stock-type trailer made its way down the road in front of Stormy Hill. It was not uncommon to see horse vans on these roads at all hours of the night or day as they transported horses from one farm to another or to one of the nearby tracks. However, this one appeared to have some kind of trouble as its engine did not sound quite right. As it belched out what could only be described as a final choking gasp, the driver pulled it off the road and onto a dirt lane used for farm vehicles going into an adjoining hay field. This particular path just happened to border the property owned by Stormy Hill.

An angry driver got out and pulled up the hood on the truck cab, disappearing beneath it as he searched for the problem. Seconds later, a voice from the passenger side called out, impatiently, "Can't you fix it faster? I don't like this, not one bit. We could be seen from here. Suppose someone stops to help?"

His companion's head popped up as he glared at his partner. "Then I suggest you get over here and help. Then maybe we'll be on our way quicker." He returned to tinkering under the hood.

Reluctantly, the other man stepped down from the cab. "Aw, Louie," he whined. "You know I don't know nothin' about engines. What good would I be anyway? I'm just scared we'll get caught, that's all."

"Yeah? Well so'm I," came a muffled reply from beneath the hood. "So, if you can't help me, just stay out of my way. Go check on the horses or something. You're making me too nervous, Ralph, just standing there."

Ralph backed away. Following Louie's suggestion, he walked around the side of the trailer and peered in to observe the horses. Everything was quiet and all seemed relaxed, for which he was grateful. He knew enough about horses to know that this was not always the case when one is transporting a group of horses unfamiliar with each other and in a strange rig. But for now all were content.

He then cast a furtive glance up and down the road, glad to see that all was dark. It was quite late at night and nobody seemed to be on this back road at this hour. Then he heard a soft whinny coming from nearby. He walked around the trailer until he spied the pasture fence running alongside the dirt road into which they had pulled. In the darkness, he could barely make out the black form of a horse standing there, head turned curiously toward them.

"Well, fella, are we disturbing your quiet evening?" Ralph genuinely liked horses. He crossed over to the fence to pat this one, who moved his head closer, asking for more when he stopped. This gesture caused Ralph to chuckle softly. "Like it, huh?" he said. "Someone's made quite a pet out of you." He continued his stroking of the friendly young horse.

Lightning had heard the truck enter the side path not far from where he stood grazing in his pasture. Being the curious young fellow he was, he naturally began to move down the field to see what was going on. His acute hearing picked up voices. People! To a colt raised by hand and treated very much like an overgrown lap dog by his loving mistress, Lightning felt no fear toward these strangers. He came closer. Perhaps someone had come to give him some attention. As he stood near the fence, a voice spoke to him. He moved closer still and received a gentle patting hand as a reward. The stranger began to rub his neck, looking for and finding the tender, itchy spots. He was enjoying this immensely.

While Ralph scratched the colt's neck, a plan began to take shape in his mind.

"Hey, I've fixed the problem," Louie's voice cut into his thoughts, returning him to their present situation. "Come on. Let's get out of here. Don't know how much longer our luck'll hold before we're spotted." He slammed the hood down and hopped into the cab, starting the engine, which sprang to life with a much healthier sound this time. Lightning started at the loud bang of the hood, but quickly settled when he sensed no further danger. Ralph continued to pat him in a reassuring way.

"Wait," he called out. ""Look what I've got here."

Louie impatiently stuck his head out of the cab. "Yeah, so? It's a horse. We've got plenty of them back there." He nodded toward the trailer. "Forget it and let's git. We've been here too long already. Chances are good they're on to us by now. 'Sides, you were the one so impatient to get going."

"I was. That is, until I saw this guy. He's a looker all right. And so gentle. We've got one more space. Why not take him, too?"

"Are you nuts? We don't know anything about him. And we don't have the time to fool around."

"I know. But, just think. He's pretty enough to bring a fair dollar, and this one would be all ours. No sharing with anyone else."

Louie started to argue, but he did see the sense in what his partner was saying. Though he thought it was foolish to take any more chances, he killed the motor and jumped back down. One look at the black youngster and even he knew this was no ordinary colt. "Okay, but only if he comes easily. We don't want to attract any attention."

Ralph grabbed quickly for an extra halter and rope he knew was hanging up in the cab next to the door, while Louie hastened to open the back door. Lightning stood patiently, never flinching when the halter was placed over his head. Ralph started to lower the rails in front of him, but as he reached out to the top rail, his eyes caught the faint glimmer of a metal gate just up the lane. While it was mostly buried under weeds, and a bit rusty on the hinges from infrequent use, it did open without too much trouble. Leaving it ajar, he hastily drew Lightning through and led him to the trailer. The colt entered the strange vehicle without hesitation, just as he had been trained to do.

"See?" Ralph told Louie, triumphantly. "Nothing to it." He and Louie swiftly closed the back door to the stock trailer and locked it tight. "We have one more horse and this one's a beauty. With his looks and manners, he'll bring a good price."

"Yeah, sure, now let's get out of here," was all his partner would comment, though he was secretly pleased to add the handsome youngster to their string.

They both leaped into the cab and Louie started the engine. The road behind them was dark and empty. During the time they had parked there no car had been down it. Carefully, Louie backed his big rig out of the lane and pulled back onto the road, heading west. Hours later, as the sun came up, they were many miles from Bluegrass country.

Dawn was just breaking when Ann arose. She had barely been able to sleep. Today's the day, she thought as she slid out of bed and pulled on her jeans. Today I get to ride Lightning at last. She slipped out of her bedroom window because it was quicker and ran lightly across the lawn toward the pasture just beyond it. In the early light she could already see the three geldings grazing off to one side, near the driveway, but she did not see Lightning right away. Not alarmed, she hurried up to the fence and whistled for him. When there was no immediate response, she ducked through the rails and stepped into the pasture, whistling again. Still no colt.

At first Ann was exasperated. This was so unlike him. Usually he came the minute he saw her, and while he did not always stay with the geldings, he seldom strayed too far from them. As she walked out farther, she attracted their attention and the three stopped grazing to come up for some petting. Absentmindedly she gave it to them, stroking the brown, the bay and the black head each in his turn.

"Where is he?" she asked each of them, as if they could give her an answer. "Where's my boy, huh fellas?" But there was no response from the errant colt.

Alarmed now, Ann began to gaze frantically about the huge pasture, looking for any sign of him. Thinking that he had been hurt, she started to search on foot until it occurred to her that she could move faster on horseback. Swinging up on Banshee she guided him with her hands against his neck, moving out across the field in a wild search for the colt.

A half hour later she had covered every inch of the sprawling pasture. The sun was now completely up and there were no dark areas left in which a black colt could remain unseen. Still, there was no Lightning. He had somehow magically disappeared. Then a sudden thought crossed her mind. Perhaps Jock or Scotty had decided to bring him in after all, without bothering to tell her. After all, they were planning to ride him today. That must be it! Hastily she vaulted off Banshee and ran for the barn. Just as she entered the stallion barn, she saw Jock coming down the aisle.

"Did you bring Lightning in already?" she questioned, running up to his stall but finding it empty.

"No, he's still out in the pasture with the others, why?" Jock answered her.

"No, he's not."

"What do you mean, he's not?" Jock abruptly looked concerned.

"Just what I said. He's not there. I've searched everywhere for him. I'm telling you, he's not in the front pasture!" Her voice rose in sudden panic.

"Calm down, Ann. He's got to be somewhere. I mean we just can't misplace a colt like him on this farm."

"Hey, you two. What's all the fuss?" asked Scotty, coming onto the scene to find a frantic-eyed Ann shouting at Jock who seemed equally distraught.

"Where's Lightning?" they both turned to him and shouted together.

"Why out in the house pasture, where else?"

"No he's not!" they replied in unison again to a baffled Scotty.

"Look, come and see for yourself," Ann added, grabbing his arm. "He's not there!"

"Impossible," Scotty argued. "He was out there last night. I saw him."

"Well, he's not now! I just searched all over the pasture—everywhere, even rode Banshee all around to look even closer. I thought he might be hurt or something. The other three are there but no Lightning!"

"Then let's go see what happened," the still slightly skeptical Scotty allowed himself to be led by the two of them out to the pasture where they were once again greeted by the three geldings. Lightning remained absent, however. Before they could all conduct another search, they were joined by Michael, who asked what was going on. Immediately concerned, he, too, joined the hunt. Yet once again they drew a blank. The horse seemed to have indeed disappeared.

The one thing they did find, however, on this more thorough scrutiny, was the gate standing wide open. Upon closer examination they noticed hoof prints around the gate, both inside and out.

"Now, who would leave this gate open?" Michael queried. "No one's used this gate in years. Probably not since we sold that hay field off," he was referring to the next field over, "have any of us had a need to use it."

"Then Lightning must have found it," Ann surmised. "He's so inquisitive. He probably got out and went wandering. We'd better get back to the house and alert all the neighbors. Hopefully he hasn't gotten far. I'll take Banshee and go look for him." She began to grow excited thinking about what had to be done. After all, if he got out he most likely would seek the company of other horses after a while. And there were plenty of those around here. Why, even now he was probably safe and sound in someone's barn, waiting to be rescued.

"I'll help you look," Jock volunteered. "I can use Tag."

"Wait, you two," Scotty said. "Michael, come see this." He had been poking around the gate as Ann had been talking and seemed to have discovered something. "Look at this, Michael. Doesn't this gate look like it's been deliberately opened. The weeds are either crushed or pulled out. It's been opened wide enough to get a horse through and then left that way."

113

"Lucky for us, we found it before the rest of the horses got out, too."

Jock, upon hearing his father's theory about the gate, had resumed his investigations, this time on the other side of the gate. He stopped suddenly. "No wait. Lightning didn't just walk out of here on his own. He was led out."

"Led?" Michael asked incredulously, as if he couldn't fathom the idea. "Who would want to …."

"Maybe the same person who left these boot prints in the soil up here by the path," Jock added. "The ground's damp here."

Suddenly Ann let out a cry. She had followed Jock's revelations a step further. "And here, look at these." She pointed to the overgrown lane beyond the gate where the grass had been crushed by some heavy vehicle. "Doesn't this look like tire tracks to you?"

They all came over, careful as to where they stepped. Indisputably here was the evidence they needed. Indeed the tire tracks showed that a large truck had pulled in here and backed out again. The tracks were clear enough to have been made recently, possibly the night before. And within the tracks lay a pile of fresh horse manure, as if a door had been opened or a ramp let down and it had been flung out. They all stared at the tracks as the thought began to form in each of their minds as to what really happened to their colt. Could he have been taken—stolen? And if so, why?

Michael was the first one to speak. "I'm calling the police," he said. "I think this is a matter for their hands now."

Scotty agreed. "Yes, and I think we'd better leave all of this till they can examine it. They'll be able to figure it out better than we amateur detectives."

"But, Lightning," Ann wailed. "Do you think he's been stolen? What about him? Why would anyone take him?"

She was so distraught, Jock put his arm around her shoulders, saying, "We don't know yet that anyone has him. Perhaps it's all coincidence and he actually did get out. I think we should still call all the farms around here to see if they've come up with a stray horse. Likely, if he's loose and wandering, he'll head for the companionship of other horses."

"Jock's right, Ann," Michael added, hugging her. "Let's not jump to any conclusions yet. Perhaps he's only gone for a walk. Let's all go back to the house and call around first." He began to lead a still very upset Ann back toward the house, as she tried vainly to choke back the tears.

"Jock and I'll join you at the house after we put the geldings in another field, at least until the police get done and we can close that gate." Scotty and Jock left them and headed for the three horses grazing at the far end of the long pasture, down by the drive.

Ann followed her father back to the house, her mind numb with shock. Just the idea that Lightning might have been stolen scared her to death. She could not even imagine what he could be going through if strangers had him. He'd never been away from her and the farm since he was born. What would he feel and how would he be treated? She paled at the thought. Better to believe that the tracks were all a coincidence, that he'd really wandered out the open gate and was in the neighborhood somewhere.

But after several calls to nearby farms, with no sign of a loose horse reported, their original suspicions were confirmed. No colt matching Lightning's description had been spotted. Worse than that, however, was the depressing news that several farms in the area were reporting missing horses, also. Already the police had been alerted and were even now making the rounds, investigating this unusual set of circumstances. They promised to send out a squad car within the morning.

By the time Michael got off the phone from the last call, Ann had worked herself into a state of complete depression. "Not again," she kept moaning to herself. "This can't be happening to me again. It's not possible."

Jock sat with her trying to comfort her, though he knew she scarcely heard him. Lost in her own suffering, she could not relate to any offer of comfort, well meaning though it was.

After making his phone calls and reporting his findings to the rest of the family, Michael was at a loss as to what to do next. But Scotty mobilized all of them into action by suggesting they get their morning chores done before the police showed up. Jessica invited Ann to help her in the kitchen, but Ann elected to keep busy by being with the horses. She needed stronger activity to keep a tight rein on her emotions.

By the time the morning work was done, the police had arrived. Michael got to the car first, trailed by the rest of them. "Hello, Sergeant Palmer," he said. "Thank you for getting here so quick."

"Michael," the sergeant acknowledged, getting out of his squad car and nodding to the rest of them. His partner removed himself from the passenger side, also nodding to each of them. "It's been a busy morning. A number of farms such as yours have reported missing or possibly stolen horses. Looks like we have a modern day horse rustler on our hands, I'm afraid."

Ann let out a little cry and her father reached out, placing his arm around her shoulders, holding her tightly. He could feel her tension. This was not the news he wished to hear. Already Ann was so brittle, it was as though the slightest movement and she would shatter into a million pieces. "Are you sure the others were taken?" he queried.

"Evidence points in that direction. In each case, though, the ones taken have been riding horses, not brood stock."

"Why would that be?" Jock asked.

"We think they probably plan to resell them at an auction."

"Oh, no," Ann moaned, distraught at the idea.

The sergeant turned to her, seeing her pain and wishing to ease it somewhat, he said, "Actually, that might be the best thing to happen. We're more apt to recover stolen horses that way. But I'm getting ahead of myself. First, tell me about your horse. Then I want you to show me where he disappeared."

Michael introduced Ann to him. "Sergeant Palmer, this is my daughter, Ann," he explained. "Lightning was her horse, a black yearling colt. Big for his age."

"He had a crooked white strip down his forehead," Ann added. "It looked like lightning. That's how he got his name. It was the only white on him. And he was so gentle and sweet. He'd been an orphan, you see. I hand-raised him. That's why. He was just like a big puppy always following me about," She ended in a choked sob, remembering. "I was going to ride him today, for the first time...."

"Well, unfortunately if he was so manageable, that would make him an easy horse to take."

"Oh, he was easy, all right," Ann agreed proudly. "Anyone could handle him." Suddenly she stopped, realizing the path the sergeant was taking. "Oh, dear, I guess you're right. He would be no trouble at all, even for a stranger to handle. And he's been taught to load in a van. He always had such good manners. I never thought I'd be sorry for it."

"Well, look at it this way," Scotty intervened. "If he's an obedient horse for them, they are more likely to treat him well." At Scotty's words Ann brightened somewhat. She hadn't thought of that.

"We'd like to see where he was taken," the sergeant interrupted, not unkindly. He, too, had a young daughter who loved horses and he could well sympathize with what this young girl was going through. "I'm afraid we have much more to do today and must be on our way soon. Who first noticed him missing?"

"My daughter did," Michael told him. "We'll take you to the spot. It's this way."

Ann led them across the front pasture, noting that the sergeant and his partner observed everything as they went, occasionally stopping to make note of one thing or another. His partner held a pad in his hand and took quick notes. Upon coming to the gate, still standing ajar, they both took extra pains not to disturb anything, motioning them back so as not to destroy any footprints. Carefully Sgt. Palmer went through the gate and checked all around the tire tracks, pacing off the area to get the most accurate dimensions. His expert eyes did not seem to miss a clue. They all stood back in silence, watching.

At one point he groped in the bushes alongside the path and came up with an empty bottle of engine oil. His partner pulled out an clean plastic bag for it.

Finally Sgt. Palmer spoke, "I'll want the lab men to come out and make copies of these footprints and tire tracks," he said. "Until then leave everything as it is. I know it'll be an inconvenience for you not to use this field," he glanced at Michael, "but it should not be long. I want it done by this afternoon while they're still fresh."

"No problem," Michael assured him. "We can do without this field for now. And we certainly want to help as much as we can."

"What do you think, sergeant," Jock asked anxiously, "Now that you've seen this?"

"Well, I would say you folks are mighty good detectives. I think you guessed it pretty close. Looks like our thieves pulled off here, possibly because of engine trouble," he held up the bag containing the empty can of oil, "and when they got out to see to the truck, they saw your colt. If he's friendly and likes attention, he might have been drawn here by their presence, being curious as most youngsters are. And if he's as good looking as you say, the thought probably occurred to them to add him to their collection. The gate and his cooperation made it simple. Once they fixed their engine problem, they had but to load him and be on their way. They could have as much as a ten-hour jump on us by now. Even accounting for a heavy trailer to pull, that would put them quite a distance from here already."

"Can you catch them?" Ann asked, stricken.

Seeing her distraught face, he assured her. "Most likely. We've already got an APB out on their vehicle. We figure they've got at least eight, maybe nine horses. That's a good-sized rig to pull. Probably using a stock trailer by the looks of those tire tracks. The lab can tell us for sure. Anyway, that's the first step."

"And if you don't spot it?" she continued in a desperate need to know.

"We will carefully monitor horse auctions around the country. These horses are all identifiable in some way. Most are tattooed. They should be easy to spot if a load of horses as valuable as these comes through. Most of the others taken were competitive horses used in events and shows. These men knew what to look for all right. Even without papers, at an auction block they'll bring top dollar. And we suspect they've gone to this much trouble, they probably have fake papers to use with each of them."

"Wow," Ann sighed, "I never thought …."

"No, most people wouldn't. But this is our job. We've got to cover all angles."

"Why are you so sure they'll try to sell them through an auction?"

""It's the quickest way to get rid of stolen goods. We suspect this could be part of a wider chain of horse thieving. They obviously have a ready market for selling them as keeping them any long period of time requires feeding them and that eats into their profits. So most likely they have an auctioneer in their pay who is willing to look the other way about where these horses come from as long as he receives his cut." Ann looked so completely shocked that such a thing might be going on that he added, "I know, it's not a pretty picture, but if your colt is in such hands, you can rest assured they'll treat him well. He's worth money to them only if he's looking his best. And as soon as they try to sell him, and the rest, we've got them." He looked at his watch, "Oh, dear, I've got to run. The lab fellas will be out soon and when they're done, the pasture's all yours again. Sorry about the inconvenience."

"No trouble," Michael said a second time. "We just want you to find our horse. Anything we can do to help, we'll be only too glad."

"Believe me, we want to find your horse, all these horses, as much as you do." Ann let out a choking sob. "And we will, little lady," he spoke to her as he got into his patrol car. "Count on it."

As his car pulled out of the lane, Ann found herself hanging onto his words as one would a lifeline. For without Lightning, she felt she could have no life.

At first Lightning did not mind the trailer. Even though strange hands had led him in here, he'd been taught well. Ann had taken him in and out of their horse van many times. Sometimes he'd been left to stand in the stall, but he'd hardly minded it when there was sweet clover hay on which to munch. They had even taken him for short trips so he would get used to the trailer's sway. These times there had always been another well-trained, mannerly horse alongside him for comfort. Lightning had no fear of trailers.

He was aware of other horses in this one, too. Their quiet presence also calmed him. They all stood in a line, lead ropes tied snugly to the sides of the stock trailer. Occasionally there would be the thump of a hoof as one or another sought his balance, but the fact that they were packed tightly made it easy to stand during the motion of the vehicle. Lightning, used only to the stalls in a van, had never ridden in this type of conveyance before, but still he did not object. The only thing he missed was the lack of hay to munch on as they rode. The big chestnut gelding beside him was placid traveler and offered comfort for him to lean against.

They did not stop until well past noon. By that time they had crossed the Mississippi River, leaving Kentucky far behind. At this point Ralph and Louie felt to travel main roads or highways was too risky. Surely by now the owners of the missing horses had alerted authorities and at the very least the state police would have been notified to be on the look out for the stolen horses. They rightly guessed that an all-points bulletin would be in effect for a vehicle fitting their description. The back roads may take longer, but would be much safer to avoid detection.

They chose to stop for lunch at an out-of-the-way little diner and gas stop, situated in a grove of trees to the side of a large dirt parking area. Several picnic tables invited passersby to relax a bit under the shade. Woods spread out around the way station, making no other buildings visible.

After filling the gas tank, Louie parked the truck toward the far end of the parking area and went inside to order them some food, while Ralph opened the back door to the trailer. The horses began to whinny, sensing freedom from their close confines. Lightning, too, let out a sharp whinny, turning expectantly for Ann's touch. Instead a stranger untied his lead rope and asked him to step down from the trailer. Used to a ramp instead, Lightning, nevertheless, hesitated only slightly before stepping off the trailer, straining his neck all the while for a glimpse of his beloved mistress, whom he was sure was not far away.

Instead he was taken around to the side where he was again tied, this time to an outside hook. He started to paw restlessly but was soon rewarded with a flake of hay. Immensely hungry by now, he turned to the food and was soon indulging in the sweet-tasting hay, unmindful of his surroundings.

Ralph did the same for each of the other eight horses, tying them to the trailer and offering them a hay net. By the time he was done, Louie was back with their food. They sat at a nearby picnic table where they could observe the horses and the road while they ate lunch.

The place they had chosen was remote enough that few cars passed by and even fewer stopped while they were there, most of these only getting gas. No one spoke to them or even acknowledged their presence. That was fine with them. The less attraction they caused, the better.

Just as they were finishing and starting to reload the horses to continue on their way, a family stopped and children began pouring from the car, intent on securing one of the picnic tables. The two older children stopped upon seeing the horses and began to show interest, making noises to their parents that they wanted to come over and see them.

Hastily Ralph and Louie finished loading the last horse and slammed the door shut, fearful that any interaction among strangers might be remembered later. Quickly they went over last minute safety precautions, checking lead rope ties, before gathering any unused hay to be stuffed back into the side door at the front of the trailer. Jumping into the cab, they started the engine and pulled out onto the road, leaving several disappointed children staring in their wake.

As the rig gained momentum, Louie let out a pent up sigh of relief. "Whew, that was close. Another minute and we'd have had a whole tribe of curiosity seekers buzzing about us, asking silly questions. We'd be forever getting away from them." Ralph only nodded. "I don't think it's wise taking them out during the daylight like that. Causes too much interest."

"But, Louie, they gotta eat. Can't go all day without …."

"Then tie up hay bags for them. No more taking them out each stop. 'Sides it takes up too much time."

"What about exercise?" Ralph continued, unabated.

"They'll get plenty where we're stopping tonight, if we get that far. We're behind schedule now, what with being forced to take these back roads. I want to make Jake's place by dusk. They can graze in his field all they want then. Stop babying them. They're horses, for Pete's sake."

Ralph knew when to keep his mouth shut. Louie could have a wicked temper when provoked, he knew. With that they pushed westward, getting farther and farther from Kentucky and Lightning's home.

—⁓—

By nightfall, the Collins family had heard nothing of the stolen horses. A lab crew had come that afternoon, taking back with them all the prints they needed, confirming that a large stock trailer was indeed used. However, stock trailers were hardly uncommon to their part of the country, and with no license plate to go on, they were no closer to capturing the thieves then they had been.

Though road blocks had gone into effect soon after the horses were reported missing, and many such stock trailers had been stopped at various points, all checked out as legal. It truly was as if the ground had opened up and swallowed the trailer and its contents.

As each report came back negative, Ann's tenuous grip on the faint hope that the police would indeed be able get her Lightning back began slipping away. She fell deeper and deeper into a depression as she began to realize that he might actually be lost to her. Unable to sleep, she lay in bed searching for answers, answers that eluded her, leaving her unfulfilled.

—∿—

While Ann pondered the whereabouts of her missing colt, Lightning and the other horses were being removed from the trailer and turned out together in a large field, located many miles from where he'd begun his journey. At first the young colt stood at the gate, whinnying for his mistress, but the smell of fresh grass soon drew his attention back to the other horses. Eventually he joined them. All grazed their fill as night settled upon them.

Meanwhile, Louie and Ralph cleaned out the trailer and followed their friend, Jake, into his small secluded cabin for a plain but filling meal.

"Looks like you boys have some real fine horse flesh this trip," Jake commented, as they sat over coffee, following their meal. "Ought to get a pretty penny for this bunch."

Louie only nodded, not filling Jake in on any details. The less he knew, the better for him. While Jake suspected that what Louie and his partner did was not quite legal, he did not know, nor did he want to know, the full extent of their 'business.' He never asked, and Louie never volunteered any more than was necessary. Periodically the two men came through with a trailer load of horses to sell, which was all he was aware, that and the money Louie left behind for his 'inconvenience.'

By morning, the horses, albeit rested from a night of grazing and stretching their legs, were again loaded into the trailer and driven out the long dirt road leading from Jake's remote hideaway. Turning onto the paved road, once again Louie headed the rig west. For the next several days this became the pattern, that is until the trailer crossed into Oklahoma. After traveling only one hundred miles or so, they came to their final stop, a ranch located several miles from the nearest town.

Chapter Eleven

Flight!

So far Lightning had willingly accepted the trip, giving them very little trouble. Most of the time Ralph had been the one to handle him and Ralph had a quiet hand with horses, due to the fact that he genuinely liked them. They in turn responded well for him. Several times as he lead the young colt in or out of the trailer, Lightning had stopped, as a tremor would pass through him and he would look off into the distance, whinnying fretfully. He was looking for Ann, though of course Ralph would have no way of knowing that. But sensing the colt's increasing frustration at an obvious loss, he sought to soothe the colt before continuing. After a bit Lightning always heeded, submitting reluctantly but quietly to his captor's request.

Louie, on the other hand, had none of the patience his partner had. If he saw one of the horses balk, he would yell to Ralph to hurry it up, not willing to show any patience toward a recalcitrant animal. He led the horses in and out impatiently and it was only their good training and normally gentle natures that kept them from open rebellion. Once when he tried to hasten Lightning and the colt stopped in confusion, he tried to punish his disobedience. More confused than ever, Lightning, who'd never known pain or any kind of reprimand in his short life, only resisted further. Angrily, Louie had used a crop on him until Ralph stepped in and took the colt from him. Under his quiet reassuring hand he finally settled and proceeded as desired. This only served to anger Louie more, as he did not like anything to get the best of him.

Finally Ralph took over exclusively the handling of the colt, much to Louie's disgust. Though he remained silent about it, he secretly resented the colt's fickle preferences. Lightning in turn gave him wide berth, mistrusting a human hand for the first time in his young life.

When they arrived at the ranch that was to be their temporary home until they would be taken to a nearby auction to be sold, they were turned into a large paddock and given enough hay to eat to keep them content for a while. Eager also to stretch their legs, the small group readily quit the trailer for the open surroundings the paddock offered. Having traveled together for nearly a week, they had formed a bond where all got along. Only Lightning continued to show reluctance to settle and be content in his new environment. Periodically he would stop eating and throw up his head, letting out a sharp whinny as he paced up and down the fence. But no familiar form came into his line of vision to ease his discomfort.

For the next week Lightning and the rest of the horses were left pretty much alone. Besides the two men that had become familiar to them, another man came up to the fence to observe them. Sometimes he offered them hay to eat and they all became used to his presence. Unbeknownst to them, he was the owner of the ranch.

After a few days in the paddock, the gate into a bigger pasture was left open, permitting them to come and go at will. The grass was green and plentiful in the bigger field, thus helping them regain any of the weight they had lost in traveling. Within a week all the horses had taken on a fat, sleek look to their coats.

For two weeks each day was pretty much the same. Then one morning the horses were herded into the paddock and the

125

gate was closed. One by one they were removed to a smaller corral. There was a great deal of activity as each horse was saddled and worked individually. Besides Louie, Ralph and the ranch owner, two strangers were also in attendance, though they mainly stood outside the fence and observed the process in silence. At the end of each performance the horse was brought to them for examination. Comments were exchanged concerning each individual's abilities and possible value, before the horse in question was removed to the stable nearby. There he would be groomed preparatory to leaving for the auction block. Anxious to unload the stolen horses as soon as possible, Louie and Ralph had wasted no time getting them commissioned for the next sale.

Lightning was the last horse to be brought into the corral, partly because, while they had known something of the other horses' capabilities, having researched each background carefully before taking them, Lightning was an unknown factor. He had been picked up as an afterthought and they were as yet unsure of exactly how they would offer him for sale to prospective buyers.

As Ralph led him into the corral preliminary to tacking him up, one of the strangers leaning against the fence, let out a whistle. "Whew-EE, boys, that youngster's a real looker. But isn't he a bit young? Doesn't look more than a two year old to me. Bring him over here." He entered the ring and walked up to the black colt, prying his mouth open, none to gently. Unused to force, Lightning rolled his eyeballs and fought back against the sudden intrusion. When released he shook his head defiantly, trying to rid himself of the touch.

"Why, this baby's not quite two yet," the stranger exclaimed. "I doubt if he's even broke, big as he is."

"We'll soon know, won't we?" Louie muttered, hauling a heavy stock saddle out toward the now reluctant colt. Lightning, under normal circumstances, would not have minded being tacked up for he had learned to stand quietly while Ann slipped the light racing saddle on his back and tightened the girth. She had always been gentle as she inserted the bit and slid the bridle over his head. None of his training had ever been anything but kind and loving.

But Louie's methods were another thing altogether. In the three weeks Louie had been around the young colt, Lightning had learned to be wary and mistrusting of the man. Often impatient and hasty in his movements, Louie only added to this apprehension by his lack of understanding as to how to handle all but the calmest of horses. Even now, as he came toward Lightning with the heavy saddle, he was too quick, allowing straps to flap and stirrups to bang along the ground in a noisy, unnecessary way, guaranteed to upset the already nervous youngster.

"Hold him steady," Louie called out to Ralph, who stood at the colt's head. "We'll soon see how much training this guy's had."

"Perhaps it would be better if I ..." Ralph began hesitantly, seeing the colt's obvious unwillingness.

"No," Louie spat out angrily, annoyed that once again this colt was trying to get the best of him. "You just hold him. I've got a score to settle with this one. No horse will make me look bad." Without a further word, he swiftly moved toward the skittery colt, bringing the blanket up to flap across his back. Almost simultaneously he heaved the stock saddle in place, reaching to cinch the girth before Lightning knew what was happening. As he pulled the cinch tight, the colt just stood there shivering, unable to comprehend at first what took place. Before he knew it, a thick hard bit was shoved into his tender mouth and the bridle dragged roughly over his ears. "There now, nothing to that, was there?" Louie stated triumphantly.

Ralph, seeing the colt's fear in his wildly rolling eyes, started to suggest that he ride him instead, but upon seeing Louie's almost savage gleam as he contemplated the conquest of the handsome colt, he thought better of it. Having seen examples of Louie's anger too often in the past, he had no desire to be on the receiving end. Silently, he held the reins as Louie vaulted heavily into the saddle. "Okay, turn him loose," he muttered, panting from exertion, or possibly from anticipation.

At first Lightning stood still. The only weight he had ever known on his back had been Ann's, so light he had barely felt her. And that had been for brief periods of time. She had always eased up gradually until he hardly noticed the difference.

This sensation was totally alien to any he'd ever known. This man was better than twice the weight of his mistress and he had landed hard, throwing himself into the saddle. Unable to react at first, Lightning just stood trembling.

Thinking he had the horse conquered already, Louie let out a whoop and at the same moment jabbed his sharp spurs into the colt's tender sides. It was the worst thing he could have done. Reacting without hesitation, Lightning suddenly came alive. The normally placid, well-mannered, friendly colt exploded. He leapt straight up into the air, coming down with a bone-jar-ring stiff legged landing, almost on top of the surprised Ralph, who barely scrambled out of the way in time. Even so, the colt may have stopped there, for he was anything but mean, had it not been for two things happening simultaneously. One was the sound let out by the men observing the contest.

"Hey, we got us a rodeo horse here!" one cried gleefully in an ear-splitting yell.

"Ride 'em, Cowboy!" the other returned, his voice equally loud.

That noise startling Lightning, coupled with another hurt-ful jab with the spurs, made him conscious of the fact that his tormentor was still on his back. Suddenly all he could think of was to rid himself of the unaccustomed weight he carried and thus be free of the pain. He promptly went into a series of bucks and twists that would have unseated the best of riders. Louie was far from that. He only lasted through two of them before he was catapulted into the air, coming to rest up against the fence as the colt continued to plunge furiously. It took him several more gyrations before he realized he was riderless, finally coming to a halt at the far end of the corral, eyeing the men, especially Louie, with a wild-eyed look of total distrust. He stood there blowing hard, sweat running off him in great streams.

Louie stood up and shook himself off angrily, starting to go after him, when one of the men called him back.

"Forget it for now," he told him. "We can't use that horse. It's obvious he hasn't been broken yet. We'll take the others, though. Get them ready for tonight's auction. Leave him. We'll pick him up next trip, when you've had time to work him." They turned away, not giving Louie a chance to argue.

"This is a nice lot, even without that colt," the other was saying as they walked away. "Sure to get plenty as it is for the rest, especially with the papers we got made up."

Louie watched them go, undecided as to whether to attempt to persuade them to change their minds and take the colt or let it go. Then, with a grunt of disgust he gave Lightning a parting glance. "I'll settle with you later," he said, as he followed Ralph out to the stable to prepare the other horses for the sale block. Lightning was left standing there, ignored.

He was not to be given much of a reprieve. The trailer had no sooner pulled out of the yard with the rest of the horses on board when Louie returned to the corral where the black colt stood, still wearing the unfamiliar western tack that felt so strange to him. He had calmed down some but upon seeing the return of the man he now associated with pain, he began to tremble violently all over again.

"Ah, now we'll see who is boss," Louie told him as he entered the corral once more. This time he held a quirt in one hand, a vicious gleam in his eyes as he anticipated conquering the young colt who continued to stand fearfully in the far corner. Lightning, ears flattened, watched his every move.

Moving cautiously toward the colt, Louie continued, "There's no one to stop me now." His face took on a fiendish flush as he contemplated with pleasure the task ahead, determined to break the spirit of this youngster who had made such a fool of him. "I even sent Ralph with the rest of them. He's too soft. Always wants to coddle horses. Humph, that's not the way to treat a dumb beast. *This* is the way you should be treated." He leapt forward, catching Lightning's trailing reins and bringing him up short with a spiteful jab to his mouth as he tried to pull away.

Jerking him again for good measure, he brought the colt to a shaky stand still. "See, you're learning already," he gloated, giving him a slap with the quirt.

In one swift move he vaulted onto the colt's back, settling quickly and sending those hateful spurs raking across his sides once more as he struck him with the quirt. Trying to escape the pain, Lightning jumped ahead, only to be brought up hard against the bit as it sawed his sensitive mouth. Foam mixed with blood flowed freely now from it, as he attempted to escape the pressure by flinging his head from side to side. But the man on his back only sawed harder, cutting his tender mouth and causing greater discomfort. Once again he applied the quirt.

Seeking to free himself of the hated weight he'd begun to connect with his intense suffering, he lunged forward again trying to outrun the pain Louie inflicted. Unfortunately that only served to gain him another vicious tug on his mouth.

Thoroughly confused by the punishment each of his movements brought him, Lightning responded in anger, exploding in a series of gut-wrenching bucks as he sought to unseat his rider. He continued to plunge and twist, ignoring the pain as his fury mounted. He struck out with the newfound instincts of a wild, untamed stallion, much as his desert-bred ancestors may have.

Louie only lasted into the fourth buck before he was thrown clear, leaping to his feet to scramble out of the way of the now-maddened young stallion-colt. As soon as Lightning realized he was free, however, he plunged to a stop and stood in the center of the corral, his sides heaving with exertion, sweat pouring freely from all parts of his body.

His tormentor did not give him a chance to recover. As soon as Lightning came to a stop, Louie grabbed for his reins and again leapt aboard the colt, more determined than ever to conquer this horse. He was beyond all rational thought, blinded by the compulsion to win at all costs. Once again the piercing rowels of his spurs slashed Lightning's sensitive sides followed by the quirt against his flanks. And again Lightning fought back, but this time he was not as quick as before. His young body was tiring. All his life he had known only kindness and love from humans. He was inexperienced in fighting against man.

Things might have ended differently had not fate stepped in, for truly Louie was determined to break the colt's spirit and bend his will to his own. Lightning was beginning to lose ground in his fight, the strain telling on him, when unexpectedly the cinch gave way with a loud pop, flinging Louie, saddle and all, into the dirt. The sudden motion panicked the black colt anew, sending him wildly fleeing across the corral. As he reached the fence, fear forced him to leap the five-foot barrier, as he sought to put more distance between him and the human he feared. The loose reins began to slap against his neck, spooking him to maximum speed as he raced toward the distant hills. He was not yet aware that he was free. His only desire now was escape from the pain.

Extricating himself from the entangling saddle, Louie raised himself off the ground. Unhurt of all but his pride, he watched helplessly as the black colt disappeared over the first hill. They'd be lucky indeed if they got that one back once he lost himself in the wilderness beyond, he thought dejectedly, slapping his hat against his leg in disgust.

—w—

The phone was ringing incessantly as Ann entered the house upon returning from school. She threw her books down on the table and looked at the clock on the kitchen wall. It read 3:30. Realizing no one was in the house, she went over to answer it, identifying herself to the caller.

"Hi, Ann," the now familiar voice of Sgt. Palmer came on. "Is your dad around?"

"I'm afraid not. He's still down at the store, sergeant," she replied. "He won't be in until after 5:00 I'd guess. He usually takes inventory on Friday so he knows what to order."

"Too bad. I guess I'll have to call back then."

"Wait, before you hang up, do you have any word on Lightning?" she asked hopefully.

131

"Not specifically about your colt unfortunately, but we have had a major breakthrough on this case."

"Really? Oh, please tell me now. I won't be able to wait for you to talk to Dad."

"Well, like we figured, our thieves did try to sell the stolen horses. They tried to pass them off with false papers at a sale in Tulsa, Oklahoma."

"Oklahoma! How did they get that far away?" Ann was stunned.

"Near as we could figure they took back roads and avoided all our road blocks. Anyway, most of the horses have been recovered. Your horse was not among them, though."

"Not with them?" she gasped. "Why? Do you know where he is?"

"Not yet, but we should have an explanation presently. One of the guys who was involved, came to the auction with the horses where he was caught. He's been brought in for questioning so we should know something more soon. And, of course we'll let you know as soon as we hear from the officers out there."

"Oh, I hope it's soon. I can't stand all this waiting for news. I feel so helpless and wish there was something more I could do to get Lightning back quicker."

"Believe me, so do I, honey," the sergeant assured her. "It isn't much easier for us. But we should have the full story soon so we can plan our next step. Meanwhile, I'd appreciate it if you'd pass on the message to your dad that I called and will get back to him tonight in any case."

"I will. Thanks for calling," she added as she hung up the phone, her mind reeling with this new bit of news. She knew she should be glad for this latest report on the plight of the stolen horses, but for some reason she felt a gloom descend over her. While it sounded like it would only be a matter of time before Lightning would be recovered, too, she couldn't help fearing the worst. Lightning not among them! That could only mean that they'd dumped him somewhere along the way. Where, oh, where was he? she pondered, eager for the next phone call but dreading it at the same time. Something was not right. Would she ever see her beautiful black colt again?

That night, shortly after her father got home, a familiar police car pulled up to the house. As Sgt. Palmer got out, Ann rushed across the courtyard at meet him.

"Any more news? Did they find Lightning yet?"

"I'm afraid not," the police officer replied, with genuine regret, "but I do have the whole story now. Why don't you gather everyone together and I'll tell you what I know."

Moments later the members of Stormy Hill's family were assembled around the kitchen table. While Jessica served coffee and fresh-baked cookies to them, Sgt. Palmer related the story as much as they'd been able to piece together. "So when they tried to unload the horses at the auction, one of the men we had posted spotted them and the consignor was arrested on the spot. All the horses taken were recovered but yours."

"Where is he?" Ann broke in. "Where's my Lightning?"

"Ann," her mother admonished, "don't be rude. Let Sgt. Palmer finish his story, please."

"I'm sorry. You're right, I shouldn't have interrupted," she said.

"We found out most of what we know from the man arrested at the auction. Once in custody, he was most eager to squeal on his partner. The other one involved was still at the ranch where they had been keeping the horses. Your colt was kept from the sale because he wasn't broken yet." Ann began to shake her head in denial, then thinking better of it, she stopped, not wanting to interrupt again. The officer continued, "They figured they'd get more money for him if they broke him first, is the reason he gave."

"Oh, no!" Ann wailed, as visions of Lightning's confusion to strangers' hands passed through her mind. "Did they try?" If they abused him...

"Officers were dispatched immediately to arrest the other thief. He was still at the ranch when they found him. He'd been saddling up one of the horses. At first it was thought he may

133

have gotten tipped off and was making a run for it. However, he admitted he'd tried to ride your colt and the colt had gotten away from him. He was actually getting ready to recapture him when he was caught."

"Lightning loose? Whatever did he do to him to make him run off? How rough was he? Poor Lightning's never known anything but kindness." Ann was near hysteria upon hearing this. Horrible images kept racing through her head. She couldn't accept the thought of her precious colt being mistreated.

Sgt. Palmer thought it best not to worry the young girl further with the details he knew of the fight between her horse and his captor. Instead he tried to reassure her. "I don't think he was hurt. From what we found out, the cinch on the saddle broke and spooked your horse. He fled into the hills behind the ranch. Since its pretty dense country around there, it may take a while to round him up."

"They are going after him, aren't they?" Ann sobbed. This news was worse than not knowing. "He's not a wild horse. He wouldn't know how to survive by himself."

"Of course. There are searchers out even now looking for him," the officer told her. "And all the nearby ranches have been alerted to watch for him."

"Why is that?" she questioned.

Scotty cut in. "Good idea. Ann, lass, you're right that he's no wild horse. And that very fact should get him back faster. He's not going to want to stay out in the wilds by himself. When he calms down he's going to feel the need for the company of other horses. Besides, he's always been taken care of all his life. He's used to being around people. Natural instincts will drive him back to what he knows. Sooner or later he'll show up at someone's place, hanging about, looking for food and the fellowship of his own kind. Any one of the ranches in that area would provide that."

Ann brightened somewhat. "You think so?"

"I'm sure of it. We'll get him back. As long as people around there know he's missing, he's bound to show up."

"That's right, Scotty," Sgt. Palmer said. He had not looked forward to this visit, wishing to have more hopeful news to give this family, especially this young girl who cared so much. "It may take some time, though, as the country around there is pretty remote, but he'll show up eventually."

"Oh, I hope so."

"Remember there are also men already out riding the area, searching for him. I'm sure we'll get him back."

But later Ann, alone with her thoughts, did not feel so confident. She kept thinking about all the dangers he'd be facing in a remote harsh country. Lightning had never had to fend for himself. He'd been spoiled and pampered all his young life. What did he know of survival in the wilds? His only hope was to seek other horses and thus find his way back to a ranch. She was sure, gentle as he was, he'd come to anyone who found him.

Little did she know that the sheer terror that Louie's vicious handling had instilled in his brain had made a profound lasting impression. One he would not soon forget.

CHAPTER TWELVE

Freedom

Lightning covered considerable ground before he began to tire. By the time he'd dropped to a walk, he'd traveled many miles from the ranch that had held him captive. Unbeknownst to him his flight had taken an easterly direction, as if some instinct was guiding him with an unforeseen hand. Unfortunately, though, his path had taken him to a wilder, rougher territory of canyons and hills, unsettled and forbidding. This was totally unlike the gentle countryside where he'd grown up. As he wandered about amidst the dense underbrush, no familiar scent of other horses came to him.

At first the companionship of his own kind was the least of his immediate concerns. His wild flight had left him thirsty and he forged on, dropping down to a trot as he sniffed the air for a nearby source of water. No longer spooked by the flapping reins, he shook his head every now and then at the minor annoyance.

Instinct finally led him to a small, slow running creek where he bent down to drink his fill. The bridle bit hindered him only slightly, causing him to shake his head once again. This proved to be his undoing as he had chosen to enter the water next to a thick cluster of bushes. As he flung his head around, the reins tangled in the branches and became fast.

Lightning did not realize he was caught until he finished his drink and began to move away, only to be brought up short by the tangled reins. He stopped and turned, puzzled, when he failed to make a connection between the taut rein and a person holding it. There was no one there, yet he was held fast. His past training, still strong within him, bade him to stand quietly, waiting patiently for release. He had been taught well. The immediate memory of the hateful man was replaced by lessons of a gentler hand. And so the colt stood in anticipation of the release that never came.

By nightfall, Lightning began to grow restless. He had long since devoured all the leaves within reach, and was starting to get really hungry. Totally domesticated and used to meals fed on time, he missed the nightly grain that he'd always received. Now he began to stamp and paw at the ground, occasionally whinnying to let someone know of his dissatisfaction.

Someone did hear his angry snorts, but it was far from the desired response he wanted. A band of roving coyotes on their nightly forage, hearing the solitary whinny of a horse, sought to investigate. What they found peaked their curiosity further. They began to surround the colt, silently stalking, ever cautious of the imminent danger of his powerful hooves. When the young colt failed to flee immediately from the threat they posed, they began to slowly creep forward.

Lightning smelled the predators and raised his head, ears twitching, as he sought to identify the danger. While he was well used to domestic dogs as pets, Stormy Hill after all had several dogs on the farm, he somehow sensed that these coyotes were a danger to his safety. He began to pace restlessly back and forth, snorting through flared nostrils but still held fast by the reins twisted in the bush.

The coyotes started to slowly circle, drawing ever closer. Lightning pawed the ground again and again, as fear began to build in him. When one bold coyote moved in a little too near, he kicked out a hind foot, barely missing the beast. Rather than deter them, the coyotes only grew braver, moving ever closer, keeping a watchful eye out for the power behind those sharp hooves.

Suddenly one, larger than the rest and distinctly the leader, leaped at the colt, snapping at his flank with his powerful jaws. Though the bite barely broke the skin, the sting frightened Lightning into quick retaliation. He reared up, striking out to get away from the pain. His right hoof grazed the coyote, causing him to howl and further sending the colt into a frenzy of bucking and kicking. Unable to take the strain of the colt's wild movements, the bridle snapped apart, thus freeing the young horse. Realizing he was loose, Lightning responded in the way of his kind, once more fleeing the danger in a full mad gallop that left his enemies far behind, staring disappointedly after their would-be dinner.

Again it was miles before he slowed his frenzied flight. By the time he stopped out of shear exhaustion he was far into the wild backcountry, many miles from his original starting point, well beyond where anyone would think to look for him. In this desolate country he would have to learn to fend for himself.

Once again he sought water, but far more carefully this time, his senses fully alert for possible dangers. He drank greedily, unencumbered by the weight of the heavy bit in his mouth. Then he settled down to graze his fill before dozing.

Morning found him seeking out a field rich with tall thick grass. He ate his way across the long, narrow strip, seemingly content to stay. But by nightfall, some inner voice was telling him to move on, as he began what was to become a pattern, seeking out good grazing land by day, but wandering on each night, dozing in between. His travels appeared to be random, yet he was moving in an easterly direction, often hampered by the ruggedness of the area through which he traveled.

As the days passed, Lightning began a slow metamorphous from the once gentle young colt, thoroughly domesticated and totally dependent on people for his needs. Instead a new horse was forming. His near brush with death when attacked by the coyotes had left him very sensitive and cautious about the terrain through which he journeyed. He took on a suspicious nature, sticking to more open ground, suspecting danger in unfamiliar territory. This heedfulness saved his life more than once.

Physically he was growing stronger, taking on new muscle strength, as his chest and lungs expanded to keep up with this more demanding lifestyle. Winter was fast approaching, the nights growing colder with the first hint of snow in the upper regions. Lightning's coat too reflected the change in weather as it grew in thicker until it fit him like black velvet fur, shiny with health. His muscles took on new definition, lengthening and hardening with the limitless exercise he received. He'd be two years old at the end of the month. His gawky, coltish appearance was slowly taking on a newer, more mature look.

In the last several weeks, Lightning had learned to exist on his own. Always a pampered, spoiled darling of an indulgent mistress, he had to learn to survive by his own wits. The lessons received were not without danger. His brush with the coyotes had taught him to avoid any close contact with other animals of the wild. He had begun to rely on his nose and ears to sense the presence of possible predators. And he learned to run when anything seemed amiss. He found his hooves to be valuable assets toward warding off animals that might pose a threat to his safety.

The land he traveled through was a far cry from the level rolling hills of his native bluegrass. Learning the hard way by taking a few falls, he realized the necessity of moving more sure-footedly through the uneven, rocky terrain of sharply rising mountains and steep, broken canyons.

Lightning had been traveling for better than a month when the landscape about him began to take on a subtle difference. It became flatter and not as rugged. Lightning did not know it but he'd crossed into the foothills. He was now several hundred miles east of where he'd escaped his captors. All he knew was that the grass was thicker and more plentiful here. He moved more slowly, enjoying the virtually unlimited supply of good grazing land.

Toward dawn of the third day, he was awakened by a familiar smell. The wind had shifted and brought with it the scent of horses. Lightning was instantly alert and whinnied low. Though there was no response, he began to trot in that direction, drawn by loneliness to seek out his own kind.

Just over the hill, he spotted dark shapes standing in a cluster within a huge pasture. They had been grazing, moving slowly, tails twitching almost in rhythm, but at the sight of the black horse coming over the hill, they stopped, raising their heads, ears pricked in curiosity. One or two whinnied expectantly.

Lightning only hesitated briefly before taking off down the slope in full gallop only to be brought up short by the fence. At first he trotted back and forth, calling to the other horses in a frantic voice. Several responded with equally nervous neighs. Finding no break in the fence, Lightning became highly frustrated. He was a colt who had spent his whole life among other horses. The past month alone had left him even more eager to return to his own kind. He had found other equines again, but was unable to reach them.

Finally, in desperation, he ran back up the hill, turned and flew at the fence, rising up at the last moment to clear it easily. Coming down, he shook his head, as though disdaining such a flimsy barrier, and ran over to where the now startled horses stood restlessly. After much sniffing, neighing and occasional pawing, the small band, fortunately made up of mares and geldings, settled back down and allowed him to join their numbers. They all returned to their grazing in the chilly morning air, under a sky grown heavy with snow clouds.

As the morning wore on the wind began to rise, blowing relentlessly across the bleak landscape. Sensing the impending storm, the horses began to circle about restlessly, huddling closer together, tails to the wind. Above them the snow clouds piled up as though chasing one another across the sky. A major blizzard was brewing.

CHAPTER THIRTEEN

The Girl

By late morning snow had begun to fall in large swirling flakes. The small herd stopped entirely attempting to graze and huddled tightly together for protection from the ever-increasing snowfall. One mare, clearly the pasture boss, began to move instinctively toward a far gate, no longer visible through the thickly falling snow. Soon the others joined her as they sought the familiar protection of the distant barns. Lightning, reluctant to leave his newfound friends, followed.

Before they had gone far, however, they were met by the ranch owner and his daughter. They'd come out to round up their herd and drive them into one of the paddocks close to the ranch buildings where there was a run-in shed for protection. In the ensuing melee of circling horses amidst the swirling snow, Lightning's presence went unnoticed. Hats pulled down tight on their heads and collars turned up against the cold biting wind, the two riders only concentrated on getting the herd rounded up. They were unaware of the extra horse.

Once moving, the band struck out eagerly, anticipating the warmth of the long shed, keeping them out of the wind and offering good winter hay while they waited for the storm to abate.

By the time the horses came through the last gate, the snow had begun to accumulate in great shifting drifts. The horses, sensing shelter was near, broke into a run as they caught sight of the long run-in shed, pushing and jostling each other in their eagerness to taste the hay they knew awaited them. Lightning, remembering his former domestic life, followed suit.

Bent on accomplishing their task of corralling the horses as swiftly as possible before the storm grew much worse, the two riders hastened to shut the paddock gate. The wind-driven snow made it nearly impossible to do a head count on their herd, even if they were so inclined. As it was they were more concerned with getting their riding mounts to an adjoining barn where they quickly stripped them of their tack and settled them into clean stalls. By the time that was done, the snow was driving sideways so thickly, they could only see a faint outline as they headed toward the nearby ranch house. Eager to reach the warmth it promised, neither the ranch owner nor his daughter hesitated as they scooted across the yard, stopping on the long, low verandah only long enough to shake most of the snow from their clothing.

They were greeted at the door by the rancher's wife, holding a husky, pink-cheeked, gurgling baby boy. On the floor in the nearby front room sat two young girls, obviously twins, arguing loudly over possession of a slightly mangled toy doll.

"Come in quick," she said, shutting the door with a slam before any more snow could find its way in. "I've got plenty of soup and hot coffee made in the kitchen. And Janie, dear," she addressed the girl, "here's a warm, dry sweater to put on after you peal off those wet clothes."

"Thanks, Ma," Janie said, with a smile matching that of her mother. "That sure sounds good after what we've been through."

"Did you get all the horses in okay?"

Janie's father answered with an affirmative nod as he headed for the kitchen and some hot coffee. "Looks like they're all there," he told her. "Snow was blowing so hard we couldn't tell for sure. We'll do a head count once this storm lets up, though." Thus Lightning's presence continued to go unnoticed.

143

Janie and her family, the Baileys, had a struggling little ranch on the edge of the foothills, far from neighbors. The nearest town was twenty miles away. It was their very remoteness that had brought Lightning to them, yet it was this very inaccessibility that left them a poor family, barely able to scratch out a living doing all sorts of odd jobs. They raised a few head of beef cattle, the usual chickens, pigs for pork, and Pa Bailey did some repair work on just about anything as he was quite good with his hands. Many of the surrounding ranchers brought their leather repairs to him for he had a reputation for fixing anything leather. But mostly they derived their income from supplying horses to dude ranches. This, then, was the purpose behind keeping the small herd of horses that attracted Lightning.

Mostly they bought horses for very little, then retrained or broke them and resold them at a profit. Janie, though still young, showed considerable talent with the inexperienced horses, and proved an invaluable help to her father with this.

On the third day the snow finally let up enough to allow them to get outside and tend to the horses' needs. The sun came out, warming the air and beginning to melt the considerable snow left behind.

Janie followed her father out of the house, smiling broadly when she saw that the sun had drawn the band of horses out of the shed where they were milling about the paddock, now and then pawing the ground in an attempt to find something to eat. She ran up to the fence to greet them when she spied the strange black colt. He stood a little apart from the rest, off to one side, eyeing the two humans curiously. Janie's breath caught in her throat.

"Who is he?" she asked her father excitedly. "Pa, look! He's not one of ours, is he?"

"No, definitely not," her father sputtered, becoming aware of the handsome youngster for the first time.

Janie could only stare. "What a horse!" she exclaimed.

"Well, a horse like that must belong to somebody," her father mused aloud. "Wonder how he got in with our band?"

Janie took note of the colt's size and finely chiseled features. "He's big, real big, but I don't think he's any older than a two year old. His head reminds me of an Arab but with that size he's got to be at least part Thoroughbred. Who do you know around here that could be breeding anything like him?"

"Can't say as I recall anybody off hand, but I'll make a few calls around to see if anyone's missing a horse." Then he remembered. "Oh, drat, the lines are down, thanks to this storm. Guess we'll have to wait till they can get out here to us. Might be a while, though."

"Gosh, I don't mind that at all. He's so beautiful. I wonder if he's used to handling and if he's broke yet?" Janie swung up onto the fence to get a better look at the colt that stood at a distance, watching them. As she did her hood was knocked backward off her head. Unconsciously she reached up and pulled her hair free. It fell in tangled waves, so dark as to be nearly black, all the way to her waist.

Lightning noted this action and his head suddenly shot up. Something about the girl triggered a reflex in his brain. He remembered a girl like this one, someone very special in his past life. He let out a low nicker, the one he had used so often when Ann was near. Then with a louder neigh he trotted across the paddock and up to the fence where Janie sat. Eagerly he thrust his head against her, nearly unseating her in his joy at finding his beloved mistress once more.

Janie returned his interest, sliding off the fence so she could stroke him more thoroughly. "So, you think you know me, huh, fella?" she murmured in wonder, thrilled at the greeting this beautiful colt was giving her.

Suddenly he stopped his snuffling. This was *not* his beloved Ann. His head came up and he stared at her as if she was responsible for tricking him. He shifted his feet and moved away. When she reached out to touch him again, he whirled back, circling undecidedly. She began to talk to him in a quiet soothing voice. He relaxed a bit and allowed her to come closer. All the while she continued to talk to him in a soft, patient tone.

As she sought his confidence she was admiring the colt before her. She was well aware of his long legs, both clean and straight, the deep chest and sloping hindquarters, the shoulders set well back to make room for a powerful curved neck. His long tail, sadly snarled with sticks and brush he'd picked up, was held high as he switched it across muscular flanks. That proud carriage coupled with a smallish, very refined head made her think of an Arab somewhere in his background. Certainly the large, deep-seeing eyes and small tapered muzzle depicted it.

His mane was thick, growing long and tangled also from his wild, unkempt existence. She longed to comb through his knots and mats until his mane, and his tail, flowed long and straight again. In fact what he needed was a good grooming to make his coat gleam like velvet once more. As she ran her hands across his neck and back, he seemed to respond as though he had once accepted such treatment as a way of life.

"I remind you of someone, that much is clear," she mused aloud. "I wonder who that someone is and how you came to be separated from her. It's obvious you're well bred. Someone must have considered you very valuable, I think. Perhaps we can find out whom and reunite you with your rightful owner. Like that, boy?" All the while she talked, Lightning stood, accepting her attention, relaxing slowly his alertness. After all, he'd only been wild a short time. Prior to that he'd known kind, gentle treatment for a far longer period. It felt good to be loved again.

Janie's father started to step forward to hand her a halter for the colt. But as he approached, Lightning became alert, snorting and backing up, showing signs of fear.

"Wait, Pa," Janie signaled. "Better just throw it to me. I don't think he likes or trusts men." Her pa stopped and lightly tossed the halter to her. It fell softly a few feet behind her. Janie reached slowly out and scooped it up. Lightning eyed her warily. "There, boy, it's only a halter. Nothing you haven't seen before," she correctly guessed. She held it up to him. He sniffed it cautiously but finding it indeed familiar, he settled back down. Very slowly she inched it over his head. He shook his head once, but continued to stand.

"See, no problem. You've worn one of these before." She gave a slight tug on the halter and he took a step forward. "Yes, I see you know what this means. Well, that's all for today." She offered him a carrot, which he took and ate eagerly. Then she released him. "Go and play with your friends. I'll see you later for more lessons." Lightning scampered off, darting between the other horses. Janie's father stood by the gate leading to the large home pasture. As he swung it open, the horses jostled one another in their enthusiasm to reach it. Lightning burst past them, running swift as the wind in his exhilaration to be free once more. Several times he ran in giant circles about the field, kicking up clouds of snow. Janie held her breath for fear he would try to jump the fence and escape to the wild country beyond, but he showed no inclination to return from whence he'd probably come. Instead, seemingly content to remain with others of his own kind, he ran until he'd had his fill. Yet when he finally stopped they were quick to notice he was barely blowing. Nor was he wet.

"What a race horse he'd make," Janie commented, "or perhaps a long distance horse. He looks like he could go all day and have plenty left over." Boy would she love to have a horse like that.

Her father came over and broke into her train of thought before she could continue her daydreams. "Well as soon as the lines are restored, I'll begin to make some inquiries as to who owns this fellow. By the looks of him, someone must be frantic with concern."

"I'm sure," Janie nodded, looking wistfully at the youngster. Already she was thinking what she'd do with a colt like this, if he were hers.

It was nearly a week before power was restored to their ranch and Pa Bailey could contact the neighboring ranchers concerning the black colt's ownership. Janie used the time well, gaining the colt's trust, though he was still skittish around others, especially men. He accepted her touch and allowed her to brush him, actually appearing to enjoy it. By now Janie was convinced his former owner had been a girl much like herself. The colt responded far too significantly to her attentions to be otherwise.

And she was just as sure that somewhere in his background, a man had abused him. Her father, though he had shown no signs of aggression toward him, still could not get near the colt. When the phone was finally back to working order and several ranchers stopped by to see the stray, trying to determine to whom he belonged, the results were always the same. Only Janie could handle him, with any men standing at a distance. Too close and he immediately became agitated.

After several days, no one had come forward with positive identification on the black colt. Those who saw him suspected, along with Janie, that he had mostly Arab blood in him because of his distinct head qualities but he was already bigger than the Arabs they'd seen and by his youthful appearance it was plain he wasn't done growing yet.

As each day went by without an owner to claim the handsome colt, Janie grew more and more hopeful that perhaps they'd end up keeping him themselves. She was growing more attached to him by the day and she rather felt he was responding with a trust of his own. Though deep down inside she knew such a fine animal as he must belong to someone, she began to hope that perhaps his owner would not show up after all.

Though word of the sudden appearance of a strange black colt had been spread among the ranches within the Bailey's immediate area, no owner was found. The distance Lightning had traveled since escaping from his captors was so great that it put him out of range of the area where people had been searching for him. No one thought that a two-year-old colt, raised as nothing more than a pampered pet, could possibly cross the wild terrain of mountains and canyons such as he had done.

—ɷ—

About the time the Baileys were asking their neighbors about the mysterious horse found in their pasture, Ann and her family were being given an update on the search for the missing colt. After nearly two months of searching, no signs of him had been found. It was as if he just disappeared. Search parties had covered the surrounding area, even riding up into the mountainous wild country, but no signs of the colt had been found. Ranchers about those parts feared he had fallen prey to wild predators, and if that were the case, they might never find so much as a carcass for proof.

Ann refused to think of the possibility. Even when the search was formally called off, she kept hoping that her colt would eventually seek out other horses and someone would be able to catch him. She would not believe that he could have succumbed to wild animals. Somewhere out there Lightning was alive. She just knew it.

—ww—

Two weeks had passed without any clue to the identity of the lost colt. Janie began to be hopeful that perhaps no one would come forward to claim him and that she might be able to keep him for herself. All her spare time she spent working with him, grooming, handling and practicing with him on the ground. She had brought out a western saddle, setting it on the fence for him to see, but he showed such fear of it, that she finally removed it. Instead she found a lighter, English type saddle that had been thrown casually in a corner of the tack room and she tried this.

At first Lightning was suspicious and snorted at it, pawing the ground as if ready to run. So she laid it across the fence rail and ignored it. When he began to show no interest in it she picked it up and took it to him. Though he snorted excitedly and rolled his eyes, he finally sniffed it and settled down.

The following day, when she lay it across his back, he stood quietly, only showing restlessness when she tried to cinch it. But within a couple more days, she was even able to do this.

After that the bridling came easier than she expected it would. She used a light snaffle bit that would not irritate his mouth, and eased it in. He accepted it without a fuss.

When she could saddle and bridle the colt easily, she knew all the groundwork had been done and the next step was to mount up. Eagerly, Janie approached her father on the subject.

"Pa, tomorrow, after we're done with the chores, I'd like to try riding Storm." She had named him that since he had come to them during the worst blizzard of the winter so far. "Will you help me?"

"Don't know why you're bothering," he grumbled. "Seems like you're getting too attached to that colt already. You get used to riding him and thinkin' he's your own and sure enough his owner'll show up. Then where'll you be?"

"I know that. I'm aware I'm only taking care of him till his owner comes. But, I'm sure they won't mind if I continue his training. "Besides he's so beautiful, I just have to see what it would be like to ride him. At least give me that."

Her father saw the desire in her eyes and couldn't help smiling. He pitied his young daughter for they were always forced to sell the horses they trained. Janie would put her whole heart into breaking and training some youngster, only to lose it in the end. So often he had seen her grit her teeth and hold back the tears, as a horse she'd worked so hard on was loaded into a strange trailer and taken away. She was destined never to have a horse she could call her own. He looked into her eyes, all shining with hope and eagerness, and thought, why not? Let her have this one chance. They were so poor, there was little else he could give her.

"Sure, honey," he agreed finally. "I'll help you. Just remember that you may be doing all this work for nothing when the owner shows up."

"I don't mind. It's just that I have to know what a horse of his quality feels like, just once. I'll bet he can fly like the wind."

Her father sighed. Perhaps, for her sake, no one would claim the colt after all and she would be able to keep him. But in his heart he knew he was only kidding himself. That was very unlikely to happen.

The next morning Janie flew through her chores. By now, she could saddle and bridle the colt without a problem. When her father appeared, she was ready.

"Just give me a leg up," she said, "and we'll see how it goes." They were in the small circular paddock used for breaking and training the green horses. The surface was deep sand, should she land on it, a distinct possibility when training young horses, and the fence was high and solid. There was a hitching post in the center for snubbing the most recalcitrant youngsters. But Lightning would not need that. He stood quietly, until Janie's father came near to help her up. Then with fear in his eyes, he began to sidle around her. Patiently she soothed him. When her father drew near enough to stroke his neck, he quivered all over, but remained still.

"Boy, some man did a number on this boy," she commented. "Pa, you should spend more time around him to get him over his fear of men."

"I'll try, when I can find the time," he replied, giving her a boost. She settled gently into the saddle, so light he barely felt the difference.

At first he did nothing, then as she gently nudged him forward, his head came up and he sidled away from her heels, expecting the pain to start. Instead she sat quietly and waited it out, her hands holding the reins slack, barely connecting with his mouth so that there'd be no unnecessary jab. She had already guessed that this colt had known some rough treatment lately and she didn't want to cause him any pain from her. This youngster would have to be brought along slowly at his own pace.

After a few minutes of restless moving about the small round pen, Lightning began to settle. The man had left the arena, which made him more comfortable, thus he began to relax.

Carefully Janie gathered up the reins and nudged him forward at a walk again. This time he did walk a few steps. He was rewarded with a pat on the neck and a soothing voice praising him. After he'd walked about the ring for a few minutes, Janie tried signaling him to stop. The second cue brought him to an impatient halt, but a halt nevertheless. For this he was rewarded profusely. Again she sent him forward at a walk, reversing the direction. This time he did it nicely. Though he'd not been ridden before this, Lightning had had all the groundwork so that stepping off with a rider was the next natural step. Janie, sensing his inexperience, knew enough about training youngsters to bring him along slowly, much as Ann would have.

151

After a bit more walking and halting, Janie stopped and slid off him, patting his neck as she did. "That's it for today, Storm," she told him, scratching his neck where she'd learned he liked it. "Lesson's over."

She stripped him down and turned him loose in the large pasture with the other horses. As he ran off to join them, she idly watched him go, thinking how good he'd been today. It wouldn't take too long to really ride him, she thought. This colt had been trained with a gentle hand before he'd been abused, of that much she was sure. She'd like to get her hands on whoever mistreated such an incredible horse.

Another thought hit her. Suppose his *current* owner was the abusive one. How could she ever surrender this youngster to someone who would abuse him all over again. Here she was making progress, getting him to trust people again and what if the owner showed up and he turned out to be the very person who'd nearly ruined Storm? She just couldn't give him back to someone like that.

Later, she approached her father with her thoughts. But he had no ready answer for her. "If … when his owner shows up, we'll have to let him go. We have no right to keep another person's property, you know." He thought a minute. "Of course, there'll have to be proof that colt belongs to him before I'll release him. Colt's obviously valuable. I wouldn't let him go without proof of ownership."

"Someone might try to claim him dishonestly, you mean?"

"Exactly. Well, it hasn't happened yet, so stop worrying till the time comes. In the meantime if you want to go on riding the colt, go ahead. I don't see what harm it can do."

"Thanks, Pa," she replied, relieved that he understood.

Over the next few days, Janie continued to school Lightning in the small pen. He responded well to her gentle touch. He even began to lose his fear when her father came around him. By the end of the week he was trotting nicely in both directions, stopping on cue and even backing well. Eagerly, she began to teach him the signal to canter and by the end of the following week he was responding perfectly to that as well.

The first day she took him into the larger field, her father came with her, just in case he should take off and throw her. They walked the whole perimeter of the field before she tried it at a trot. Lightning was willing and eager but he did not attempt to take the bit in his teeth and run, not until he was sent into a canter.

Then instinct took over. Lightning was born to run. The big open space of the field lent itself to the stretching of his legs as a sudden burst of energy took over. Up came the tail and as his stride lengthened, he shoved his nose forward, nostrils flaring as he drank in the wind. Before Janie knew it, he had increased his speed to a flat out gallop. Unable to pull him in, she just sat back and enjoyed the ride. She had never gone that fast on a horse before. His speed was exhilarating. It was like flying. She sat deeper into the saddle and held on.

Lightning ran the full perimeter of the field before he began to slow. Even as he responded to her reins he was barely winded. He came prancing back to Pa Bailey, still anxious to run, nostrils flaring. Janie's face was flushed from the wind, but the smile of joy filled her expression.

"Wow!" she exclaimed. "What a horse! Can he ever run! I bet he'd make a fine race horse with speed like that."

"Sure can run," Pa nodded. "I was afraid for you though when he took off, but you stuck him good, honey."

Janie patted the colt's neck. "Well, I didn't have much choice, did I? By the time I realized what he was doing, it was too late to stop him. Besides," she added, " by then I didn't want to. That was some ride."

"I don't know though, perhaps he's too much horse for you. Maybe you shouldn't be riding him."

"Oh, Pa, don't say that. He'll be fine, once I learn to channel his energy. Besides, I liked it. I can't wait to do it again."

"I don't know. You could get hurt."

"No worse than me breaking the green horses around here. This colt is quite gentle normally. Now that I know what he's capable of, I promise I'll only turn him loose when it is safe to do so."

153

"I suppose. Don't think I could keep you off him anyway. Go ahead, but remember one of these days his rightful owner's bound to show up and want him back. I hate to see you so attached that you'll be heartbroken when he leaves."

"Only if the one who abused him comes looking for him," she said meaning it. But secretly she did worry that one day this colt would be taken from her, as had every other horse with whom she'd gotten attached. But until that day, he was hers to enjoy, and enjoy him she would.

During the following month, she looked forward to spending all her spare time with the black colt. Lightning relished the attention, and progressed quite nicely under her tutelage. He accepted her as his person, and though there was not fully the bond he had had with Ann, he was very responsive to her as his rider. After awhile she felt confident enough in his training to ride him off the ranch and up into the surrounding hills. Together they explored trails and found straight-aways with good footing where she could let him run. She loved the thrill of the wind in her face as he sped along, flattening out in a flying run. How she would love to race him for real. She just knew he'd win. Nothing could touch him, she was sure.

But always fearful that any exposure of that kind could lead to the solving of his identity, she kept his speed her own secret and was content with her dreams. By now she knew she would be devastated to have to return him, though she did not express those thoughts to her parents. She greatly feared that the colt's true owner was someone who should not have horses in his care.

The longer the time passed without an owner showing up, the more hopeful Janie became. She now considered him her colt. When possible buyers came to look at the other horses they had for sale, she always put him out in the farthest pasture so he wouldn't be seen. Though she knew it was wrong, the less talk about him the better, she decided. It was too painful for her to relate the story of his sudden appearance over and over. Still she was aware that the more people who knew about him the better the chance they'd have of finding his owner.

Between her and her father there was no talk about the other option, that of offering him for sale. Pa Bailey was an honest man, and while he could have gotten a top price for such a colt, even without papers, money that would be very useful to them, he also knew that this colt was not his to sell. While it was becoming less and less likely as each day passed that his owner would show up, he could see the bond forming between his daughter and this horse. Janie had never really had a horse she could call her own. Every horse they had was for sale, should a buyer come along. The Bailey's were in the business of training and selling horses. That was their living. They could not afford the sentiment of getting attached to any of them. Janie knew this but she was still a kid. Her father, adoring her as he did and unable to give her much else in life, never considered letting this colt go. He would be hers for as long as they were destined to keep him. He no longer made inquiries in town about the colt's identity. Better than two months had passed and nothing had turned up. What will be, will be, he decided.

—⁓—

Ann would have been relieved to know that her beloved Lightning was at least in good hands and being well cared for. As it was, she had no such reassurance on which to go. With no more news, by now she feared the worst. The general assumption was that he'd gotten lost out in the wild country beyond where he'd escaped, and probably succumbed to the elements of winter or wild predators. In any event, nothing was seen or heard of him. Officially the search had been called off. She still kept alive a faint hope that he would turn up, but she no longer talked about it with anyone, not even her closest friend, Jock. The pain was too great.

Then, as if the Collins family hadn't had enough tragedy in their lives, came the news of Si'ad's fate.

Spring was rapidly breaking when Michael got a call from the ranch in Arizona where Si'ad was standing at stud. They called to relate the unusual circumstances leading to Si'ad's

155

disappearance. In shocked horror Michael described the tragic story to his family.

During the previous night a fire had started in the main barn that housed their office, a large indoor arena and most of their horses, including Si'ad. Because it was night, no one noticed it for some time, until one of the grooms, whose apartment was at the far end, awoke to the smell of smoke. By then the fire was spreading rapidly. Much of the barn was consumed by smoke. Frantically he sounded the alarm and he, along with the first helpers to arrive, tried to pull the horses to safety. Many were rescued, including Si'ad, who was one of the first to get out. However, and this was where the confusion came, he, like most of the other rescued horses, was shoved hastily into one of several paddocks that were used for daytime exercise. Yet when the fire was finally contained and they were left with the smoldering ruins, they began to account for each horse that had been in the barn and Si'ad was nowhere to be found. The groom who'd originally gotten him free protested positively that he'd put him in the farthest paddock before rushing back to save another horse, but the paddock was empty.

One of the people involved swore he'd seen a grey horse running loose, during the height of the fire. He was quite sure the horse ran back into the burning inferno. If it was indeed Si'ad, then surely he had perished in the blaze. But there could be no actual proof of which horses were lost until the fire cooled and they could sift through the rubble. Until then it could only be assumed that Si'ad had died, too.

When Michael was done repeating the story, he was met with only stunned silence. All of them were in shock upon hearing the news. It couldn't be. First Lightning gone, now Si'ad. It was too much to take in all at once. Though they'd given up Si'ad over a year ago, they all knew that someday he would be returning to Stormy Hill for good. Now even that hope was shattered.

All at once, Ann let out an awful scream of sheer despair and collapsed into her mother's arms. "Not again," she wailed, sobbing hysterically. Her mother tried to comfort her, but she herself felt as bad as any of them. More so, since she alone must bear the pain for all of them and be the strength they would need if they were to get through this latest catastrophe. Right at that moment Jessica doubted very much if she had that ability within her.

"Ann, honey," Michael tried to tell her. "They aren't positive he was lost in the fire. We don't know for sure."

But she would not be dissuaded. "But they don't have him, do they? He hasn't been accounted for. What other explanation could there be? Someone saw a horse like him run back into the fire. He wasn't where they put him. I know Si'ad. He could have jumped out. He was a good jumper. You remember I used to jump him." She choked on her tears, unable to go on.

"Don't, Ann," her mother begged, holding her. "Don't talk like that. They could be wrong. We don't know for sure what happened to him."

But Ann knew. Deep down inside she knew. First Lightning was taken from her. Now Si'ad was gone, too. Nothing would ever be the same for her again.

CHAPTER FOURTEEN

The Whip

But, Pa, I don't want to ride just any horse for the Ozark ride. I want to take Storm," Janie argued with her father. They were out in the barn discussing the upcoming trail ride through the Ozark Mountains that was always held the last weekend in March. It had become a tradition for many of the neighboring ranchers, including the Baileys, to attend. Folks trailered their horses to the prescribed meeting place several hundred miles east, at the foothills of the Ozarks, where the following day they would be led in by a qualified guide who knew the area. The trail boss they chose was the same one each year, now considered an old friend, who picked a leisurely ride up into the mountains to a scenic location where they would spend the night, returning a couple of days later.

The highlight of the trip was always arriving at the campsite. While pack animals carried the food for the huge cookout, as well as breakfast the next morning, each rider carried saddle-bags and a bedroll equipped with his own basic necessities. It was a real old-fashioned trail ride, sleeping under the stars and eating over an open fire. Janie, like everyone else, loved it and look forward to the ride each year.

But this year she had an extra reason to go. Storm had been doing so well, she wanted to take him along as her mount. She felt he was ready to handle it. She now thought of him as her horse, sometimes even forgetting the strange circumstances which brought him to her.

"I just don't know," her father argued. "You say he's ready, but I wonder. He's never been off this ranch since he came. There'll be lots of strange horses to deal with, for one thing."

"He's real good around other horses. His manners are impeccable. He no longer shows any apprehension around you or other men who come to the ranch."

"I suppose. Look, how about a compromise. We'll try loading him and taking him for a ride. We could take him over to Mort's place. There's always a lot of activity there. Besides that bunch is going on this ride, too."

"That's a great idea. Perhaps we could ride out from their place using the horses they're going to take. That way Storm will be used to them when we get to the Ozarks."

"Now don't get too excited, honey," he admonished. "Not until we see how it goes. If he can handle it, then I guess you can take him."

"Thanks, Pa," she hugged him. "Storm will do fine. You'll see." She ran off to tell the black colt the good news. Her father just shook his head, smiling. In the back of his mind, however, was the nagging doubt that exposing him to such a ride may not be in his daughter's best interests. How would they explain their possession of a horse of his caliber? The Baileys weren't noted for having particularly high quality horseflesh on their place. Surely people would question how they came by this magnificent youngster. There would be a lot of participants on this ride with them. Suppose someone recognized him? He seldom thought anymore about the owner of this colt showing up, though back in his mind there still lingered the fear that someday, someone would show up to claim him. Janie had become so attached to Storm. It would be devastating for her to lose him now. Still, he feared it was already too late to stop the inevitable.

The following weekend, Janie and her father loaded the black colt and the horse he was taking in the old, worn trailer and drove the few miles over to a neighboring ranch. Lightning gave them no trouble getting on or traveling in the trailer, for he was well used to them and had never known abuse connected with trailering.

Upon arriving at the new place, he stepped out of the trailer alert and very excited. He danced about whinnying to the other horses, eager to be off. Janie had some trouble getting him tacked up, but other than not wanting to stand still, he was not too bad.

Riding out amidst company, however, he behaved reasonably well. Though spirited and anxious to go faster, he obeyed Janie's hands when she asked him to walk. Even at faster gaits he did not try to run away with her, seemingly content to remain with the others. Pa Bailey was impressed enough to allow her to take him on the upcoming ride, much to Janie's delight.

In anticipation of the event, Janie spent her remaining time teaching the black colt to carry extra equipment. Though he didn't like it at first, Lightning grew used to it. She tried a heavier stock saddle but he acted so frightened of it and distrustful, that she quickly went back to the lighter English one she'd been using, modifying it to accommodate her saddlebags and bedroll.

Finally the morning of their departure arrived. Janie, so excited she could barely contain herself, helped her father load their horses in the still-black pre-dawn. Pa Bailey pulled the old battered truck, packed the night before with their gear, into the long driveway leading to the main road as Janie waved goodbye to her mother. Minutes later they reached the proposed spot where they were joined by several other trucks pulling horse trailers and the small group began their caravan that would eventually bring them to the place where the ride would start. It was dark when they reached their destination so horses were quickly unloaded and turned into awaiting stalls or paddocks provided by the company organizing such rides. Then gear was unloaded and accounted for before the riders partook of a hasty but nutritious meal. A long, low cabin called the bunkhouse furnished makeshift beds. All were eager to lay their sleeping bags down on them and turn in early for it had been a lengthy, tiring trip just to get there. Tomorrow would be a busy day.

The sun was just peaking through the trees when everyone mounted up in anticipation of leaving the next morning. Lightning was unusually agitated by the activity going on around him and gave Janie some trouble saddling up. Consequently they were the last ones to be ready. In the commotion of preparing to leave the base camp, the other riders hardly noticed the black colt until they were well out on the trail. By this time, Lightning was more relaxed as he settled into the ride. The horses he was immediately near were all seasoned trail horses whose calm manners quieted him also.

Janie was just beginning to relax and enjoy the beautiful scenery herself when a stranger swung up beside her.

"Beautiful horse you have, miss," he said, as Lightning side-stepped away from his nearness. "What is he?"

Janie started at the question. "Part Arab, I think. I'm not really sure." she answered without thinking. Then blasted herself when her vague answer led to further questions.

"You don't know? Surely you must have papers on a horse as handsome as he is."

"N-no. He was, well, he was just found in our pasture one day, a couple of months ago." She decided to be honest. After all, too many people on this ride knew the real story. "No one came forth to claim him so we kept him," she finished rather lamely, a weak smile on her face.

"I can't believe it! No one claimed him, you say. A looker such as him? Unbelievable."

"Well we did quite a bit of searching for his rightful owner," she added, self-defensively. "Lots of people came to look at him but no one could identify him."

"Oh, I believe you. Still, you'd think someone's looking for a colt of his quality," he added, sympathetically.

"You would, wouldn't you. But no one has," she finished, to let him know the subject was closed.

But the stranger continued, "So now he's yours."

"That's right, at least until his rightful owner shows up, if he ever does," she stated, moving away as Lightning chose that moment to shy at something. Actually she had nudged him on the offside so that he acted up. Taking advantage of what appeared to be bad behavior, she pretended to work at getting him under control, thus drawing farther away from the stranger and making it impossible to continue their conversation that was becoming more uncomfortable by the minute.

Suddenly, Janie wished she had not insisted on bringing the black colt for this ride. There were too many people, she realized, who did not know her colt's story. If she had to repeat it to every one of them, she'd be pretty miserable. But worse, supposing one of them had heard of his disappearance and could trace his owner? How sorry she'd be then for bringing him here.

Well, the damage was done. There was nothing she could do about it now. She really couldn't have lied about his background, but she could have just said he was an Arab and let it go at that. Hopefully the stranger wouldn't repeat their conversation to the others after all. Might as well relax and enjoy the ride.

Even so, Janie found herself keeping close to her father and their neighbors for the duration of the day. Fortunately no one came up to her with any pointed questions she felt reluctant to discuss, so when they pulled into the camp that night she had nearly forgotten the incident and was ready to chow down with the rest. The smell of the steaks cooking over a hot open fire filled the air and made them all realize how hungry they were after a long day in the saddle. Lunch had only been cold sandwiches on the side of the trail, but this was a feast worth the wait.

Later, after all the food had been consumed, except for a few diehards roasting marshmallows over the glowing coals, they all sat around the campfire, leaning against their saddles, drinking black coffee, and feeling very much like cowboys of old. One of the guides pulled out his harmonica and began to play softly. Soon everyone was humming or singing along. This led to a music-fest as they began to suggest songs.

But the exhaustion of the day caught up with them and individually or in small groups they turned in, asleep almost before they settled into their sleeping bags.

Janie went out to the picket line to check on her horse one last time. Lightning stood contentedly, munching the hay that had been brought out for them. He had long since finished his grain so she removed his feed bucket and checked his ties, though he seemed content to stand between her father's horse and another quiet horse. Confident that he was all right, she gave him a quick pat and turned in, asleep immediately.

Sometime after midnight, one of the trail guides rose and went over to check on the horses. He had heard what sounded like an animal thrashing in the bushes and he wanted to make sure everything was okay. As he moved through the dark, he stumbled over something on the ground and leaned over to see what it was. It was a riding crop. Assuming one of their party had dropped it, he picked it up, thinking to carry it back to the campsite and locate its owner in the morning. As he walked toward the string of horses, easily visible as they were standing in a clearing, bathed in moonlight, he hummed a tune, keeping time by unconsciously slapping the crop against his leg as he walked.

Down the line he went, inspecting each horse before moving on to the next. He stopped before Lightning. "My, aren't you a handsome guy," he murmured. Even in the dark, there was enough moonlight to see that this was no ordinary horse. Admiring good horseflesh, he reached up to pet him, momentarily forgetting he held the crop.

Something snapped in Lightning as the whip came toward him. He had watched the man coming across the clearing, carrying the crop, which he kept slapping against his leg. The sight of it jogged his memory back to another man, one who also held a whip in his hand. Only that one had been used against him and it had hurt. Even before this one accidentally touched him, though the man sought to stop his hand in mid-flight, Lightning's nostrils flared in fear.

Nancy Clarke

Not realizing it was the whip he feared, the man tried to calm him, but still holding the crop, he only made things worse. In an abrupt movement, Lightning reared back to escape what he thought was sure punishment. As he did so, the power of his quick actions, broke the halter in two, setting him free. Perhaps if Janie had been there at that moment he may not have run, but all he saw was what he perceived in his now fear-crazed mind to be his old enemy. The crop was the stimulus triggering the pain

164

he had known under those hands and now his only thought was to get away from it.

The man jumped forward to grab the colt before he got away, but he was too late. Lightning was already moving. As he broke free of the restraining halter, he flew backwards, turned and was gone, thrashing through the woods in full flight. The instincts of a once-wild horse kept him from immediate danger as he sensed fallen obstacles to avoid or vault over depending on the terrain. Within minutes he had covered quite a distance from the campsite and was still moving.

The commotion he had caused had awakened most of the campers who came running to see what was wrong. Other horses on the picket line had become upset by Lightning's actions and needed to be calmed.

Alerted to the cry of 'loose horse,' Janie asked one of the guides which one. When told it was a black colt, she immediately guessed it was hers. The broken halter confirmed it. With a sob, she started into the woods after him, but her father pulled her back.

"Janie, wait," he argued as she struggled against him. "Don't go after him yet. This is rough country up here. We're on the top of a mountain. You'll never find him in the dark and risk getting lost yourself. Then we'd have to rescue you and that would not help your colt's cause."

"But I can't just let him go. What if he gets hurt?"

"I know how you feel, but there's nothing any of us can do until daybreak when we can see and form a search party."

The trail boss agreed. "Chances are good, when he slows down he'll get lonesome for his buddies. Most horses do. Most likely he'll come back by morning anyway."

"I don't think so," Janie said, doubtfully. "He was wild once." Quickly she explained the circumstances under which they had acquired him.

But that only gave the trail boss more hope. "Then that's in his favor. If he's survived as a wild horse before, its most likely he knows enough not to get hurt until we can round him up. If it will make you feel better, we'll organize now so we're ready by daybreak."

165

The other riders were eager to help search for the missing colt and offered their assistance. No one could sleep anyway so they set about making a plan. Janie was grateful for their help.

"Gus, here, is a top-notch tracker," the boss told her. "He'll find his tracks if anyone can. Your colt is, after all, a trained horse. I'm betting that he'll run his fill, then return here looking for companionship. Who knows, he may just be back here at dawn waiting for us to serve him breakfast," he repeated again.

"Maybe," she half-smiled, though not really believing it. "I just wonder what spooked him to make him run off like that."

Others said the same thing, but no mention was made of any association of the sight of the whip and his panicked response. Even the man who'd actually caused his terror-filled flight did not connect the event with the crop he had had in his hand. Since most riders carried quirts or crops of some kind he assumed this horse was used to one, also.

At dawn all the riders were saddled up and, if not in a cheerful mood, were at least in a hopeful one as they headed out. At first the trail seemed to lead down the mountain in a fairly straight line, and most of them expected to see the colt quickly. But as the sun rose higher in the sky, the search became more difficult. The colt had sought out a mountain stream, which he obviously crossed more than once. At first they were able to locate the trail on the other side but lost it once again in the stream. It appeared that he'd picked his way through the streambed and possibly across a rocky flat, but no amount of crisscrossing could pick up the trail from this point. Riders branched out to cover more territory but even as they straggled back to base camp, each hoping perhaps the colt had actually returned, they were met with rejection. A whole day's search had turned up nothing.

Janie and her father opted to stay there overnight and continue looking for the colt. Several other riders volunteered to stay with them. The base camp boss loaned Janie a horse to ride and sent a couple of his guides with them both to help look and, more important, to keep them from getting lost. Still, after three more days of searching, they were all forced to call it off. No sign of the colt had been found and the others had to get back to their respective lives. Even Pa Bailey could not afford any more time away from his ranch, much as he'd like to stay and continue the search. Janie was very reluctant to leave but finally relented when the trail boss assured her that he had many more trail rides scheduled into the Ozarks. For him the season had just begun. Surely, some sign of her missing horse would surface before long and they'd get him back.

"I never should have brought him here in the first place," Janie told her father on the way home, the trailer one horse lighter.

"Perhaps it was meant to be," her father reasoned. "Think about this. He was never our horse to begin with. We both knew he really belonged to someone else. One day his owner was bound to show up and you'd have lost him anyway."

"But then, at least, I'd have known where he went and what happened to him. Now I'll never know."

Her father had no answer to that.

Lightning, by then, had covered quite a bit of ground. Initially, as in the past, he had no desire to stop until he was completely exhausted. The fear that drove him now was not unlike the other fear he had felt before. The sight of that crop had reaffirmed in his mind once again that people were not to be trusted, certainly not men. The girl may have been kind but she was not there now, and he had a vague gnawing feeling about someone else in his past he needed to reach. Once again an instinct inside him drove him onward in an easterly direction as he sought that goal. By daybreak of the first day he was miles from the campsite, well beyond any area the search party would be covering.

Each day he continued to travel eastward, slowly coming out of the Ozarks and into the foothills. Once again he thrived on living in the wilds. He fell easily to living by his own devices this time, as his body toughened and his muscles hardened.

He had been traveling over a week when he began to cross into arid grazing land. Cattle now moved in distant fields. Occasionally he'd see signs of people but he gave them wide berth. He'd learned strong lessons. People were to be feared.

But he did long for one type of companionship, that of his own kind. He began to feel the need to be with other horses again. Thus on one early morning, about two weeks after his second escape, when he scented horses in the wind, he did not hesitate. He followed the scent to a huge field where in the distance grazed a number of horses, most of them mares. The scent of mares drove him on. The young colt, now past two, was developing into a stallion.

A wire fence stood between him and the mares. Lightning jumped it effortlessly and ran toward the distant horses. They milled about uneasily at the sight of him. He circled, sniffing and nudging at each one. But there was no stallion heading this band. The few geldings did not dispute his inclusion so things settled down and one by one each horse went back to eating. Lightning had joined the herd without a fuss.

Lightning had been with the herd for several days when he noticed riders approaching from a distance. Immediately he raised his head and began to pace back and forth nervously. The sight of people again brought back fearsome memories. When they began to spread out and circle the herd, Lightning took flight. Unfortunately he had waited too long. Instantly one of the riders broke away and headed after him.

He had chosen rocky, uneven ground for his retreat, making it impossible to reach his full speed, while the wily, tough little cowpony chasing him was able to catch him and drive him back into the herd before he realized what had happened. Boxed in by the other horses, he was unable to make another attempt at an escape.

The herd was driven down a long, low-lying valley to a waiting holding pen at the end. Lightning was swept into the gate before he could turn away. Once in the pen all the horses milled around, stirring up dust clouds. This corral was much smaller than they'd been used to so it took awhile before they began to relax. All but Lightning. He kept eyeing the top rails as though he was going to jump, but this fence was close to six feet, much higher than any he'd cleared before. Finally he gave up and settled down with the rest, who by now were munching contentedly on the hay that had been distributed about the pen. Not seeing any initial threat, he grew less restive and resumed eating, though he maintained a watchful eye on his captors. However, after assuring themselves that the horses had plenty to eat and water to drink, they departed.

The next day, two men returned in a truck. They came up to the fence and stood talking as they looked over the herd.

"Nice bunch Harry's got for us this time," one man, the taller, lankier one remarked.

"They ought to bring a decent price at the auction next week," the other commented, nodding his head so that his longish dark hair bobbed in all directions. He was shorter, heavy-set, and walked with a slight limp. "Funny, I could have sworn he told us he had twenty head in this back pasture to haul. Maybe I'm counting wrong but I keep coming up with an extra one."

"Ah, you know Harry. He's a bit addle-brained at times. Probably doesn't even know what he's got back here. Never did have no business sense, he did."

"Nope, but he does know his horses. Too bad he's laid up with that busted leg. I'd like to make sure we got all the right ones."

"Won't make no difference. He said to take all the ones in this lot and sell them, so I guess he knows what he's talking about." He turned back to the truck. "We'll bring the stock trailer out beginning tomorrow and get this bunch moved to the holding pens at the auction. That way they'll be good and settled before the sale."

"Sounds fine to me. Must say," the other man added, climbing into the truck, "them horses are in mighty good weight. Nice and rounded out. Harry should be pleased with what he gets this time."

The following day a stock trailer arrived to load some of the horses. Lightning stayed well back in the herd, eager to avoid human contact. That day he was not among those picked to transport. Nor the next. However, by the third trip, there were only five horses left and there was no avoiding the trailer this time. Lightning tried to escape but he was lassoed and forced to load with the remaining horses. These were experienced cow-boys who dealt with horses for a living and had learned not to take any nonsense from them. Lightning lacked the experience of a true rebel. Reluctantly he finally went on, gaining some comfort from the company of the other horses.

The trailer trip took several hours. By the time they stopped and unloaded the horses, all were eager to get out and stretch their legs. They were driven into a pen, much like the one they had just left, except that this was one of many, most containing horses like themselves. Again hay was plentiful and soon they had all settled back into the routine of eating and milling about.

This lasted for several days. Occasionally men passed by, sometimes stopping to observe the different horses in the pens, but things didn't pick up until the end of the week. From after-noon into evening more and more people came by, stopping, making comments, then walking on. A few jotted down notes on paper before moving on to the next pen. Lightning stayed to the back of the pen, taking no notice unless a young woman came up, but after the first several disappointments he stopped showing interest in any of the visitors.

By dusk the crowds had grown. Most had taken seats in the auction building where tack was being sold first. Finally, the first horses were led out. One by one the pens began to empty. The lot Lightning was with was one of the last to cross the auc-tion block. By then the crowds had begun to thin out as the hour grew late.

Lightning shied away from the two men who entered his pen, but highly skilled in catching recalcitrant horses, they were quick to seize him and place a halter over his head. He tried to balk as one led him out into the narrow aisle, but the man just slid a chain over his nose. The chain cut into his tender flesh and forced him forward. Nervously, he sidestepped into the arena, the bright lights spooking him after the semi-darkness of the back lot. His nostrils flared and he swirled around, wide-eyed, staring at the crowds in sheer terror. The man who held him grew angry at his disobedience and gave his lead rope a vicious yank. Lightning felt the sharp pain to his already sore nose and immediately rebelled, rearing straight up to escape from the agony. This only got him another jolt. Angry now, as well as hurting, he tried to rear again, striking out with his feet.

By now there was tittering from the audience as shouts of "Gee-haw, get him, cowboy," and "Got you a rodeo horse there, son!" could be heard.

The show ended quickly when another man entered the arena, bullwhip in hand. Using it with a lasso, he snubbed the colt and brought him in line. Shuttering with fear but temporarily subdued, Lightning stood still.

Quickly the auctioneer bid him up, taking the first bid that seemed reasonable for a colt of his quality, then hustled on to the next sale. Horses with attitudes like his were bad for business.

As the gavel sounded, Lightning was led out the gate and into one of the sales pens. There he stood trembling, wild-eyed, as sweat pored from his body. But for the moment he was left alone.

Sometime later two men appeared at his fence, watching him. Though neither showed interest in entering the pen, Lightning remained watchful, remaining at the farthest point from them.

"Don't know what made you include him in your lot, Johnny," the one said. "He's petrified of us. Poor thing, can't trust no one."

"Yeah, that's the very reason I claimed him. He's been abused," his friend replied. "Besides, if I didn't grab him, I'm afraid he'd have gone to the butchers. No one else was bidding on him."

"That's no reason to get soft and bid on him. We can't take home every sad case we see. It's just not practical."

"I know that but there's something special about that colt. Look at his conformation. Even without papers, he's quite the looker. And I got him for a steal. Think what he'll be worth when we get some training into him."

"Ya gotta tame him first," the other man scoffed.

"That's the point. What he needs is gentling not more abuse. I think we can bring him around once we get him back to the farm. Make one heck of a horse if we do."

"Take time."

"We've got plenty of that. Look, give him time to settle in. He hasn't been cut yet. That'll make a difference, too. Anyway, our trainer's pretty good at what he does. That's what we pay him for. This colt just may be the bargain of a lifetime for us."

The discussion continued, but to Lightning all he cared about was to be rid of this place and away from all who'd hurt him. The following morning he got his wish, as he was once again loaded into a van where, together with other horses bought at the sale, he was hauled off to his new home.

Chapter Fifteen

Kentucky

There's been a possible breakthrough on Lightning's disappearance," Michael announced to his family on the same night that the black colt was crossing the auction block. Quickly everyone gathered around, anxious for news.

"Did they find him?" Ann begged, her eyes lighting up.

"'Fraid not, but an incident occurred clear in the Ozark Mountains of Arkansas that may have something to do with our colt. There's this place at the base of the mountains that advertises trail rides. You can rent their horses or bring your own. They supply guides, food and lead rides up into the Ozarks. Anyway, about a couple of weeks ago, a large group of folks did an overnighter with them. They came from quite a distance and brought their own horses. During the night one of their horses got loose from the picket line and ran off into the mountains. Quite a search was made to find him but as of yet nothing has turned up."

"What makes this have anything to do with our missing colt?" Scotty asked.

"Because the horse in question, the one that got lost, is a black, solid black with only a crooked blaze. That is how the guides and folks involved are describing him."

"Lightning!" Ann screeched, excitedly. "Yes, it's got to be him! Who else could it be?"

"Wait, there's more," her father continued. "The story goes that he was being ridden by a young girl who came with her father for the ride. She was heard talking to one of the others about how her horse just appeared at their ranch one day. They had checked everywhere but no one could identify him. So they kept him."

"Now I know it's him," Ann's face lit up as hope spread through her. Could it be that Lightning was still alive, out there somewhere, waiting for her to find him? She longed to go to the Ozarks herself to search for him.

"Wait a minute," Jock cut in. "There's something here I don't understand. How could these people not know we've been looking for him? We were able to trace him all the way to Oklahoma before losing him."

"I know, Jock," Michael explained. "That's exactly what I thought, but these folks who had him, or a dead ringer for him, live in a remote part of the country, many miles from where our Lightning escaped. Too far away to hear about our missing colt in any event."

"So now what?" interjected Scotty. "If this is Lightning who's running loose in the Ozarks, what next?"

"After the initial search turned up nothing, they alerted all the guides who lead groups up there to be on the lookout for him. Also, any property owners in the area, especially those who own horses. It seems most likely at this point that once he gets done running, he'll seek out pastured horses, like he did the last time."

"If he doesn't get hurt," Ann suddenly moaned. "Isn't that pretty wild country up there?"

"No worse than what he's survived already," Scotty reassured her. "That was pretty rugged country back in Oklahoma that he came through and survived. He seems to be managing quite well for a pampered pet," he smiled and squeezed her shoulder. She managed a half-hearted smile back.

"Most likely," her father added, comfortingly, "he'll seek out the company of other horses and if the folks in that area are aware of his identity, we stand a good chance of getting him back."

"Think positive, Ann," her mother soothed her. "This is the best news we've had in a long time. I believe we're going to get him back, after all. Have a little faith."

"But shouldn't we be doing something?" Ann asked, plaintively.

"Like?"

"Like going up there. Going after him. Perhaps if I was up there he'd come to me?"

"Oh, Ann," her father sighed. "It's not that easy. He's been loose three weeks or better. He could be anywhere by now. Where would we look? The Ozarks are a huge mountain range, and quite a distance from here."

"Oh, but, I can't just wait here hoping for someone to spot him," she wailed. " I've got to do something!"

"I understand, honey, but I don't know what else to do until he's sighted. But I can promise you this. When a report comes through that he's been spotted, you and I will drop everything and go out there to look for him. How's that?"

"Great, Dad," she hugged him. "That's infinitely better than just sitting around doing nothing."

"Fine, then, that's what we'll do. And we'll take Jock along to help, agreed?"

Jock immediately jumped at the chance. He'd been feeling pretty helpless thus far, and this way he could do something useful. The two young people looked at each other and smiled. It was the first genuine smile for Ann since Lightning had disappeared. She would not have smiled, though, if she'd known that at that very minute, her beloved Lightning was once again riding in a horse van, as his newest owner took him miles from where this latest search for him was being conducted.

Of Si'ad there had been no word at all. It was now assumed that he had been lost in the tragic fire along with several others, though, due to the extensive damage it had caused, no positive identification was possible.

The van carrying Lightning traveled most of the day at a steady pace, stopping only for gas. Lightning and his five other traveling companions settled easily into the routine, contentedly munching their hay. Lightning had always been a good traveler, not minding the slight sway of the vehicle. He only became alert when they stopped and one of the men poked his head in to check on the horses. But since no one came in, he easily went back to eating.

Unbeknownst to him, they rolled over the wide Mississippi and passed into Tennessee. Later they crossed the border and entered the state of Kentucky. Each mile was bringing him closer to his old home but Lightning had no way of knowing that.

It was getting on toward dusk when the van finally stopped for good. The ramp was lowered and the horses gazed out onto a green expanse of perfectly manicured rolling hills and miles of brilliant white fences. The barn lay directly in front of them, a long, low affair, painted white with maroon trim, spotlessly clean and well kept. One by one, each horse was led out and taken to an awaiting stall. Finally only Lightning was left.

"Take it easy with that one," the man who'd bid for him admonished. "He's been roughed up some and he's very nervous. I'd put him in the end stall for tonight. Want him to settle well before we try to work with him. Such a shame," he added. "The horse is a real beauty, too. Sure hope we can reclaim him. He looks like he could be a superb jumper prospect."

His partner watched as they unloaded the fractious black colt. Lightning threw up his head, whinnying continually as he circled about, anxious to see where he was. There was something familiar about this place. Even after he was led unwillingly to a stall, he continued to pace, unable to settle. An image lodged in his memory would not go away. His nostrils flared in and out, absorbing the distinctly recognizable smells as he searched for an answer. He was unaware of what a dramatic picture he made as he circled the large stall, head and tail up, neck arched.

"I can see now why you bought him, though," Lonnie, the partner, said. "It would have been a shame to let the killers have him. You're right. In spite of his problems, he was well worth the price."

"Yeah, I think I did all right by him. He should settle, too, after he's cut. They usually do when they're young like this."

"I'd hate to cut a fine horse like him. What a stallion he'd make."

"But useless without papers, remember?"

"I know, I know. But still." He left the thought unsaid.

Lightning, ignorant of their plans for him, resumed pacing about the stall, stopping every so often as if listening. He could not shake the feeling that this place gave him. The need to always travel in an easterly direction had returned, stronger than ever. Something was out there he needed to find. The urge to run was nearly overpowering. Tired from the trip as he was, it was a long time before he settled.

The following day, he was turned out in a small paddock behind his stall. It did not give much freedom but at least he could move around more, which he did. At first he eyed the fence, but at six feet of strong oak, it was nearly insurmountable. Thus he developed a pattern of pacing back and forth against the back fence, occasionally stopping to test the air. Every so often he would return to his stall to eat some hay, but after a while, back he would go to stand in the corner and gaze off to the east, head and tail up, nostrils flaring. Then he would let out a sharp whinny and begin to pace again. While his new owners noted his behavior, they attributed it to his newness in strange surroundings, expecting him to calm down eventually.

By the end of the week he seemed much better, enough that they chose to put him in one of the larger pastures toward the back of the farm, away from the clamor of this busy hunter-jumper facility. Thinking he just needed to rest further before beginning their work with him, they turned him out with several other horses, all quiet, older reliable horses, whom they felt would help him to relax and accept the farm faster.

They were able to catch him without too much trouble this time as he was willing to be led as long as the chain lead was not used across his nose. He was actually eager to be put in the bigger pasture. Seeing the horses in the distance he called to them, picking up their scent. The horses raised their heads as he entered the field. Once released, he began to trot in their direction, sniffing the wind.

His trot turned into a gallop as he bore down upon them, running around the clustered horses, snorting enthusiastically. Then he slowed and one by one he sniffed each, finally turning away as if disappointed that he did not recognize them.

Misunderstanding his motives, the men laughed at his antics. "I think he'll be all right now," Lonnie said.

Indeed Lightning had expected to know at least one of the horses turned out in this wide, grass-filled field, rolling gently up a slope then down to meet a slowly meandering stream passing through it. The young horse was recalling another similar pasture where he'd spent so much of his time. The similarities were remarkable, but then so many of the horse farms in Kentucky bore an almost repetitious likeness. And Lightning was truly home in his beloved bluegrass once more.

The yearning within him grew stronger as the days passed. Rather than settle more, Lightning had taken to pacing off every inch of the borders around his field. He was drawn to something still vague in his mind, but there nevertheless.

It was May now and for the most part the horses would be left out at night, unless they were in training and needed on a daily basis. It was felt that Lightning would be safe to turn out with the rest as he'd been there long enough to make the adjustment.

"We'll leave him where he is tonight," Johnny remarked one evening to one of his grooms. "But bring him in early. Tomorrow morning the vet's coming and I think I'll have him gelded while he's here. Perhaps that'll remove these urges to pace he has."

So that night Lightning was not brought in as he always had been, but left out with the rest. They thought his willingness to stay with the other horses would overcome any desire for freedom. They were wrong. At first he seemed content to graze along with the rest, but by dusk a stiff breeze had come up, making Lightning extremely restless once again. Whether it carried with it the scent of something in his past or just instinct telling him to move on, whatever it was, the black colt began to run back and forth alongside the outer fence line, repeatedly casting his head in the same direction, always toward the east. It was as though he could see the home that had evaded him for so long. Every once in a while he would stop and whinny low in his throat as though calling to something or someone.

Suddenly he made a decision. Without hesitation he turned and galloped straight for a low spot in the fence. His leap was an effortless curve up and over without breaking stride. If the owners of the farm would have seen it, they would have gloried in his potential as a jumper. However, they would not discover his disappearance until morning. By then it would be too late.

This time Lightning struck out across the land with a different purpose. The instinct that had driven him since his first escape, grew stronger by the minute as he covered the miles between him and the one place that to him was home. Whether he understood what he was seeking or not, he was being driven to keep moving until he found it.

For the most part, he avoided any possible contact with people by skirting barns and buildings and staying pretty much in the woods or close to the tree line along the fields, leaping fences if necessary to cross long open spaces. His black color blended with the night shadows. If he was seen crossing the country roads, he was not recognized for what he was, but rather as some night creature, a shadow melting into the forest before its identity could be made. As the first rays of dawn spread across the rich green fields, Lightning made his way unerringly toward his goal, miles from where he had started.

CHAPTER SIXTEEN

Derby Day

For a brief moment, Ann regretted not joining the rest of her family for Derby Day. It was a Kentucky tradition she'd never missed until today. Still, by the time five o'clock rolled around, she found herself drawn to the television set as she watched with the same avid interest of every other race fan.

The warm, sunny day had indeed brought out the much-touted capacity crowds. The cameras flashed across an infield ablaze with color, packed with people so close together as to be virtually unable to move. Some of the more hardy picnickers tried to hold impromptu football tosses and the like, but were hard put to find any available space to play their games. Most settled for the space of a blanket or a beach towel and spent the rest of the day trying to keep people from stepping on it. Ann, watching in amusement, wondered why any of them bothered to come at all. It was most likely they'd never get close enough to the rail to see even one horse go by. But like so many other events in life, some just wanted to say they'd been there. For others, it was merely an excuse for a party.

Not so with Ann. Her soul interest lay in the horses, the real stars of this huge pageant that took place every first Saturday in May, America's oldest continuous sporting event, the one day all eyes were on Kentucky. For Ann, there was no other event like it.

Each year the finest three-year olds prepared for the premier race, the one that held all the mystique, the charm and the glory that no other race had ever equaled, the Kentucky Derby. Just its name evoked pictures of pillared southern plantation homes, rolling green fields, white plank fences, and spreading oaks where gentlemen and ladies with parasols strolled gracefully among gardens, riotous with color. For years they had arrived in horse drawn carriages to see their favorite horses run, while sipping mint juleps in frosted glasses, sitting in their boxes. Now the spectators arrived in cars, parking wherever they could find room. For Churchill Downs had never anticipated the crowds that were to come, and the parking lots filled to overflowing long before the grandstand seats were taken. And while much of the crowd came only for the party atmosphere, there would always be the true devotees of horse racing to make up the bulk of the crowd.

The backbone of the racing world would always be the farm owners and breeders. They, along with their trainers and special friends, usually chose to watch the race from their box seats. Most of them were unaffected and probably unaware of the masses of milling crowds, as they stayed in their own insular world, meeting in the exclusive clubhouse, or being served from their boxes by white uniformed waiters. These boxes were limited in number and as such had been jealously guarded within each family, hastily renewed each year at premier prices, even if they were only used once on Derby Day. For to lose your box meant it would be gone for good. The waiting list was a long one. Among the oldest families of the Bluegrass, boxes were passed down from generation to generation. It was with a sense of pride that one boasted of how many years his family had held a box on Derby Day.

The Collinses, having lived at Stormy Hill for five generations, were one of these families. In spite of hard times recently besetting them, Michael never had considered not renewing his family box year after year. Personal setbacks not withstanding, it was a sign of Southern culture that they were still one with the rest of the horse people living on estates far grander than Stormy Hill. They lived in what many would refer to as genteel poverty, but they were pure Kentucky all the way, and for that reason the elite horse world would never turn their backs on the Collinses.

Thus, on the first Saturday in May, Michael Collins and his family joined the thousands of others who had come to watch the annual running of the Kentucky Derby. All, that is, except Ann. She had not been able to bring herself to go this year and infect the others with her depression. Still, she could not stay away altogether, so by late afternoon she was watching like everyone else for the horses to take the track.

She watched and imagined herself there, as she had so many times in the past. Churchill Downs was a familiar place of which she held a strong fondness. She loved the old buildings kept pretty much as they had been, the landmark twin spires that dominated the track much as a beacon might, and the warm, homey feel of the stabling area along the backstretch, the place that housed both famous and soon-to-be famous without distinction.

In her dreams she had always pictured that one day she and Lightning would share this week together, as she readied him for the big race. She had longed to be part of the excitement, the festivities leading up to the big day. She could visualize Lightning running in his own Derby, running to win, making them proud, putting Stormy Hill back in the top ranks of major horse farms again, as it had been so long ago in the days of her great-grandfather. And winning! Winning the one race that none of the fine Stormy Hill horses had been able to capture—vindication for the race Stormy Hill, himself, had lost. How fitting that this colt, a direct descendant, win it for him.

And in her dreams, Ann always saw herself on Lightning as he ran the famous mile and a quarter. She knew that part was only a dream, girls couldn't be jockeys, maybe someday, but not now. Still, she always saw it just that way in her mind.

Just then she was brought back to reality as the announcer told his TV audience that the horses were coming out onto the track. She shook herself back to the present. There was no

Lightning. He was gone. No sightings had been reported from the Ozarks. It had just been another false hope. She must face the fact that he was never coming back and get over it. For them, he, and Si'ad, were no more. And yet she could not put away her dream of Lightning as a racehorse, certainly not on a day like today, Derby Day.

"The horses are at the gate!" came the announcer's voice. Even Ann was caught up in the frenzy of excitement as she, along with everyone else, held a collective breath for the release of the gates.

"They're off!" With a clang, the gates burst open and as one, the horses leapt forward. Another Kentucky Derby had begun. As Ann watched, she let herself feel the excitement, the tension mounting as they flew down the track. She was one with the jockeys, feeling the rise and fall of the horse beneath her, hearing the pounding of hooves from all around, tasting the dust stirred up by many feet. There was the roar of the crowds, a veritable wall of noise as they came down the homestretch, making their final play for position. She could feel the hot surge of straining muscles as each horse struggled to give his all to be the first to cross the finish line.

Too soon it was over. Horses flashed across the finish line. A number flashed up on the scoreboard and a giant cheer went up from the crowds. The victorious horse, a bright coppery-red chestnut, slowed off the backside and turned his white-blazed head to the camera as he cantered back to the winner's circle.

Ann only half listened to the commentary as the awards were presented and the race was replayed with the winning jockey giving his interpretation. The Kentucky Derby was now history, one more down in the record books. Already speculation had begun as to the chances of this colt winning the coveted Triple Crown. To do that he would have to win the Preakness, run at Pimlico in Maryland in two weeks and, if lucky enough, the third jewel, the Belmont Stakes three weeks later. Only a handful of horses had ever done that.

Lightning would have been good at all of these, she thought. Now he'd never get the chance. Neither Scotty nor her father had ever discussed the possibility of running him, at least not in her or Jock's presence, but that hadn't stopped her. She'd known when the time came, she'd be able to talk them into it. She gave a long sigh for what would never be.

The race was over. Ann flipped off the set. She was restless, too restless to stay in the house. The family wouldn't be home for hours yet, she supposed, and she didn't feel like waiting around inside for them.

I'll go riding, she thought, and headed out to the barn. Once there she was indecisive as to which to ride. There was her mother's old hunter, Cedardale, but he was so predictable. No challenge there. Of course she could ride Jock's gelding, Tag-along. As a retired racehorse he could still open up and run, but he was, after all, Jock's horse. That only left Banshee or one of the broodmares. She sighed, not much choice to that, and started to get Banshee's tack.

On the way to the tack room she passed one newly occupied stall and stopped. Just last week her dad had acquired a new mare for the farm, Bit O'Ginger by name. The liver chestnut mare had come as partial payment of a rather large feed bill owed at Michael's store. At first Michael had been reluctant to take her when he really needed the money more, but softhearted as he was, he finally agreed. She did, after all, have a nice pedigree, was bred for a foal next year and they could always use more broodmares.

Bit O'Ginger proved to be living up to her name, however. She had not yet adjusted to her new home and remained flighty and nervous. Scotty and Michael said they would not be surprised if she slipped this foal by the way she was acting. Consequently, no plans had been made for her yet.

Ann and Jock had ridden her around the paddock right after she came so they knew she was saddle broke, but neither had tried her outside yet.

No time like the present to find out, Ann thought, as she shifted gears and went to pick up a saddle and bridle for her. Besides restless and moody as Ann was right now, this mare's temperament would be just what she needed—a challenge.

Ginger sidestepped nervously away from the saddle as Ann went to place it on her back, but she was distracted and did not seem to notice or to mind. She waited patiently for the mare to take the bit. Finally, she led her out into the courtyard, hopping up quickly as she circled, unwilling to stand still for mounting. Absently, Ann made a mental note of this to work on at a later time. She disliked bad manners in horses, and saw no reason for them not to be trained out.

But for now, the mare's mood suited hers and she let it go. They left the courtyard at a jigging pace that brought them to the back gate in no time. She looked at the gate distastefully, remembering a time when, on Si'ad, they would together fly over it as if it weren't there. Any one of the geldings would stand quietly for her to open and close it. She doubted if Ginger would do either. Reluctantly she dismounted and led the mare through it, shutting it behind her. She was beginning to regret her impulsive decision to ride the mare.

Getting back on her was difficult at best as all the mare wanted to do was circle. Finally Ann resorted to vaulting on her. Ginger was off before she settled into the saddle. This time, she let her go, easing her into a steady hand gallop as they chose the path lined with trees that took them to the farthest reaches of Stormy Hill. Eventually it wound its way up Flat Top. The mare was damp with sweat long before they reached the summit, more from nerves than the heat though it had turned very humid and quite warm, even for early May.

Ann slowed the mare back to a walk as they began the gradual assent to the table top of the rise overlooking the surrounding horse farms. There she stopped and Ginger, having exhausted her initial need to stretch her legs, seemed content to stand still for once. Good, Ann thought, because she was rapidly losing her desire to ride such an unpredictable horse.

Instead she stood looking out over the Bluegrass country she loved. Soon her thoughts were far away, lost in dreams that could never be. Again she relived the running of the Derby, placing herself and her beloved black colt in the starring roles. One more time, she wondered, as she had done so many times

185

before, just what had happened to him and if she'd ever see him again. Life seemed so empty without him. Perhaps it would have been easier for her if he'd never survived the foaling than to have pulled him through, raised him, trained him, only to lose him like this in the end.

Again she pondered, could the horse that had gotten loose in the Ozarks indeed be her colt? She reviewed the facts she knew. Reports said a young girl had been riding him, but no name was given. This fact made her curious. She'd like to find and talk to the girl about her horse. If it were Lightning, she'd know instantly by the description. Surely the group that led the rides knew her name. She'd have left it with them so they'd contact her should the horse be found. By all means she'd want him back.

That's what she'd do when she got back, Ann thought excitedly. Ask her father to find out who the girl was and see if she could talk to her. At least they could identify if this was her Lightning who'd been found by the girl and her father and was running loose a second time.

Suddenly she was jolted out of her reverie. A distant clap of thunder rumbled in the thickening air and the mare spooked. One minute she was quietly standing, the next she whirled around, twisting in mid-air and rearing straight up. Ann may have held on had she been alert to Ginger's warnings, but she was deep in thought, miles away, when the mare bolted and before she could get a firm grip on the saddle, she felt the mare rear. Grasping for anything on which to hang, all she came up with was air. Before she knew it, she was rolling backwards, falling in a heap on the ground, her ankle twisted painfully beneath her. Spooked further by the sudden lightness of the saddle, Ginger took full advantage of her freedom and bolted for home before Ann could assess the situation and make a grab for the reins. Within seconds, the chestnut mare had disappeared down the well-worn path they had come.

But Ann, having the wind knocked out of her by the abrupt fall, just lay there a moment, catching her breath. As she took tally of her various body parts she realized she was basically all right, except for the sharp throbbing in her right ankle. Realizing that it had absorbed most of the fall, she shifted her weight to ease the ankle some, wondering how bad it was hurt. Mostly, she just felt very angry toward herself for allowing this to happen.

Certainly she of all people, knew how flighty Ginger was. Why hadn't she paid more attention to what she was doing? Now here she was, thrown like some kind of greenhorn beginner and forced to walk home, probably on a hurt ankle to boot. Another clap of thunder reminded her of why the mare had spooked in the first place. Looking at the sky, she grimaced. The sky was very purple to the west where distant flashes of lightning could be seen.

"On top of everything else, I'm going to get soaked," she groaned, not liking the prospect at all. Then she remembered another black thought. By the time she should get home, her family would probably be back also. If Ginger should be wandering loose about the back gate, assuming she got that far, they'd be terribly concerned about her, at least till she showed up in one piece. But Jock, oh, he'd have a field day with this. He'd be ribbing her forever about falling off. She'd never live it down. Darn.

She made an attempt to stand. There was a sharp jolt of pain in her ankle and she was forced to sit back down, rubbing it. Now she was in a real fix. What if she really couldn't walk on it, she'd have to wait for someone to come and get her. She certainly didn't like that outlook at all.

She was about to try again to stand when a movement in the distant bushes stopped her. She glanced up. Now what, she mused, somewhat annoyed at the whole chain of events that had taken place. What she saw was probably the last thing she ever expected to see. A huge, coal-black horse stepped into the clearing, head up, nostrils testing the building wind.

Ann had dreamt and thought of little else except Lightning so much that at first she was sure she was only envisioning a mirage conjured up in her mind or at the very least as a result of her fall. She blinked, shaking her head to clear it, but when she looked again, he was still there.

"Lightning?" she whispered, hardly daring to hope, frozen to the spot. The great black horse turned his head toward the soft noise, nostrils flaring as he strove to catch the scent. As he stared straight toward her, she saw the crooked blaze, so familiar she'd know it anywhere.

"Lightning!" she exclaimed. "Is it you? But you're so much bigger then when you ..." her voice broke and she couldn't go on. Suddenly all the emotions kept inside her from the day he disappeared, were caught in her throat and she couldn't do anything but stare at her long-lost colt.

Lightning heard her voice and caught her scent. He continued to stand there as old memories came flooding back to him and gradually he began to realize who called to him. This was the scent he'd been seeking all this time, this was the voice he had loved and lost, and this was the person to whom his instincts had led him to find again.

He lowered his head, reaching out to Ann, whinnying low in his throat, just as he had many times in the past when he saw her.

"Lightning?" Ann again called his name, her voice hardly more than a whisper, so filled with emotion was she.

The young stallion, for indeed he could hardly be called a colt after all he'd been through, trotted across the clearing, closing the distance that separated them. As he drew close he dropped his head and sniffed her hair. Ann rose up on her knees, ignoring the painful ankle. She reached out to touch him. Yes, he was real! This was no ghost, no figment of a vivid imagination. He was really here! With a great sigh, she threw her arms around his neck, hugging him.

Startled at first, Lightning raised his head, carrying her with him and lifting her to a standing position. She continued to alternate between hugging his neck and stroking him, all the while crooning to him in a soft voice, still unable to believe this was actually happening to her.

Yes, he was her colt but how much he had changed! He was a colt no longer. The metamorphosis was complete. For the first time in her life she felt dwarfed by him. He stood over sixteen hands tall. But it was more than that. He'd filled out, gained

muscle from the hard life of living on his own. His broader chest and well-rounded hindquarters had only been an immature hint of promise the last time she saw him.

He appeared to be well-fed, she also noted, pleased, as she ran her hands along his well-muscled neck and through the thick, though tangled, mane. Though his coat was glossy from obvious good health, she was instantly aware of the attention it needed. She couldn't wait to give him a thorough grooming, especially removing the knots from his mane and tail. She marveled at their length and thickness. Even his forelock came down black and thick over his eyes, obscuring much of his thin, jagged blaze.

She began to check every inch of him, making sure he was as sound and fit as he appeared. She marveled again that his legs had remained clean and that there were no lasting scars anywhere.

"Oh, Lightning," she murmured. "If you could only talk. How I'd love to know what has happened to you since you were stolen from me. It's only been months but it seems like forever. And here you are and I don't even know how you came to be here. I may never know the whole story." Yet right now none of that mattered to her. She could only think of how wonderful it was that he was back.

Lightning responded to her touch by turning and rubbing his head against her chest. In every way a horse could express his delight at finding her again, he showed her. If a horse could sigh, he would have, but he had to be content with soft whickerings. Long shudders ran through his large body. All throughout his lengthy ordeal he had never lost the instinct to return to his beloved mistress. The drive within him that had always drawn him east, had eventually reunited him with the one person he loved. The pressing need had been fulfilled. He was home.

A sudden flash in the sky, followed by a louder clap of thunder interrupted their reunion. Ann became belatedly aware of the oncoming storm. She jolted herself back to their immediate plight. They must start for home, even though she knew they'd never make it on foot before the storm broke. But as she took a step forward her ankle nearly buckled beneath her, making her wince with pain.

"Darn," she told her horse, "I'll never get back with this stupid foot. Now what?"

The thought came to her as Lightning pressed against her, lowering his head to nuzzle her. "Hey, I know. I can ride you," she said. Why not? He'd been broke to ride before he left, even though she'd not done so. Obviously from the stories connecting his whereabouts, others had, at least one girl. A stab of jealousy ran through her. She should have been the first. He was *her* horse.

"Okay, Lightning, why should I walk when I've got you?" But how to get up was a problem. He was so tall now. And her ankle forbid her trying to vault on. She looked around for a rock on which to climb. Taking a hunk of his thick mane she used his strength to hobble over to one and stand on it. Now Lightning's back was within reach. Quickly she scrambled on board. The ankle would not hinder her now.

Lightning stood quietly, as she had trained him to do, awaiting her signal. She was surprised. After all this time he had not forgotten his manners! Oh, but, it felt good to finally sit on his back. She reveled at the feeling of power beneath her as she nudged him forward.

"Okay, fella. Let's see what you can do." He broke into a light, springy walk, the kind that covered ground quickly.

Not quick enough. Another clap of thunder threatened them. Ann let Lightning break into a canter as they wound down the path to the base of Flat Top. She delighted in the sheer strength and raw potential beneath her. As they came off the hill and onto level ground, Ann felt the first drop of rain. There was no holding back now, she thought. Besides she *had* to know what he could do. And she trusted Lightning. Perhaps he'd been wild for a time, but already she sensed the renewal of the bond they had shared. He would never deliberately place her in danger. Of that she was certain.

"Go for it, Lightning!" she cried into his mane, bending down low and wrapping her legs tightly around his barrel. "Take us home!" A thrill ran down her spine as he burst forward, all restraint broken as he increased his speed, his unerring sense of direction taking them home. Ann let out a whoop of pure joy. Certainly this horse was like no other. Even his own sire, Si'ad, could not run like him. She was sure of it. She was on the ride of her life.

With blinding speed, the stallion ate up the distance between Flat Top and home. He was running free and unrestrained, running because he loved to run. Ann had never known anything like it. She clung to him like a burr, almost obscured in his mane. This was the most breathtaking experience of her life.

Soon they were approaching the gate leading to the lane behind the house. Ann continued to let Lightning have his head for she wanted to see just what he would do. He slowed somewhat but only to judge his pace as he maintained a ground-eating gallop straight for the gate. She prepared herself for the jump to come but he flew over it so effortlessly she felt as if they were flying.

"Oh, Lightning, you are the greatest horse ever," she cried out, happily. "Is there anything you can't do?" The stallion-colt came down the lane at a fast gallop, bursting into the courtyard, as the first drops of serious rain caught up with them. He slid to a half-rearing halt before a surprised group of people, all standing around an unfamiliar horse van. There in their midst stood a very familiar grey horse, his halter held by a strange blond-haired boy.

Lightning saw the horse first and immediately identifying him as another stallion, pawed the ground, screaming a challenge, just as Ann became aware of the other horse's presence. The grey stallion responded to the potential threat by whirling toward him and issuing a challenge of his own. The boy holding his halter struggled to keep him back. Ann, fighting to gain control of her horse, without benefit of bridle, could not help but recognize the other stallion.

"That's Si'ad!" she shouted above the din. "Where did he come from?"

Suddenly everyone was shouting at once. "Ann, what happened to you?" her father called out, turning toward her. "And who is this you're riding?"

"Why Lightning, of course!" she shouted back, circling the restless horse to keep him from getting near Si'ad. "Don't you recognize him?"

"But where? How?" Jock asked in amazement, before Scotty cut him off.

"Let's talk later!" he yelled above a clap of thunder. "Get these two studs into the barn before we have a fight on our hands. Besides, I'm getting wet here. In case you folks haven't realized, we're in the midst of a thunderstorm."

At his words they all galvanized into action. Jock assisted the stranger who, with the van driver, managed to get Si'ad into the barn and into one of the empty stalls at the far end. Meanwhile, Ann continued to sit astride Lightning while Scotty went to get a lead rope to use, but as soon as he drew near, the stallion balked and sidled away from him, his eyes rolling in fear. Nor could Michael get any closer. It was plain he had not recognized either of them.

"He doesn't remember you yet, I think," Ann said. "I'll get down and lead him." But as she leaped off she landed on her sore ankle, which nearly buckled under her as she winced in pain.

"What happened? How did you hurt your ankle?" her father wanted to know, coming to her side. Lightning immediately laid his ears back and shifted away from them. In spite of the pain, Ann moved with him, taking the lead rope from Scotty and sliding it around Lightning's neck. Immediately the stallion calmed under her hands.

"Fell off Ginger," she explained shortly. "Oh, my gosh! Ginger! I forgot all about her. Is she all right?"

"Don't worry. She's fine. She was standing at the back gate when we got home from the Derby, saddle and bridle still on her. We figured something had happened to you and were just going to head out to look for you when this van pulled into the driveway."

"That's a relief," Ann said. "Angry as I was with her, I surely didn't want her hurt."

"Hurry," Scotty reminded them. "We're getting wetter by the minute."

"Sure thing," she answered, taking up the lead rope, looped around his neck and using the giant stallion for support, limped into the barn where she put him into a stall on the opposite side from Si'ad. He followed her like a friendly puppy.

Jock, observing the scene as he returned from Si'ad's stall, remarked, "How did you do that?"

"Do what? Oh, he remembers me. He's still my Lightning after all. He never forgot his first mother." She rubbed his neck and he responded by pushing against her.

"I can see that," Scotty watched over the stall door. "Now tell us what happened to you and how did you find Lightning?"

193

"First, let me look at that ankle," Jessica admonished, pushing her way into the stall with Ann. Oddly enough Lightning showed no discomfort at her presence.

"Oh, I'll be fine, Mom. It hurts but I can stand on it." Her mother insisted on looking at it anyway. While she did, Ann explained briefly how she was reunited with Lightning. When she had finished her father spoke up.

"Ann, taking the new mare out on your own with none of us here was not very smart," he admonished. "But I don't have to tell you that, do I?" She looked a bit sheepish, knowing well what might have happened. "Still, at least you're okay, though you'll have your ankle to remind you of your folly for a few days."

"Sure would love to know how Lightning came to be on Flat Top," Scotty commented, changing the subject now that Ann's ankle seemed to be just a sprain. "Wonder if we'll ever piece together what really happened to him?" he mused. "Bet if he could talk, he'd have some story to tell."

"The main thing is that he's back," Michael said. "And looking better than ever. Wherever he's been, it's agreed with him. He's developed into one fine stallion." They all were leaning over the stall now, admiring him.

"And look how he's grown," Jock whistled, appreciatively. "He's quite a beauty. Who would've thought Ann's little orphan would turn out so fine," he added for her benefit, ducking her punch.

Scotty smiled at both of them. Things were back to normal. "Well, since everything seems to be all right with this guy, let's check on Si'ad before we retire to the kitchen to hear Ted's story."

"Ted?" Ann asked, confused.

"Why the young man who brought Si'ad back to us. At least we can find out what happened to him."

"Of course, I'm sorry," she said acknowledging the blond-haired boy for the first time. "I'm so wrapped up in getting Lightning back, I nearly forgot." Giving her horse one last pat, she moved out of the stall and hobbled the short distance to where Si'ad had been stabled, observing him briefly before slipping into the stall and going to him. "We thought you were lost in the fire..." she murmured, stroking him. The stallion turned his grey head away from the hay he was munching, and acknowledged her with a soft nuzzle.

"See," she called out, excitedly, "he remembers me, too. Don't you, Si'ad, huh, boy? Oh, it's so good having both of them back." She continued to stroke the stallion's neck. Her reunion with him was interrupted when the boy, Ted, entered the stall. Immediately, Si'ad left her to go nuzzle the stranger instead. He smiled, glancing over at her. Did she imagine a slight touch of resentment on his part, perhaps jealousy? In any event, it was obvious, at least to her, that these two had developed a strong bond, much as the one she shared with Lightning. Suddenly she was able to forgive him his need for possessiveness.

Watching them, she noticed Ted for the first time. He was of slender build, not much taller than her, but wiry and muscular as from an active physical life, though a bit too skinny for his size. He had an unruly shock of straw-colored hair that seemed to fall everywhere and was much in need of trimming, or at the very least, combing. But it was his eyes she really noticed. They were a deep sea blue, honest and open as though she could see right into his soul and know what he was thinking. Ann recognized immediately his bond with horses and felt a kindred spirit with him. Still there was something else, she sensed, a fear she couldn't place. Something was troubling him intensely, though he was trying hard to hide it. As he looked lovingly at the stallion, she caught a glimpse and thought she knew what it was.

Her thoughts were interrupted when Michael spoke, "Come on, everyone. These horses appear fine to me. Let's all go in the house for a cup of coffee and let Ted tell his story." He included the van driver, who up to this point had been simply a curious witness.

As they gathered around the large, old oak table, after removing wet outerwear, Jessica quickly prepared coffee and rummaged up a cake to go with it. When everyone was settled, Ted began his tale.

CHAPTER SEVENTEEN

Ted's Story

Better bring Si'ad in tonight," Bart, the head stud manager, requested one night in late winter. "He's got a mare to breed first thing in the morning. Give him the end stall. It's vacant and I think it's all prepared."

"Sure thing," Ted went to get the grey. As he led him to the main barn, he told him, "I know you'd prefer to be outside but we need you up here. You've got a lady love visiting tomorrow and you wouldn't want to look untidy for her now, would you?" The stallion just nickered and pushed against him in happy contentment. Ted left him deep in new clean bedding, munching on his hay.

Ted went to bed that night thinking about how perfect his life was. He had a job he loved as a stud groom at an Arabian farm, a place to stay, and best of all, the most wonderful horse in the world in his care. He awoke to a nightmare.

He was jolted awake by the screams of horses and cries of "Fire!" Hastily pulling on his clothes, he ran for the door of the trailer. The groom who shared it with him was already through, the door banging in his wake.

Si'ad was Ted's immediate concern as he ran toward the main barn, already alive with flames shooting out from the roof. Horrified, Ted bolted for the end of the building where he had put Si'ad only hours before. Smoke billowed from the doorway as he ran blindly into the blazing inferno. He was almost run over by a groom leading a terror-stricken horse, his head wrapped in rags to keep him from panicking and bolting back into the blaze.

Taking extra precautions, Ted shoved his hands out in front of him, feeling for the wall to his right. "Ouch!" he smacked his knuckles on the side bar used to hold blankets. Groping, he found the lead rope laying over it and pulled it to him.

"Si'ad!" he called out. An answering high-pitched whinny told him the horse was somewhere near. He found the stall door and flung it open, but it was empty. He had gone too far! As swiftly as possible he struggled back to the left, so blinded by smoke he could barely see, and opened the next stall. Already his lungs were screaming in protest, but this stall was occupied. A grey form appeared thrusting against him. It was Si'ad!

"Quick, boy! You've got to follow me." He hastily clipped the lead rope to his halter and tugged the stallion forward. But as he entered the hallway, Si'ad panicked and tried to return to his stall. He nearly got away from Ted, but the boy hung on desperately. Frantically he fumbled about trying to find a rag, blanket, anything to cover his eyes. There was nothing. As a last resort, Ted tugged his shirt off and wrapped it across the stallion's face, hiding his eyes. Si'ad quieted sufficiently to allow himself to be led down the aisle and out to safety. When they were at last clear of the burning barn, Ted stopped only long enough to cough the smoke out of his lungs before dragging the reluctant stallion farther away.

Only when he was a distance from the building, now totally engulfed in flames, did he feel safe. As he stood, holding tightly to the stallion's halter, he heard a shout. "Quick, the annex! It's going next! We've got to get those horses out, too!"

Ted realized he was right. The two long sheds extending from the main barn were in danger of burning next and there were horses in each one of those stalls, as well. He must help!

But what to do with Si'ad? He looked about but everything was in chaos. There was no one to ask. Then he got an idea.

197

Si'ad would be safe in one of the back pastures, at least for now. Hurriedly, he ran down the path between the various paddocks, Si'ad trotting beside him. He did not stop until he came to the very last one, farthest from the fire. He should be fine here, he thought, opening the gate and turning him loose. With a quick pat on the neck, he told him, "You'll be safe here. I'll be back soon as I can." Shutting the gate securely, he double-checked it before running back to the burning barn.

In the next few hours, Ted lost track of how many trips he made back and forth, pulling horses to freedom. It was just about dawn before the danger was over and the fire was finally under control. When at last they stopped to survey the damage, the scene before them was awesome. Most of the main barn, which had also housed the office, Bart's apartment, and feed and tack rooms, in addition to two rows of stalls and the indoor arena, lay in ruins. Nothing remained intact. On the other hand, the two shed rows coming from each side of the big barn, were basically saved, thanks to the quick thinking firemen who kept the roofs doused with water. The horses that'd been stabled there, along with the horses they'd saved from the main barn, were everywhere.

In the previous night's panic, every conceivable place to stick a horse temporarily had been used. All the paddocks now housed horses, still milling about in confused disarray. They had doubled up wherever they could, but with stallions and mares alike, that had not always been possible. A couple had been shoved in horse trailers when they stood, devouring the hay left from the last trip. One was found in the manager's fenced back yard, contentedly eating the grass growing between his wife's flowerbeds. Others were tied to nearby fences where volunteers were keeping their eyes on them.

The parking area in front of the main barn was literally littered with whatever could be dragged or thrown from the burning building. Books, office records, a file drawer, a sulky cart, various pieces of tack, a couple of blankets, buckets, a lunge line, all of these lay strewn across the parking lot. Someone had tried to knock down hay bales, probably to keep the fire from spreading, and they, too, lay scattered amidst the melee. It was a huge mess.

Still, as soon as the threat of fire was over, everyone congratulated themselves on what they did save. It could have been a far greater disaster than it was, but for the quick thinking of all involved. Without stopping to rest, they began to take into account what must be done immediately. As the sun climbed higher in the sky, the members of Desert Sun Ranch began to put their lives back together.

First the needs of the horses must be met. While they were accessing the monumental problem of what to do with the large number of horses left homeless by the fire, as well as identifying which ones were missing and presumed perished, Ted excused himself to go check on Si'ad.

The empty pasture startled him. Knowing he had put the stallion in this particular paddock, he, nevertheless, checked all the others just to make sure he hadn't made a mistake in the furor of the moment. But there was no sign of the grey stallion. Si'ad was not among the other horses. Confused, he went back to the original field and checked the gate, which was as secure as he had left it. Where was Si'ad?

When he returned to report the stallion's disappearance to the manager, Jim, one of the grooms overheard their conversation.

"I saw a grey horse running loose," the groom told them. "Could have been your stallion. He came out of nowhere. Ran right back into the barn, he did. We tried to chase him back, but he got past us."

"You sure it was him?" Ted questioned, alarmed.

"Can't be sure of anything in that chaos last night. But it sure looked like him. Big and grey, definitely a stud."

"But we got lots of horses around here that match that description," Ted went on. "Grey's a pretty common color for an Arab." He was almost hysterical at the thought. He didn't risk his life to save Si'ad only to have him run back into the fire.

"Well, I couldn't be a hundred per cent sure," the groom hedged. "Just thought it looked like him, that's all."

"You sure he ran back into the barn? After all, there was so much smoke, you could have thought you saw him run that way."

"Looked like he did. I had my hands full at the time, trying to bring out one of the youngsters. I did the best I could but … he got by me." The groom broke down then. "Ah, look, kid, I'm sorry. I tried to save him, too. It was awful... Those poor horses! I—we tried to save all of them. But it happened so fast, then ..." He stopped, tears running down his face, as he relived the horror of the previous night. He knew he'd hear the screams of the doomed horses in his nightmares for a long time to come.

Ted could not blame him. As upset as he, he went and put his arm around the man's shoulders. "I'm not blaming you. I know you did what you could. We all did. I, too, wish we could have saved them all," he reflected. "But, well, I did save Si'ad once. I just don't understand what could have happened to him. Maybe he jumped the fence, but then where is he now?"

"If he got loose," Jim speculated, picking his words carefully, "it's very possible he could have run back into the barn. Horses do that for some reason, thinking they're safe. That's why they need to be blindfolded."

"Well, I'm going to find out for sure," Ted said decisively. I'll go back to the field and comb every inch of it till I see if I can find out what happened."

Ted did that. Carefully he searched for some sign that Si'ad had escaped over or through the fence. There was no break in the wire. That meant only one thing. Si'ad had to have jumped the fence. About to give up and assume he'd jumped, he finally stumbled on something. Along the back, facing the desert, he found a sandy patch that had been scuffed up a bit, like a horse had done some pacing back and forth. He bent over looking for hoof marks, noting that this part of the fence was slightly lower. Then he saw two deeper impressions as if he had dug in, though sand had drifted in and he wasn't quite sure.

But on the other side it was easy to see where a horse had landed. The dirt left two deep impressions. This was how Si'ad had gotten out. He jumped!

Triumphant, Ted started to follow the hoof prints. They appeared to go up, away from the ranch and out toward the mountains. Maybe he hadn't gone back to the burning building after all. Perhaps the horse they saw was another one. Encouraged, Ted headed back to tell the others what he'd found.

But the manager was not convinced. "You can prove he got out of the field all right, but I'm not at all sure he didn't double back here."

"I know he didn't. The tracks lead away from the ranch. He's always been half wild. Bet he's out there now, wandering about, just waiting for us to find him. Let me go after him. I'll get him back."

"If he's out there he'll either come back on his own or show up at someone else's ranch. Half wild or not, he's domesticated enough now to seek out other horses. I doubt he'll go far."

"At least let me look for him."

"Sorry, Ted. I need you here for now. There's too much work to do."

Chafing to ride out and look for him, Ted reluctantly saw the wisdom in staying where he was so badly needed. All the horse owners in the valley were notified in case Si'ad should show up. Ted held to the hope that he'd be spotted, but by the end of the day, there had been no report of any loose horse fitting Si'ad's description.

All the rest of the horses had been accounted for, one way or another. It took a couple more days before they knew for sure, but the end count was that they had lost only eight horses, including Si'ad, who was still missing. Though any loss was awful enough, when they thought how much worse it could have been, they realized they were unbelievably lucky. The cause was finally attributed to a loose wire shorting out, causing a spark, which smoldered for some time before bursting into flames. By then it had traveled far from its source, through much of the ceiling area, and the barn went up quickly. By all reports they were fortunate to save what they did.

When after several days, the whereabouts of Si'ad continued to be a mystery, it was presumed that he must have run back into the burning barn and his remains were too charred to positively identify him. This was the story told his owners back in Kentucky, and everyone more or less believed it to be true. All, that is, except Ted.

Then five days after the fire, Ted's theory was somewhat vindicated, from a rather unlikely source. The night of the fire the young daughter of the ranch owner had seen what she thought was a horse, running loose, heading away from the ranch and toward the Superstition Mountains. Thinking her elders would only laugh at her, she told no one about this incident until she heard of Ted's theory. Even so, it took her, a child of seven, at least one more day before she told anyone what she'd seen. That person was Ted and he immediately believed her. He was convinced the 'ghost horse' was Si'ad.

"Let me at least look for him," he begged her father, Mr. Haines. "We've got to know for sure and you can spare me for a couple weeks, whatever it takes. If it's him, I'll find him and bring him back."

"How can you be so sure? Those mountains are easy to get lost in, even for those who know the Superstitions. A horse could hide up there indefinitely and never be found."

"If he's there, he'll come to me. We have a special relationship, after all."

"Yes, I know you do. But I'm not so sure he'll want to be caught, even if you're lucky enough to find him. They can turn wild, you know, especially a stud with his temperament."

"I'll get him back. All I need is one of your mares to use and some supplies. I can do it. You'll see."

At last Mr. Haines agreed to let him go, for if indeed Si'ad was out there loose, they owed it to his owners to try every means to get him back.

The following day, Ted struck out on his borrowed mare, complete with enough supplies to hold him for at least two or three weeks. He carried a hand-made map one of the men familiar with the mountains had made him, and the good wishes of everyone on the ranch. Ted thanked them and turned the sure-footed little trail mare toward the Superstitions, smiling grimly. He would get his horse back.

CHAPTER EIGHTEEN

Si'ad

It took three days of steady riding to get deep into the mountains where he thought the stallion might be. Late on the third afternoon he found a likely spot to stop and prepare camp for the night, trusting the smells of dinner cooking would entice him down if he was in the area. He staked out the mare very carefully as he didn't want to lose her and be adrift in mountains as rough as the Superstitions were known to be.

On the way in he had marked his trail precisely, leaving signs wherever he could so that he'd find his way out. From everything he'd heard, more than one person had gotten lost in these mountains. He didn't want the same fate.

The mare remained calm all that evening so he bedded down, feeling pretty sure that no stallion was within smelling range. If Si'ad were in the area, surely she'd show some sign but he slept through the night without interruption.

The next morning he decided to move. Trying to think like a horse, he rode on, seeking out possible places that might attract a stallion. Later that day he found a canyon area that spilled out into a valley. A rare spring providing water and grass, though not plentiful, was adequate enough to sustain a horse or two for a little while. Once more he made camp.

Again he staked the mare very securely, pulling up a considerable amount of grass and bringing it to her. Only when he had enough to hold her through the night did he feel comfortable in tending to his own needs. He left her only to wash up at the spring and bring back water for cooking. As he prepared his meager fare of beans and bacon, to go with the cold biscuits he'd brought, he hoped the delicious smell from the bacon would penetrate to wherever Si'ad was hiding. He'd made camp far enough away from the spring that, should the stallion come in for water, he would not be spooked by the boy's presence.

Although Ted had had a fine rapport with Si'ad previously and the stallion had responded to him almost exclusively, he was well aware of the possibility that this semi-wild desert-bred stallion had reverted back to an independent, self-sufficient existence, and that he may need to be tamed all over again. The fact that he had failed to return to any nearby ranch, thereby seeking other equine companionship, led him to believe that it was highly probable that he chose freedom over his previous life.

Ted was prepared for this. When he found Si'ad, he planned to go very slowly, regaining his trust. There was always the chance that Si'ad would remember him, but each day he remained a wild horse the odds grew. He refused to think of what he would do if he did not find him.

Another night passed uneventfully. Ted spent the ensuing day, climbing into the hills surrounding them, searching for another likely valley containing a water source and sufficient grass to sustain life. He found nothing. Deciding to remain where he was at least one more night, he returned to the original spot. Once more he staked the mare out, giving her as much grass as he had located.

"If you don't help me find him tonight," he told her, "I'll have to spend all day tomorrow just getting enough for you to eat." Checking again to make sure she was securely tied, he turned in.

It was well past midnight when he was startled awake by a strange noise. Instantly alert, he sat up, looking first to make sure the mare was still there. She was, standing poised, head up, staring off into the distance. Her ears twitched nervously and she began to pace, stopping frequently to paw the ground. Then she let out a soft whistling sound, throwing her head up again as she tensed and stood still, waiting.

Ted recognized that sound, the call of a mare to her mate. Excitement rose within him. A stallion was near. It *must* be Si'ad.

Quickly he darted to her, catching hold of her halter lest she break free and run to him. Sliding up alongside her shoulder, he tried to remain out of sight so as not to alarm the stallion, not knowing what Si'ad's reaction to him would be.

The mare whinnied again and this time the night air was split by the scream of a stallion, the sound echoing back across the distant mountains. This was what awakened him, he realized as the mare jumped forward. Ted desperately clutched at her halter as he frantically searched the darkness for a glimpse of the stallion. Out of nowhere, the shadowy form appeared. It was Si'ad! He was sure of it.

Si'ad was alive! Seeing him in the flesh made Ted realize that up to now, he'd always harbored a small particle of doubt in the back of his mind that maybe he was chasing a dream, that perhaps he had been consumed in the fire after all, as others suggested. But no, he was right to follow his instincts. They had led him to his beloved stallion nonetheless.

The stallion shook his head, sending his heavy mane cascading out behind him as he half-reared and struck out with his forelegs. Small rocks were set tumbling down the hill below him. Again the stallion screamed and the mare answered. Ted had all he could do to hang on to her as she fought to free herself of his grasp so that she might run to him.

Just when he thought he could hold on no longer, it was over. Just as suddenly as Si'ad appeared, he was gone, leaving only the echo of retreating hoof beats ringing against barren rock. Disappointed, Ted stared after him, unwilling to believe that he was gone. Gradually the mare quieted down, as Ted continued to hold, willing Si'ad to return. He remained vigilant the rest of the night, watching, but there was no sign of the stallion again.

By dawn he had formulated a plan. Relieved that he had found Si'ad's whereabouts, he felt sure that Si'ad would return to this spot, lured by the scent of the mare and access to water. He would be ready for him, for he knew now he would not leave these mountains without the stallion in tow.

He set out early with the mare to gather as much grass as she could carry. He wanted to have enough to feed both her and to entice Si'ad into their camp. There was still a bit of sweet feed left with which he planned to train the stallion once he was caught.

On the way back to their camp, he found a likely looking tree, which he stripped and sunk into the ground near the water hole. It would be used as a snubbing post. If he was fortunate enough to get a rope around the stallion, he might need its added security to hold him should he choose to fight.

With the mare once again securely tied, contentedly eating the grass he had collected, he made a hasty meal and lay down to sleep through the afternoon heat. He doubted very much that Si'ad would show up before night fall and he wanted to be awake this time when he came.

He almost wasn't. The events of the past few days had left him more exhausted than he realized and as night fell, he slept on, unaware of the descending dark. Once again it was well past midnight when he was awakened by the soft whinny of the mare near him. Having finished all the grass provided her, she had first been content to dose, but as evening wore on, she became restless. The distant scent and sound, heard only to her ears, of the approaching stallion, alerted her. Again she whinnied. This time Ted came fully awake. Softly he moved to her side, checking to make sure she could not free herself. Then he settled down silently beside her. Si'ad was out there. Soon, very soon, he would be within sight.

After what seemed like eternity, he heard the muffled click of hooves scraping on rock. The stallion was coming along the valley floor. Encouraged, Ted reached for the rope he had placed near the mare, drawing it to him. While he had very little experience in actually lassoing anything, by keeping the mare between him and Si'ad, he hoped he could get near enough to make a pass over the horse's neck and thus catch him.

The mare snorted again, encouraging the stallion to come to her. Ted hid in her shadow, one hand on her neck, the other clutching tightly to the rope, his palms sweaty with tension. He was afraid the slightest movement on his part would startle the stallion back to the hills. He was under no illusion that Si'ad would recognize him on sight, even if he called to him. More likely the experience of the fire that had driven him up here, had caused him to revert back to his roots, living wild and free in the desert. Once caught he could be taught to relate once more to the boy who had cared for him so lovingly. But first he must catch him.

In the distance a shadow moved. Ted held his breath as the shadow took on the shape of a horse. Si'ad was close, so close the rope burned in his hand as he willed himself to be still, waiting. For what seemed like forever the stallion stood still as a statue, his attention focused on the mare. Then ever so cautiously he stretched his neck out toward her, taking one step, then another. He was now close enough for Ted to see his nostrils flare casting out thin breath on the night air. Another step and he was able to reach out and nuzzle the mare's neck. She swiveled her head toward him, smelling stallion and responding.

Ted was barely breathing now as his mind worked furiously, willing Si'ad to come within reach. Just a little more, he thought, and he'd attempt his toss. He knew he'd only get one chance. He had to make it count.

But fate stepped in. The mare swerved away from him as she tried to flirt with the stallion, exposing him face to face with Si'ad. The stallion's head jerked up as he saw the boy, catching his scent at the same time. He whirled but not fast enough. Ted reacted instinctively, throwing the rope point blank at his head, watching it settle squarely over his shoulders as the stallion jerked backward.

He did not have any time for triumph as the stallion's response put him in immediate danger of being dragged. Acting with a lightning speed that even he did not know he possessed, he darted to the snubbing post nearby and wrapped the rope

around it. Again he raced around the pole, as Si'ad flew frantically backwards, trying to escape, but brought up short by the
rope. Instead, he jumped forward, striking out at the pole, which
he considered his enemy. Ted barely missed his hooves as he
scrambled out of his way.

The fight was short but fierce before the stallion gave up,
standing with his head down, sweat poring from his body.
At first elated that he had at last caught him, Ted's reaction
immediately turned to chagrin as he observed the now conquered stallion.

"Oh, Si'ad, what have I done?" he cried out in anguish. "I'm
so sorry. I didn't mean to hurt you. It was the only way. I had to
get you back. Please forgive me. I promise I'll never be anything
but kind to you again." He longed to go the grey, check him over
to make sure he had not hurt himself, stroke him as he had once
done so often, but he knew Si'ad was not yet ready to accept
him. Instead he went to the mare and took her a safe distance
away before retying her. Then he sat down to await daylight,
giving Si'ad time to relax and submit to his recapture before he
approached him.

Only then did what he had just accomplished sink in. He
had Si'ad back! Two immediate feelings overwhelmed him.
Immensely relieved at having achieved his goal, he could not
help but be struck by the awesome power and beauty of the
stallion that really belonged to this wild setting. As he sat and
watched the grey reluctantly submitting to the feel of the rope
again, he wished somehow it could be different. All too soon
he would break camp, saddle the mare and lead this wonderful
stallion out of the hills and back to the ranch. There he would
return to the domestic life he'd led before the fire. So final. Not
the way he'd pictured it so often in his mind.

Unexpectedly an idea popped into his head as he sat there
waiting out the night. Why did he really have to return tomorrow? The folks at the ranch didn't expect him for at least another
week. They all figured it might take that long just to locate the
stallion, if he had indeed run off. Why couldn't he stay here just

a little longer, let Si'ad get to know him again? It would take time, but he had plenty of that.

He must have dozed off, because suddenly he awoke with a start. It was daylight. Glancing frantically around, he was relieved to see both the mare and Si'ad standing where he'd left them.

He jumped up and went to gather some grass from his fast dwindling pile. After giving some to the mare, he approached the stallion cautiously. "Hey there, fella," he crooned. "Remember me? I took care of you these last few months. I'm your friend, Si'ad." He went on chattering about anything or nothing, just letting the sound of his voice wash over the horse, as he had done back on the ranch. The stallion turned his head in his direction, pricking his ears, listening. Ted came closer, offering the grass.

"Hungry, boy? Yes, you must be. You haven't eaten most of the night. How about some of this?" He held the grass out to the stallion that sniffed it suspiciously. Slowly he reached and took a mouthful, munching it greedily as he realized what Ted was offering. The boy moved closer before allowing him the next bite. Soon, the horse was eating contentedly as Ted began to stroke his long neck, talking in the same tone of voice all the while. Si'ad showed no aversion to being touched but whether he recognized his old friend yet, the boy was not sure.

What he was sure about was the plan he had gone over in his mind. Sitting there observing him through the long night, he understood now that he had his beloved stallion back, he could not just ride out of here and return him as if he were merely another horse. This may very well be his one and only chance to ride Si'ad, to know what it felt like to sit on his back and feel the wind in his face. He did not even know if the horse was broke to ride. Many stallions weren't. But ride him, he must. Then once he had experienced the feeling, then he'd be ready to return him. Or so he thought . . .

Si'ad had finished his grass but he continued to stand as Ted scratched him all over, finding the tender spots that had always calmed the stallion in the past. As he relaxed under the boy's hand, Ted became more confident of his strategy. Much as he wanted to begin immediately, he held himself in check, aware of the need to move slowly. Eager as he was, it was wiser to give the stallion time, time to settle back to the subservient life of a domesticated horse. Besides he was out of grass again and must go in search of it before beginning Si'ad's training.

Leaving the rest of what he'd picked the previous day, he set out on his quest. He'd have liked to take the mare with him, but fearing Si'ad would grow restless, he left her behind. He could not bear to think of recapturing the stallion again.

He was later than he'd planned when he started back. It had taken considerably more time than he thought to gain enough to feed two horses. The sun was beginning its descent as he crested the last hill. A sudden thought struck him. Supposing the horses had somehow gotten loose and were not there. Visions of Si'ad breaking free and taking the mare with him went through his mind, lending speed to his legs as he fairly flew down the last slope.

At first he didn't see them, but suddenly they came into view. Immense relief flooded over him. He did not want to think of what he would do if they were gone.

Si'ad raised his head sharply at the sight of the boy running toward him, poised for flight. Ted realized just in time his mistake and slowed, calling out the stallion. "Si'ad! It's me! It's only me."

The mare nickered in response. Si'ad flared his nostrils, turning in Ted's direction as he listened to the familiar voice. Ted put down his bundle and went to the grey, offering him some grain that was in his pocket. Accepting the treat, the stallion sniffed him all over, inhaling his scent.

"Remembering, huh, boy?" Pleased, Ted continued, "Yes, you do know me. I'm the one who took care of you." His voice droned on, softly, using the same soothing tone he'd used in the past. This time the stallion responded further, pushing against the boy whenever he stopped scratching.

Thrilled by Si'ad's reaction, Ted now knew he was ready for his lessons. Whether he'd been ridden before or not, the boy intended to find out. He had no doubt that the horse would be wonderful to ride. This horse was too special to be otherwise. And before he left these mountains he would experience the thrill of riding Si'ad at least once.

His lessons began that afternoon. By the following day, Ted knew he had been trained to ride. He'd accepted his tack with very little fuss, only side-stepping in confusion when he felt the unfamiliar weight of the heavier stock saddle. But even that he got used to in a short time, for Ted was exceptionally patient and moved slowly through every step.

At one point he stopped his work with Si'ad to go after more grass, but this time he took the stallion with him. Remembering the fear he'd felt upon returning the day before, thinking that perhaps the stallion had gotten loose, he didn't want him out of his sight. Besides Si'ad could carry more grass than he could.

It was easier with Si'ad along. The stallion sensed the places where sparse patches of grass would be found in these desert mountains. Ted learned to trust his judgment and follow the stallion's lead. Because Si'ad was with him, he did not mind the time he spent searching for food. The bond between boy and horse was being renewed.

It was already late when they returned to their camp. The mare whinnied eagerly, anxious for something to eat. Ted took care of both horses, then himself, before bedding down. As he lay there, he thought about tomorrow. Si'ad was showing signs of his old trust having been restored. It was time to ride him. The anticipation excited him, making it hard to fall asleep. Over and over in his mind he visualized what it would be like. When he finally drifted off, he dreamed of flying over the desert on a magnificent grey stallion with wings for feet.

The next morning Si'ad stood before him, tacked up, awaiting his rider. Ted let out a deep sigh of pent up breath. Eager as he was, he willed himself to remain calm, waiting for his pulse to stop racing. It would not do to upset Si'ad unduly. He must relax and ease into the saddle as though it were completely natural. Chances were, he'd walk off just as mannerly as he suspected the stallion had been trained to do, since it was clear

he'd been trained to a saddle and bridle. So what was holding him back?

But suppose he launched into a bucking frenzy, throwing Ted, and running off into the hills again? That fear crossed his mind more than once. The boy gritted his teeth with determination. He could not afford to be thrown and risk losing Si'ad again. If he couldn't capture him the second time, he would have to return without him. How could he explain that?

There was another option. He could forget the whole idea of riding the horse and return to the ranch now, leading the stallion he had volunteered to find. There would be no risk to that decision.

But as quickly as he thought it, he dismissed it. He had come too far to turn back now. "This is it," he told the stallion, stroking his neck. "It's come down to just you and me. If you've learned to trust me at all these last few months, do so now. I'm going to ride you and I hope you'll accept me because that's what it's all about, pal. Remember, I'm your friend." With one fluid movement he was in the saddle.

Si'ad's first reaction was flight at the unaccustomed weight on his back. He forgot that this was only Ted on his back, the boy he was beginning to trust all over again. Instead fear took over. He shot forward, reaching full speed in seconds, fleeing down the valley floor, dodging obstacles in his path as he tried to outrun the thing on his back.

Ted could do no more than hang on. It took all his riding skill to maintain his balance as the stallion took a twisted path at breakneck speed. He prayed that he would just stay on, for if he were to fall he knew he'd never get the stallion back in his frightened state. He must ride him to the end. Only when Si'ad grew tired, would he ever begin to respond to him.

In the meantime he was experiencing the ride of a lifetime. Hard and fit, Si'ad did not tire easily. He flew across the desert floor, heading for the slight rise at the end, his nostrils wide and flaring as he drank the wind and ran on. Even as he headed for the hills he showed no signs of slowing.

He must have covered a couple of miles when Ted began to realize two things. One, miraculously he was still on, and two, he was enjoying it. Ted had ridden many Thoroughbreds in his young lifetime. Speed was no stranger to him. But where before they had always been on a flat, manicured track, this galloping over natural rough terrain was quite something else. Desert-bred, Si'ad was in his element here. Sure-footed, he skimmed along the hard-packed sand as though he were flight itself. Ted began to relax and move with his mount, drinking in the sensation of flying. Nothing he had dreamed of had prepared him for this. Si'ad was unbelievable. He was one in a million.

CHAPTER NINETEEN

The Return

The next day Ted moved their camp. But not before he had taken Si'ad on a brief ride. This time there was no repeat of the previous day. Instead Si'ad moved off like a well-trained saddle horse, performing each gait as Ted requested. He was actually disappointed until he realized that the power was still there. He had only to ask for it and Si'ad would once again fly across the desert, but with a little more control.

Riding Si'ad, Ted led the mare laden with his supplies such as they were. He left the route up to the stallion, knowing the semi-wild horse would seek out water when he was thirsty. Sure enough, several hours later Si'ad led them to a new spring bubbling up from the ground between a pile of rocks. Ted smiled. He never would have found this one had he not been led to it. There was even more grass growing here in this region. Eagerly he stopped and set up camp. This was a perfect spot to spend the rest of his time in the mountains.

By the time he'd staked out the horses and fixed himself something to eat, night had fallen. Tired from a full day, Ted drifted off to sleep immediately and slept soundly. He was awakened at daybreak by something tickling his face. Startled, he opened his eyes to stare into a big dark muzzle rubbing against him. Si'ad! How had he gotten loose? Swiftly, he jumped up, spooking the horse into darting backwards, but not before Ted managed to grab the dangling lead rope, lest he get away.

Then he laughed. If Si'ad had wanted to escape, he'd have done it by now. Instead, as a sign of his growing dependency on Ted, he had sought him out, waking him in the process.

"What's the matter, fella? Miss me? Wanted to make sure I'm still here? Well, I am. I'm not leaving you, Si'ad, not ever. And that's a promise," he added, knowing in his heart that no matter what, he meant to keep that promise. Hadn't Si'ad just proved his loyalty by staying around, even when he had the choice of running off? What more proof did he need? Throwing his arms around the stallion's neck, he hugged Si'ad, telling him what a good fella he was.

A thought came to him. While he was still out here, he would teach Si'ad to come when he whistled. Then he'd never have to worry about him getting away. In no time the horse learned to recognize Ted's whistle and respond, especially when he was rewarded with some of the remaining grain Ted had kept.

It was a fun game, but two days later Ted found himself glad he'd taught him this trick. He had given up using the saddle, preferring to ride bareback, as it seemed more natural. This one particular ride, they had wandered further from camp that he'd intended and night was upon them before he realized. Suddenly the countryside looked unfamiliar and Ted feared he was lost. Trying not to panic, he gave Si'ad his head. The stallion seemed to know where he was going, but as he started down a slope, he began to slide on loose shale and Ted slid off, landing unceremoniously on the ground. By the time Si'ad was able to stop, he was a distance away.

Fortunately unhurt, Ted rose to his feet, whistling for the stallion. Si'ad, true to his training, trotted back to his rider. Ted was never so relieved in his life, as he leaped back on the stallion, praising him profusely. They preceded back to camp without incident.

The time with the stallion sped by all too fast for Ted. Each day they explored their surroundings. One day they located some caves, finding some interesting carvings on the walls. Another day they came upon the remains of an old campfire, the only sign that other humans had traveled this land. They were so alone that he'd begun to think of it as their own private world.

At least until the food ran out. When there was barely enough left for one more day, he knew it was time to leave his fantasy behind and return to civilization. Reluctantly he packed the little bit left and saddled the mare. Then vaulting up on Si'ad bareback, he gathered her reins, silently saying good-bye to the place that had given him such joy. Without a backward glance, he nudged Si'ad forward in the direction leading out of the mountains.

Two days later, Ted crossed a ridge to find the Valley of the Sun laid out before him. Even so, he had a distance to go and by now he was completely out of food. The horses were more fortunate since they could forage along the way. Ted became so hungry he tried to eat along with them, but the tough desert grass was far from palatable to his digestive system. The best he could do was to suck on pieces of the inner part of the cactus plant that grew all over. The juice he derived from this method was far from tasty but it kept his mind off his growling stomach.

It was with great relief then that he spotted some buildings in the distance, though it took him a couple of more hours to reach the outskirts of what appeared to be a ranch. Finally he could make out several barns and a small house. Following the outlying fence he came across a dirt path, which led him to the nearest barn.

Suddenly a dog came out of the barn, barking furiously. He had a shaggy, merled coat and semi-erect ears. His tail was either bobbed or he'd been born without one. Ted recognized it as one of the Australian shepherds that were so popular among the local ranchers. His own ranch had a couple of them as well.

Not wanting to fret the dog unduly, Ted halted Si'ad and waited. Soon a man appeared in the doorway, yelling at the dog in a foreign tongue Ted assumed was Spanish. The dog stopped barking and slunk away. Upon seeing the rider, he turned to him. "Yes? What you want?" he spoke in broken English to the boy.

Ted started to speak but was overcome by speechlessness. This was the first human he'd seen in nearly three weeks. Suddenly he was overwhelmed by the magnitude of what he was about to say. Where to start? Then the words seemed to tumble from his mouth.

"I—do you have a phone? I have to call—I—We've just come from up there ..." he pointed back toward the Superstitions. "For nearly three weeks and—I've got to call the ranch -" Just as suddenly he ran out of steam. "And do you have any food? I'm really hungry," he finished lamely.

Regrettably, the man understood very little English, but perhaps at the speed with which Ted had spoken it was just as well, since he no doubt confused the man enough as it was. In any event he did catch the urgency with which the boy on the magnificent horse spoke and one word sunk home.

"Ah, food, yes. You wish food." He rubbed his stomach to accentuate his words, nodding in understanding.

Ted continued to point toward the mountains. "Three weeks," he said, holding up three fingers. "Camp. Hungry." Again he pointed to his stomach.

This time the Mexican nodded and exclaimed, "Tortillas. You like? Come."

At that point Ted would have eaten anything short of horse meat. He did not hesitate. Jumping off Si'ad and leading the two horses, he followed the man down the dirt road toward a house not far away. It was hardly more than a shack, but if there was food there, he would be most grateful.

As they approached, a Mexican woman came out, exclaiming in Spanish. Her husband answered her, pointing to Ted and nodding back toward the mountains. Her eyes widened, "Si, si," was all she said as she signaled him to come in.

Ted stopped, pointing to his horses. Quickly the man showed him a corral nearby he could use. He hastened to open the gate and usher him in. Ted removed the mare's saddle and turned them both loose while the helpful stranger tossed down some hay for them. Only then did Ted, after an affectionate pat to each horse, turn to the house and his own creature comforts.

Ted downed one tortilla after another. Nothing had ever tasted so good. Or perhaps he'd never been this hungry before. In any event the wife stood by grinning happily as she put another one on his plate each time he finished the last until he felt he was going to burst. Finally, laughing, he signaled enough. She replied rapidly in Spanish and though he couldn't understand the words, the intention was clear. She was obviously pleased he liked her cooking.

Ted glanced around for a phone but there was none. Again through words and gestures he tried to make his request known. Finally the man nodded. "Tel—a—phon—y? Ah, no." He shook his head sadly. Then he brightened. "Ah, yes, big house. Boss, he have tela -" he gave up trying to say the word and used a gesture instead. "Si, come, come! We go—tell Boss. He know." Ted was whisked away out the door as he was still trying to thank the wife for her generosity.

The man led him to an old relic of a truck that Ted very much doubted would even start, much less run. Reluctantly, he held back. The man misunderstood his concern. "Horses fine," he said emphatically. "Have water—hay—be fine. We go." He hopped into the truck, leaving Ted no choice but to follow. Amazingly the ancient vehicle not only started but ran, though by the sound of it he doubted it would for much longer. He need not have worried. The main house was only just around the next hill. As they coughed and sputtered their way into the yard, a man appeared on the porch. As he saw one of his employees drive up, a smile crossed his face as the old truck rolled to what sounded like a very painful stop.

"Yes, Miguel?" he asked, stepping off the porch. Miguel, he knew, to be a hard worker, if he were somewhat lacking in mechanical skills. Then he saw his passenger. Ted climbed out gingerly, appearing to be slightly shaken by the adventure he had just survived.

Miguel started to explain, but Ted stepped in, first thanking the Mexican for his help. "May I use your phone?" he asked.

" I need to call my employer right away and tell him I found the stallion." When the man looked confused, he hastened to explain, "I'm sorry. My name's Ted Winters. I work for Desert Sun. I've just spent three weeks tracking down our lost stallion. Up there." He pointed back toward the Superstitions.

"Wait a minute. You're not talking about the big fire over by Cave Creek Road that occurred about a month ago?"

Ted nodded. "That's the one. One of our stallions got loose. I went to bring him back." Briefly he related what happened. The ranch boss was quite impressed.

"Come on in. Phone's in my office. We ranchers all heard about that stud getting loose. Been quite the talk around here, that fire. Can't believe you were lucky enough to get him back. He okay?" When Ted nodded, he continued, "Hard to believe a domestic horse could survive. Rough country up there. But then I don't need to tell you. Quite a feat yourself. People have been known to get lost up there more than once." He shook his head.

Ted did not try to explain that Si'ad was no ordinary horse. He started to follow the man into the house when there was a big commotion in the yard. He turned to see a big grey horse burst around the corner, skidding to a stop when he saw Ted, then thrusting his nuzzle into the boy's chest. How he'd gotten out, Ted could only guess. No doubt he'd used his jumping ability again. Ted smiled, pleased that Si'ad didn't want to be separated from him for even a little while.

"This is the stallion that ran away," he said, unnecessarily.

The man laughed. "I guessed that but looks like he's your horse now. You left him in the paddock? How'd he get out, you suppose?"

"I hope he jumped. I'd hate to think he let the mare out, too."

"Let's go check."

But before they could move they saw, and heard, an hysterical woman coming down the lane. Miguel's wife. She stopped when she saw the stallion, then began babbling furiously in Spanish, so fast even Miguel had trouble following her. But when she gestured with her hands, they all understood. Si'ad had indeed cleared the fence, and by a considerable margin if she was to be believed. The mare was still in the paddock.

This changed things for Ted. He turned to the man. "How far away is Desert Sun?" he asked.

"About twenty miles more or less, I would guess. Why?"

"I've changed my mind. Would you call the ranch for me? Tell them what happened and to send a van out for the mare. And could you give me some food and water? I'm going to ride Si'ad back."

"You're what? Why don't you just stay here until they come for you? We don't mind. Besides, haven't you ridden enough already?"

Ted shook his head. "Sorry, this is something I need to do. This horse, Si'ad," he rubbed the stallion's nose as the horse responded in kind. "He's not mine. He doesn't even belong to Desert Sun. He's been leased to stand at stud. He belongs to some people back east. I have no way of knowing what will happen when I get back. But I do know I'm pretty attached to him."

"And he to you," the man smiled, already guessing Ted's thoughts. "So you want some more time alone with him. I understand. Sure, no problem. We'll call Desert Sun for you. And the mare can stay here until they come for her. But it's kind of late in the day to start out. Wouldn't you like to stay the night and leave first thing tomorrow?"

It sounded like a good idea to Ted. One more day with his beloved stallion before returning. Happily he agreed.

By dawn the next morning, fortified with a good night's sleep and plenty of food, including some of Miguel's wife's tortillas, Ted headed out across the desert on the last leg of his journey. With him he had a hand-drawn map to help him find his way. Determined to make the most of this last day together, he chose a course that, while heading in the general direction, kept them out on the desert as much as possible. For long moments he was able to pretend there was just the two of them in his world as he relived the things he and the stallion had shared.

Before the sun rose high in the sky, Ted found a long open stretch to let Si'ad run. Together they skimmed over the ground, the stallion's powerful strides eating up the distance as he sped across the hard-packed sand. Ted's heart sang with happiness as he watched the scenery flash by him. No horse could run like this. He let the horse slow of his own accord, sad that it was over. There was no telling if he'd ever get the chance to do this again. He wondered if his real owners knew what a powerful, exciting horse he was to ride. Broke to saddle he was, but had he ever had the chance to open up and fly with a rider on his back?

Si'ad slowed eventually and Ted walked him to cool him out. He could not risk an injury at this point. Si'ad was too valuable.

Soon the sun rose high overhead and it grew too hot to do much more than walk. Ted stopped to rest, eating his lunch and sharing his water with the stallion, letting him graze before continuing. As they drew closer to the ranch, his thoughts drifted toward the future. Had the big barn been repaired by now? If not, where would Si'ad be kept when he returned? Surely, they would let him continue on as his groom, at least until he was sent back to Kentucky. Perhaps he could suggest an outside paddock where he could stretch his legs whenever he wanted. Confinement was not for this horse.

Ted, himself, never doubted that he would not stay on at the ranch. Where else would he go? He could not think about leaving Si'ad. If all he had was feeding and caring for the horse, it would be enough. It would have to be. Si'ad was not his to choose.

All too soon their idyll was over. Climbing a slight rise, they saw Desert Sun stretched before them. A sinking feeling came over him and he fleetingly wondered if anything would be the same again. Reluctantly he walked the stallion toward the distant barns, vaguely aware of the new improvements since he'd been gone. Already the framework of the new replacement for the big barn was visible. The roof appeared completed but much of its walls were still only framed out. A pavilion-like structure dominated the scene over what was once the indoor ring. Ted realized how long he'd been gone for the area had hardly been raised before he left, the new lumber stacked neatly to one side.

221

It looked like they had been racing to get the barn completed as soon as possible.

By the time he'd reached the outer paddocks, all of which were still filled with horses awaiting the new stalls, he'd been spotted. Returning their waves, he realized they'd probably been watching out for him. Sure enough, as he rode into the main yard he was surrounded by people from the ranch, all talking at once.

"Didn't think we'd ever see this old bugger again," Jim called out, his eyes scanning the stallion critically, as Ted slid down from the horse. "I still can't believe it. When we got the call that you made it back and were on your way here, we were all shocked."

Ted could only nod, not trusting himself to speak and not sure what to say if he did. He was remarkably close to tears as he felt his throat close up. Instead he went about pulling the saddle off the stallion in order to give himself something to do. Jim tactfully chose to ignore his silence.

"Amazing," he continued, shaking his head. "He appears to be fine, too. How'd you do it? Never mind, we'll talk later. First let's get him settled, though I had to do some creative arranging just to find a place to put him. As you can see, we're still all topsy turvy around here." Jim took the saddle from Ted and led him toward one of the outside paddocks, as he added amiably, "Still don't understand why you didn't just stay at the Whitman Ranch and wait for us. You didn't need to ride all the way back."

Ted had had plenty of time on the way back to rehearse how he was going to answer Jim. "I asked to do a job for you," he replied. "To get Si'ad back. That's what I set out to do and I felt, well, I had to complete it, including delivering him right back here personally, I guess. Besides," he finished lamely, "he's kind of a special horse. I had to do it my way."

"So I see," Mr. Haines said, as he came up to join them. "Including riding him, I suppose. Interesting. We didn't even know he was broke. Guess we know now," he added, smiling to ease the guilt that appeared on Ted's face.

"I—I chose to ride him to spell the mare. It was a long ride out."

"I'm sure it was. I'm proud of you, son. Not many folks could have done what you just did, especially single-handedly. It's quite a feat." Ted felt better for the praise. "Now I think we'd better leave this fellow in peace and see about your needs. You look about done in. Rest, get a nice long shower and something to eat. Then we'll talk. Everyone's dying to hear your story, but it'll keep till you're fit."

"But Si'ad?" Ted questioned.

"He'll be fine. Besides there are enough people around here to tend to his needs."

"Please, sir. He's used to me. I'd rather, if you don't mind." As he spoke the stallion brushed against him. Mr. Haines saw the naked look of love come over the boy's face as he reached to pat the stallion and he grimaced. So that's how it was, he thought. Si'ad belonged to neither of them. He feared the boy might be in for a big disappointment ahead.

Aloud, he only said. "Sure, go ahead. Come up to the house when you're ready."

Ted released him into the paddock set aside for him. He waited while the stallion explored his new surroundings before settling down to the hay provided. Only then did Ted feel comfortable about leaving him.

Later, when he had taken care of his own needs, including visiting his old trailer for a change of clothes, he returned to the office where both Jim and Mr. Haines were waiting for him. The story he gave them was a much abbreviated version, stating only the facts without making himself out as a hero. He chose to leave out the personal for those memories belonged only to Si'ad and himself. Already he missed their freedom together. "Now what happens?" he asked when he was finished.

"Once we got word you were back, that was practically the first thing to come to our minds," Mr. Haines answered.

"So we discussed what we should do," Jim added. "There are several options, but first we'll need to contact his owners."

Ted winced even though he knew that was necessary. "Make sure you tell them that he's back sound."

Nancy Clarke

"Of course. They'll be glad to hear that. Thank goodness he wasn't seriously injured up there."

"Oh, no," Ted told them proudly. "Si'ad's tough. He adapted right back to living on the desert. Took care of himself very well. That was why it took so long to catch him," he went on. " He was like a wild horse all over again."

"All the more reason it's a miracle you got him back," the owner said. "We can't thank you enough for what you did. We owe you one."

"The only thing I want is to continue to be his groom."

"That would not be a problem if he were to continue here as per our original leasing agreement. He's supposed to remain through next year's breeding season, but in lieu of these current events, that may not be possible."

"Why not?" Ted suddenly looked concerned. He had never thought of Si'ad not remaining through his lease contract. Desert Sun had considerable money invested in him, he knew, plus several more of their mares were slated to be bred to him, not to mention this year's breeding season being interrupted by the fire and Si'ad's escape. He wasn't sure how those obligations would be met, but he always assumed that he would return to his stud duties once back at the ranch. A tinge of guilt came over him as he realized he'd kept him away an extra week unnecessarily. Still he could not have done things differently and he'd always have his memories of that glorious week with Si'ad.

"Well, for one thing, as you can see our facilities are still very much under construction and it doesn't look like they'll have this mess," he spread his hands out toward the half-completed barn, "done before breeding season ends." Ted was jolted back to the present as he contemplated for the first time what that might mean. "While you were gone we made arrangements to send the rest of the stallions to stand temporarily at nearby studs. Not only do we lack the facilities for properly housing our own stallions right now, but there's no way we could do the breedings and hope to settle the mares with all this banging and noise going on, even if we had the room for visiting mares."

"Fortunately," the manager added, " the other breeders have been most generous in offering their help. So you can see, there's no way for Si'ad to stay here and expect to perform in this chaos."

"So, we decided to cut our losses," Mr. Haines summed up, "and send Si'ad back to his rightful owner."

"What!" Ted was clearly not anticipating this solution. His face registered instant alarm.

"It's the best way for all concerned. His owners will be delighted to get him back sooner, I'm sure. They can complete his season back there for those mares still booked to him if the owners are willing to ship. Most of our mares have been bred to him already. The two who haven't dropped their foals yet can either be shipped or held off until next year."

Ted continued to look bleak at the news. Si'ad leaving?

"Anyway," Jim went on, "we both feel the fire was our personal loss, and that they shouldn't be penalized for it. So we pretty much have agreed to send him back to his owners."

"When?" Ted croaked out.

"As soon as possible. A couple of days."

"A couple of days?"

"As soon as a van is ready for the trip. And, of course, we'll have to notify Stormy Hill first. They should be elated. They still think he's dead."

"Dead?" Ted asked, shocked.

"Even though you went looking for him," Mr. Haines explained, "we weren't sure if you'd be successful so since they already thought he'd been lost in the fire, we thought it best to keep it that way, unless—until we had proof otherwise. Now that he's back safe, we can give them the real story."

"I see. And I guess there's no question that once they know he's alive, they'll want him right away. I know I would." Suddenly Ted had a thought. "You'll need to send someone with him, right? So since I'm still his groom, please send me."

They both saw the eagerness on the boy's face and smiled at each other knowingly. "Don't see why not," the owner replied. Ted's

225

face lit up. " He responds better to you than anyone. It's a long trip and he'll need looking after. I'll make the arrangements."

"Oh, thank you, thank you!" Ted exclaimed over and over, his eyes shining with gratitude.

"Why don't you go now and rest up. You must be exhausted from your ordeal. Tomorrow is plenty of time to prepare yourself and Si'ad for the trip. And if there's anything we can do, just let us know. We both owe you a lot for saving him," Mr. Haines repeated.

After Ted had gone, they looked at one another. "Don't know what really happened up in those mountains but those two got really attached to each other."

Jim agreed, "I'm afraid the kid's heading for a big disappointment when that stallion gets back to his real home. Unless they can find a place for him there."

The owner shook his head. "That's why we got Si'ad in the first place. Money problems. Still I'd hate to lose a good worker like him. Guess we'll have to wait and see. Meanwhile you'd better call Stormy Hill and let them know what's up." Leaving that task in his manager's capable hands, he left the room.

As soon as he was alone, Jim sought out the phone number of Si'ad's owner. He was about to dial when he realized just how late it was back there. Remembering the time difference he hesitated, doing quick mental calculations. No, it was far too late to call now. Leaving the number scribbled on a paper next to the phone, he planned to do it first thing in the morning.

But when morning came, he got very involved in other projects, especially the new construction that always seemed to have a myriad of problems, and forgot all about it. By the time he remembered to make the call and was near a phone, it was again too late to call. When he finally did call he got no answer. Two days later, the van was ready to pull out and he still hadn't reached anyone. Feeling extremely guilty, Jim decided to send a telegram to be sure they knew what was happening. Thinking it would be better to wire it directly to the feed store where Michael worked, he sent it there. This way he'd be sure to get it.

All would have been fine, if Michael had been at the store when it arrived. However, he was out delivering a load of hay personally, as his driver was home sick. The employee who received it, placed it on his desk with the other mail and somehow it got buried under other papers and forgotten, Michael failing to see it when he finally did return to his desk. Thus they were totally unaware that Si'ad was on his way home.

Blithely ignorant of these events, Ted began to prepare for his departure with Si'ad. First he went to visit the horse. Assuring himself that the stallion had suffered no ill effects from his adventure, he told the horse what he'd just heard. "And I've convinced them to let me go with you. I just hope I can come up with a way to stay with you when we get there." He refused to think of a future without this horse in his life.

The following couple of days were busy for him. He worked hard to outfit the van with everything he'd need for the trip. By comparison, his own personal things took no time at all. Everything of value to him fit quite easily in one duffel bag.

Checking out the vehicle they would use took the most time. The truck was gone over thoroughly to trouble-shoot any possible problems beforehand. After a couple of parts were replaced and new tires were put on, the truck was declared road-worthy.

Three days later Si'ad and Ted were ready to embark. Because the trip would be a lengthy one, they planned to stop each night to rest the horse, and themselves. They would leave at dawn.

Most of the time Ted chose to ride in back with Si'ad. Even up front he seldom spoke to the driver. He knew he was not much company, but he was unable to break out of his apathetic mood. In the end he opted to stay in the back with the horse. If the driver thought him odd, he cared not a wit.

At the end of each day, they stopped at a cheap motel where Ted took Si'ad out and walked him. However, the first night they chose one next to open countryside. Ted saw an opportunity to ride the stallion to keep him limber and fit. Though he told himself he was doing it to keep Si'ad from getting stiff, he was really doing it for himself.

227

But that first experience brought back so many memories that this became a pattern they would follow all the way cross country. Each night they would look for a motel bordering open areas. He even got up earlier each morning to exercise the stallion again before getting back on the road.

All along the way, Ted tried to postpone the inevitable, but on the fourth day they crossed the Kentucky state line and he knew it was impossible. As each mile clipped past, a sense of doom settled over him. He hardly spoke at all that day for he still didn't have a solid plan to stay with Si'ad worked out and now he feared the worst.

Late in the afternoon the van turned off the main highway and onto a narrow country road. They had been passing horse farms for some time now, large, beautifully manicured pastures that looked more like well-kept lawns, and green everywhere on this the first Saturday in May. Ted was quick to contrast the difference with the arid desert he'd left behind. He chose to sit up front this day so that he might catch the first glimpse of Si'ad's home.

"This is it," the driver suddenly commented, as he turned into a long lane beneath a battered old sign that read "Stormy Hill."

Ted's first glance was favorable. He instantly loved the long, tree shaded drive, the deep green rolling pastures on either side, several horses grazing in each. At the top of the lane, off to the right stood the main house, southern in design yet unpretentious and charming. A courtyard to the left was shaped by three barns forming a horseshoe. Ted immediately felt a sense of warmth shine through what could only be described as genteel poverty. These people were poor but proud, he'd bet.

Still his heart sunk as he looked closer seeing at second glance that this place needed a lot of work and it didn't look like they could afford to pay to get it done, either.

As he jumped down from the cab, he failed to see anyone, though a car was parked in the driveway. He went back to check on Si'ad and started to take him out when a boy about his age came down the lane next to the house, leading a saddled and bridled chestnut mare. He was followed by two men and a woman, all talking excitedly, that is until they spotted Ted and the very familiar grey stallion he held.

Suddenly everyone began talking at once but before Ted could answer their questions, a loud clap of thunder diverted their attention to an impending storm.

The boy holding the mare, called out, "Don't explain anything till I take care of Ginger. That's Si'ad and I want to hear everything! I'll be right back!" He hurried off to strip the mare of her tack and hastily put her in a stall. Meanwhile, Ted was inundated by the other three who clustered around him, patting the stallion and exclaiming disbelief at his return.

The boy was back in record time, but before they could hear Ted's story, there was another commotion from the direction of the lane. They all turned, none of them prepared for the sight of a huge black horse bursting into the courtyard, completely free of any restraining halter or tack. At first sight he appeared to be loose but as he drew closer, Ted was able to make out a rider on his back, a girl, almost completely enveloped by the long, thick mane whipping out behind him. The girl's own long black hair was flung back in an extension of that mane. The stallion came to a rearing halt and, upon seeing the other stallion, screamed a challenge. For an instant no one moved, frozen as they were. Then Si'ad came to life, fighting Ted's restraint as he responded with a challenge of his own.

CHAPTER TWENTY

Heritage

When Ted finished his story, everyone sat in stunned silence for a moment. His story seemed so incredible. They had long since given up believing Si'ad had survived the fire. But here he was, in the flesh and *very* much alive!

Ann was the first to speak. "That's one amazing story! I still can't believe he's back. But how come Desert Sun never notified us?"

"They did. I mean Jim, the manager, tried to call right away, but things got so hectic and between the time difference and no answer when he did try, he said he finally sent a telegram. You never got it?"

"Not that I know of," Michael shook his head. "I'll check down at the store Monday. Possibly it was sent there. It could have been misplaced, but something that important should have been brought to my attention. Anyway, it no longer matters. He's here now," he sighed, smiling at the boy, "and are we ever glad to see him."

"Just what this means to our family, you have no idea," Jessica added, a genuine smile of gratitude on her face. "We need Si'ad back here more than ever now. He can help make ends meet with his stud services."

Ted returned her smile but inside his heart was breaking bit by bit. It was obvious how necessary Si'ad was to this farm. There was no way these people would consider letting him go back to the ranch. Nor were they in any position to offer him a job so that he might stay here with the stallion. The disappointment showed briefly on his face before he was able to hide it.

Even so, Ann caught that look. She'd been watching him closely as he told his story and did not fail to catch the way his eyes lit up each time he mentioned Si'ad. In spite of the fact that he had left out most of the personal details when retelling his adventures, she was able to read into what he did not say. In him she recognized a kindred spirit, she realized. Si'ad means as much to him as Lightning does to her. No wonder she felt that brief tinge of jealousy when she saw how Si'ad reacted to Ted. After all, Si'ad had once been *her* horse, before Lightning took over her affections. An idea came to her.

"Ted?" she asked. "Now that you've brought him back to us, will you be going back to the ranch?"

Ted shrugged. "I suppose so. That's my job."

"Your family there, too? Arizona, I mean?"

He shook his head. "Nope, don't have any family. I live at Desert Sun now."

"I'm sorry," she murmured, saddened at the thought of being orphaned at such an early age. Why he wasn't any older than she and she couldn't imagine how she'd get along without her extended family.

"Don't be. It happened a long time ago. I'm over it."

"Well, if that's settled," Jessica jumped up, changing the subject to bring back the cheerful atmosphere. "Come on, everyone, let's finish off this food while I make another pot of coffee. Can't have anyone leaving here on an empty stomach."

Ann caught her father's eye. "Dad, can I see you for a minute?" she asked, urgency in her voice.

Seeing his daughter's intense expression, Michael nodded, following her out of the room, for once without a comment. When Ann got that look on her face he'd found it was best to hear her out. And she certainly did seem serious about something.

Ann wasted no time getting to the point. "Now that both Si'ad and Lightning are back, we're going to need more help around here. Couldn't we ask Ted to stay?"

Michael was taken back. Though he'd suspected what she might be getting at, he did not expect this. For a moment he was quiet, gauging his reply. Looking at her hopeful face, he tried to formulate an answer that would let her down gently. "Honey, we can barely support ourselves as it is. There's no money to pay someone to work for us. Besides that wouldn't be fair to Jock and Scotty."

"I didn't mean pay him. I know we can't do that. But I was thinking, well, maybe he could stay here, like Jock and Scotty do. We don't pay them but they help out in all kinds of ways."

"Scotty and Jock are different. They've grown up here. They're really like family. No, they *are* family. Besides they get spending money by working at Garrison's."

"And so could Ted. I'm sure we could find room around here for him. Why there's that old apartment in the stallion barn that's only used for storage. It could be fixed up." Already she was planning it in her mind.

"Hold on, honey," he stopped her ramblings. "You're not listening to me. We don't even know this boy and you want to take him in like some stray dog."

"Maybe not, but I do know he loves Si'ad every bit as much as I love Lightning. Anyone who feels that way about a horse is good enough for me. That's all I need to know!" she ended emphatically.

Her father smiled at his daughter's sincerity. "So on that basis you'd take him in?"

Ann nodded. "Look at what we do know. That boy went into those mountains, no mean feat, and found Si'ad, then caught him and rode him back. Somewhere along the way he gained Si'ad's trust. Not an easy thing to do, I might add. And I should know, he was my horse first. That horse adores him. I'm willing to bet Si'ad would do just about anything for him. That's all the character reference I need!" she finished honestly.

"But -"

"Besides," she cut in. "Now that he's back, someone will be needed to take charge of his stud services. Ted's already got that experience. The rest of us will be too busy taking care of the farm and getting Lightning ready to race."

"I don't doubt we could use an experienced stud manager," her father pondered aloud. Suddenly his daughter's words sunk in. "Wait a minute, what's this about racing Lightning?" he eyed her suspiciously.

Ann giggled. "Caught that, did you? Never mind, we'll discuss that later. So, what do you think?"

"About which? Racing Lightning or Ted?" her father teased. Two could play at this game. About Ted, he had already made up his mind.

"First things first. So, Ted, can he stay?" she wasn't going to let her father sidetrack her.

"My, you don't give up, do you?"

"Come on, Dad, this is really important."

"Have you considered the possibility he may have other plans? Maybe he won't want to stay under these circumstances. All we can offer him is an arrangement like Scotty and Jock have."

"Oh, I have a strong feeling that will be very acceptable. Anything would be okay if it means staying near Si'ad."

"You're *that* sure?"

Ann grinned. "Yep. Just watch." Suddenly realizing her father had said yes, she hugged him compulsively. "Thanks, Dad. This is one decision I know you won't regret."

"Don't be too sure. I'm already regretting it." But he was smiling when he said it.

Ann was smiling as if from some private joke as she entered the kitchen and sat down beside Jock. He noticed and looked at her, questioningly.

"What's up?" he asked.

"You'll know soon enough," she replied.

Then Michael came in behind her and signaled Ted that he wanted to talk to him. Thinking it was something pertaining to his departure for the ranch, he followed Michael out to the hall. Ann strained to listen for the explosion soon to come.

She was not disappointed. Only moments later, Ted let out a whoop that they all heard. Suddenly all conversation stopped as they turned to the sound.

"Guess that's a 'yes'!" Ann cried out, grinning from ear to ear.

"What is?" Jock wanted to know.

Before Ann could elaborate, Ted burst back into the kitchen, Michael right behind him. Ann jumped up. "I told you he'd say 'yes'," she told her father, hugging him again. "Who could pass up a deal like that?"

"Whatever are you talking about?" Jock insisted, confused.

"Tell them, Dad."

"I've asked Ted to join us here at Stormy Hill," Michael announced. " With Si'ad back and our broodmare band growing we'll need his help. He can be in charge of Si'ad's breedings and whatever else we need. In return, we'll fix up the old storeroom for him, and, of course there's Mother's cooking."

"Wonderful," Jessica beamed. "I do so love cooking for an appreciative audience." She had seen how quickly he had downed her cake and then shyly asked for more. "Welcome to our family." She patted him on the back.

"It'll be great having another hand around here to share the chores," Jock said, grinning deviously, "especially a male one. It can get decidedly too feminine around here at times," he added looking straight at Ann, who stuck her tongue out at him.

"Why, you! I'll get you back for that remark, Jock McDougal," she cried huffily.

"Before you do," interrupted her long suffering father, "there are a couple of things to get settled. Ted, you'll get a commission for each mare bred to Si'ad, of course, but you might want to apply for part-time work next door where Scotty and Jock work. It'll give you pin money." Ted looked up from his second helping of cake, somewhat dazed. He never expected such generosity from people who were strangers to him. But Michael wasn't done yet. "Now, what about your schooling?"

Ted looked blankly at him. "Schooling?"

"What are you, about sixteen, seventeen?" Ted nodded. "I guessed you were close to Ann's age. She's sixteen and a junior at the local high school. You didn't get to finish, did you?" He shook his head. "Perhaps you can go with her and see about getting your diploma, too. That is, if you're interested?"

"You mean it? That would be great! I've always been sorry I had to—I mean I dropped out." He looked guilty but no one seemed to notice the slip. Maybe one day he'd feel comfortable talking about his past. But not now, not when this family had been so generous to him. A chance to stay with Si'ad. Wow!

"Good, then that's settled. We'll look into it first thing Monday. Looks like the storm's finally let up. Perhaps you two would like to check on your horses?" he smiling knowingly. "And, Ted, if you'll just get your things out of the van, I'll send the driver on his way."

"No problem, Mr. Collins, I've only got my duffel bag."

"Hey, none of this 'Mr.' stuff. You'd better get used to calling me Michael like Jock does if you're going to be part of our family."

"Okay, M—Michael and thanks, for everything. You won't be sorry. I'll work hard to live here."

"I know you will. Now scat. I've got to call Desert Sun and tell them you won't be returning so they can forward your stuff."

"That won't be necessary," Ted replied as he followed Ann and Jock out the door. "I really didn't leave anything behind worth sending."

Jessica caught her husband's eye as he said the last. She was shocked. As soon as the younger trio had left, she murmured to him, "That poor boy. Imagine having so little of your own that everything of value fits in a duffel bag. We must change that soon. He seems like such a nice boy."

"Uh, oh. Do I detect the mother hen instinct coming out again, now that you have another 'child' to take care of?" He softened his words by hugging her. "Then I'm glad I decided to take him in."

"You decided?" she scoffed, pulling away from him, but not without affection. "I doubt that. More like Ann put the bug in your ear and you went along with it."

"Guilty as charged," he said sheepishly.

"Well, I'm glad you did, because if you hadn't, I would have. That poor child. Didn't he say he was an orphan? Must have been tough on him, no older than our own daughter. I hope we can give him roots."

"I'm sure if anyone can, you can, my dear. You're a sucker for a good cause. Jock and Ann have already accepted him. He's so good with horses, he'll fit right in. Another stray for you, Mother," he added, lovingly. "You were meant to have a large family."

But Jessica, who was only blessed with one, replied. "I do, I have all of you."

—⚬⚬⚬—

The storm had abated. Already the sun was out, drying up the puddles. The three teenagers hastened to get the horses out.

Ann stepped into Lightning's stall, her eyes drinking in the sight of him. The finely-chiseled black head, with its oddly endearing crooked blaze, swung toward her. Eagerly, he came forward and pushed against her. Impulsively she threw her arms around him, hugging him.

"Gosh, it's great having you back," she cried. She released him and snapped on a lead rope, leading him out into the sun, though she suspected the lead rope was not necessary. This colt would follow her anywhere.

Once through the gate to his field, she removed the halter and turned him loose. Lightning stood still a second before galvanizing into action. Flinging himself down the fence line he burst into a full, bucking run. Back and forth he galloped, running for sheer pleasure. Ann watched, fascinated by the beautiful horse he'd become. She always knew he was special, but this—he'd fulfilled her wildest dreams. Maybe the Kentucky Derby was not so hopelessly out of reach after all. It was exactly a year away. Boy, she couldn't wait to start working on her father and Scotty for that one!

Lightning got all the kinks out and settled down to grazing on the lush spring bluegrass. Ann turned away, her eyes suspiciously moist. Then she caught a glimpse of the pasture across

the courtyard where a grey stallion also grazed. He was not alone. Ann smiled, knowing well how Ted must be feeling now. As the stallion moved slowly, savoring the good grass he'd not tasted in a long time, the boy moved with him, his arm resting across the horse's back. Ann would not have interrupted their reverie for anything. Their bond was kindred to her own with Lightning. Si'ad had been her horse once, but now he was Ted's. How could she deny him that when she had Si'ad's son to take his place? Lightning meant the world to her, just as Si'ad was Ted's whole world. Maybe even more so since up until now the horse was all he had. Perhaps when he was more comfortable with her, he'd tell her about his past and what really happened up in those mountains. She suspected there was a lot more to his story than the very sketchy details he had related earlier. That must have been quite a tale to produce the strong bond that existed between them now. But until then, she'd respect his privacy.

Having Ted around would make life nicely exciting. With both Si'ad and Lightning back, the future looked bright, indeed. She turned toward the huge black colt. Something caught his eye and he raised his head to stare at it, still as a statue. Ann's breath caught in her throat as she went to him. The future was now and she couldn't wait to get started.